The Prisoner of Zurenda

Warrior from Olympus

Book One

Kent A. LeFevre

SQUARE PLATE MEDIA

Square Plate Media
www.squareplatemedia.com

Publisher's Note: This is a work of fiction. Names, characters, places, and incidents are a product of the author's imagination. Locales, products and public names are sometimes used for atmospheric purposes. Any resemblance to actual people, living or dead, other books, or to other thematic works, businesses, companies, events, and institutions is completely coincidental and is not intended.

The Prisoner of Zurenda – Book One.

Warrior from Olympus/ Kent A. LeFevre.-First Edition

ISBN 13: 978-1-7322266-0-9 (Paperback Trade)

ISBN 13: 978-1-7322266-1-6 (E-book)

ISBN 13: 978-1-7322266-2-3 (Audible)

Library of Congress Control Number, LCCN: 2018904315

Content:

Fiction, Fantasy, Sci-fi fiction, Greek Gods, Greek Mythology, Fellowship, Friendship, Adventure, Monsters, Greek Gods, Demi-Gods, Shapeshifters, Amazons, Treachery.

Ages: 13 to Adult.

Printed in the United States of America.

For Jason

Face your destiny and read this book!

Foreword:

Our story is set around the time frame of the First Millennia B.C. as a derivation stemming from the events concluding the Trojan War. Nothing short of the complete dedication, resources and the tenacity of three friends and a few helpers will overcome the raw power of evil and discord.

This book teaches the value of friendship, dedication and personal sacrifice, with the belief that a few individuals can make the world a better place.

Description:

Vanquishing the Citadel of Troy was a noble effort to be sure. However, with a twist of fate, or perhaps the shifting will of the gods, life forever changed for a warrior named Arjun and his friends, Kiera and Lycos.

Join the adventure as three friends, and four "not so normal" helpers, set out to vanquish all discord among the gods and among men. With the help of the gods, and one in particular, can they accomplish this impossible mission?

This is a story of shapeshifters, sea monsters, mythical and strange creatures, gods, demi-gods and mere mortals which will have you thinking about ancient Greek Mythology all over again.

CHAPTER ONE

Arjun

"Kiera, Kiera, Kiera!" Gasping for air, Arjun cried for help as the gaping sea monster now circled beneath him in the foaming water. Through the boiling brine, he could see the whole shape of the beast now.

The thing must have been sixty or ninety cubits in length. Substantial blazing red eyes, a giant fish-like mouth, and a head packed full of razor-sharp teeth. Arjun could see that the teeth were laced with bright drops of iridescent green poison. Mid-body, the beast sported large pectoral fins giving way to the rest of the body which had the appearance of an oversized worm or a mammoth milli-pede complete with spiny barbs at each body segment. The beast's barbs pulsated a dull yellow, and then a bright point of light shot from each of the barbed hooks. They looked like shooting stars in the water.

From Arjun's view, he could see that the beast was fit-ted with four pairs of slender whip-like stingers that no doubt were full of poison as well. *This will not be good!* Ar-jun thought to himself, trying to catch another breath as if it were his last while feeling the pressure of the water drop from beneath his feet. Finally, coming to terms with the whole situation, he realized that the beast was going to swallow him whole! Arjun gulped one last gasp of air, and a shouted skyward for anyone that could help him.

Kiera was the last name he called to, but she was in Kymi, he knew that. He was somewhere in the middle of the Aegean Sea. He felt alone because he was alone! His ship had just been destroyed by this...this Charybdis! To Arjun, it looked like all his fellow ship-mates had been or would be devoured by this beast of the deep. His only hope was Selene. In his mind, he calls for her to intervene. Meanwhile, the beast closed in on him to take its final bite.

The water around him foamed and began to form into a conical shape that immediately became, what seemed to Arjun, to be a funnel. A funnel directed toward that gap-ing mouth! Arjun could not fight against the current anymore. He knew it was useless. Instead, he let the pressure of the water flip him upside down and begin his head-long plunge into the gaping maw.

Sword in hand, and head first, there was no stopping now. He had to get past the gauntlet of dagger-sized teeth and somehow land on the beast's tongue without getting ripped to shreds in the process, or swallowed whole. *Could it be done?* Arjun had no choice; he had to do it! He took courage at the fleeting thought.

Now hurling forward toward the beast, water rushing beside him and inside the beast's mouth, he pulled his arms close together while holding his sword outstretched be-tween clenched fists as firm as he could manage it. *Only three fathoms from the beast now, I just need to head for the gaping middle, focus on the tongue,* he thought. *FOCUS!* His mind, not even thinking about the want for air at this point, only to land on that tongue!

A split second flashed by, streaks of blurred white teeth passed, the tongue was right in front of him. His sword pierced it cleanly, starting an involuntary reaction of the monster. The beast began flipping its head side to side and then backward allowing Arjun to gain a foothold on the roof the great beast's mouth.

This shaking action allowed Arjun to find a foothold on the bony middle, the corrugated section of the beast's mouth. With his left foot holding this position long enough to allow a thrust of his sword up into the roof of its serrated mouth.

Arjun was able to force the sword in all the way to its hilt, connecting he hoped, with the beast's brain.

This action will surely kill the beast! He thought to himself.

The beast started to flail and shake its body wildly from side to side, like a worm newly threaded on a fisherman's hook. *Hold onto that sword!* Arjun thought, followed by the next flash of inspiration, *it is time to get out! NOW!*

The want for air was becoming more acute. *I need a breath.* He thought, *but how do I get out of here?* Suddenly, the gills of the great fish opened as it too seemed to be gasping for one more breath.

Leaving behind the sword buried in the beast brain, Arjun pushed away from the roof of the beast's mouth. Swimming straight for the opening between the gills he managed with some effort to obtain a hold of the outside edge of the gill, pulling himself through the slit and out of the beast's mouth and to freedom. Looking up from the depths, he could see piercing rays of light near the surface of the water distantly above him. Swimming slowly and exhaling as much as he could he let himself drift to the surface. His brain and lungs were screaming for air. He could not last much longer.

However, as if by magic, out of the deep came a multitude of mermaids to lend him breath. Each siren gave him the kiss of life-sustaining breath by replenishing much-needed air into his lungs and restoring his ability to concentrate on getting to the surface.

Tense seconds passed. A few more mermaids came to lend him breath. *I'm actually going to make it!* He thought.

Ascending in a column of water, Arjun caught a glimpse of what had become of the sea monster. A lifeless worm at the bottom of the sea, even the yellow pulsating lights had stopped.

Barrowing one last breath from a mermaid, he felt the energy and the strength to break the surface of the sea.

Air never tasted so good! Arjun thought as he made the surface and took a deep breath, and then another. "Thanks to Selene!" He exclaimed to the waiting sky. He did not mind the rolling waves breaking on his back. He could breathe again! More air and more clarity of thought! He had to go now, but where?

The sea was relatively calm, but he felt lost. His ship had been destroyed. *What to do now?* Became the pressing issue in his mind. "I need more help." He called skyward.

More help came. A large section of the ship's hull came floating into view. It was a relatively big piece of lumber, big enough for him to lie down on and haul himself out of the water.

The ship's splintered wood surfaces were jagged and broken however; there were still enough edges to grasp.

After a few deep breaths, Arjun grasped on to the edge of the make-shift raft and using all his strength; he pulled himself onto the wreckage.

At first, the raft wobbled acting like it would capsize in the tide. And then, as if someone, unseen, had placed a hand upon it, the raft stabilized to a quiet lull and a steady drift.

For the first time since the attack, he was out of the water. Sunlight warmed his skin. Arjun lie there for a while and let the sun's warmth penetrate his drenched skin

He now had the time to orient himself, think about an escape plan, and at the same time catch some rest.

The afternoon passed slowly. Arjun gazed into the azure sky and then drifted off of to sleep.

His clothes were shredded to tatters after the encounter with the sea monster, but, after a quick inspection of his limbs and torso, he suffered only a few cuts and scrapes during the ordeal. He had no food, no water and it seemed like an inevitable but postponed death awaited him.

When would death come? Today? Tonight? Tomorrow? He did not know. All he knew was this: He was on a floating scrap of ship drifting somewhere around the Aegean Sea.

How did this day go so horribly wrong? Arjun asked himself as the tide drifted him further into the sea. *We had a flotilla of ships heading for Troy. My Trireme alone lost over 30 men. My men. My warriors. My friends.* This loss made his heart sink a little. *Which god did we offend to bring on this disaster, or to unleash that monster?* He wondered.

Scanning the horizon, Arjun could see no other ships. *Did all of them get destroyed by Charybdis?* He mused. *We were so close to Troy. We were so close to victory! This foray was going to be the final siege of Troy. I wanted to be there to see it fall!* Lamenting: *My men are all lost at sea. I am alone on this make-shift raft. How will I find my way back home?* No one was in sight. No other sailors and no other wreckage.

For Arjun, nothing else was in sight except a half-submerged piece of cloth. Sailcloth! Linen! At seeing this, his heart took courage. *I can make a sail and get somewhere.* He thought. Pulling the cloth onto the planks was tricky, but manageable. Each handful of material had to be rung out at the edge of the raft in order to lift it on to the planks. This process took some time, as he balanced the raft and the new load to prevent a capsize.

Arjun managed to hook two edges of the sailcloth to the leading edge of the planks. The eyelets of the sail were tied with a few strands of shredded fabric which made the connection possible. By hooking rope fragments to the planks and by lifting the rest of the sail up to his shoulder he could feel the breeze catch the sail and propel him forward. He was moving!

How did this all happen? Arjun wondered again. These and other random thoughts crossed his mind. Thoughts about his friend Kiera and his other friends back in Kymi swirled around his head like a cyclone, shredded memories of Greece.

The long day had stretched into a very long night.

Not wanting to fall off the raft, and getting thirsty for a drink of fresh water, time wore on finally giving way to a cool and quiet evening. *Almost peaceful.* Arjun's make-shift sail was working and the wisp of a breeze was pushing him to the northeast. He knew from experience that land would be found in that direction. It was just a question of when.

To keep moisture in his mouth Arjun chewed on the back of his tongue. *He may be adrift for one day, maybe two.* His thoughts turned again to Kiera. *Surely Hermes would spread the news of our maritime disaster. No doubt, news of this disaster would soon reach the shores of Greece. What would Kiera be thinking? Would she miss him as much as he missed her? Would she assume he was dead?*

The evening was coming on. He needed some rest; however, he dared not sleep for fear that he would lose his natural bearings of time and space.

The full moon began to rise over the sea just at sunset and from his perspective, the moon seemed bigger and brighter than ever before. He kept watching it rise. Was this an omen, a sign? The moon's reflection began to touch the water and glisten off the gentle waves. The reflection was punctuated by a sparkle of light here and there in the ebbing tide.

While gazing downward, he could see a shadowy reflection of a woman wearing a white robe down in the water. This being was no ordinary woman. She introduced herself as Selene! *I must be dreaming!* Arjun let the sail down on to the deck of his raft. He then stood up entirely transfixed at the image of the moon-like reflection speaking to him from the water.

"Raise your eyes, my son, Arjun." The soft feminine voice clearly pierced his mind.

Was I dreaming? I think this is real? Again Arjun questioned what was unfolding before him. The watery reflection gained some clarity and definition, as he began to look upon the Goddess, the immortal Selene revealed herself to Arjun wearing a long flowing white gown. A crown of glowing stars floating above her shimmering shoulder-length hair. Her eyes were like starlight, no shadow from the evening could hold sway in her presence. She continued to address him.

"Arjun, my Son. I saved you today from Poseidon's ravenous beast. I saved you from Poseidon's watery depths, with the assistance of my handmaids. I have saved you from your shipwreck. I am Selene, goddess of the Moon."

Arjun could scarcely look upon her as she continued to speak. "Arjun, the Gods and I have a work for you. You have proven your valor. Your mission will forever change the history of your homeland and the world as you know it."

Puzzlement filled his thoughts about the declaration of being a Son of Selene. *I was the son of Theseus, and I never knew my biological mother. I really must be dreaming!* The more he gazed upon Selene, however, the more he realized that this was not a dream.

Arjun was now paying full attention.

Arjun finally understood the message completely and asked the Goddess: "How am I counted worthy to be your son and yet I have never known thee?"

Selene did not answer directly, instead, she stated: "I shall send you to the island of Skyros. There you will meet my oracle and obtain your mission."

Before his question could be answered, a drifting cloud came between his raft and the now full moon over his head.

Arjun, looked back down into the water for Selene's image again, but the vision had faded into the night, her image was erased by the shifting lines of waves in the obscured moonlight.

Did this just happen? He thought to himself. He was left to wonder while standing on his makeshift raft and contemplating what had just happened. *What could it all mean?*

CHAPTER TWO

Eris

T he Goddess Eris started this war. After all, it was
her vanity and contempt for the will of Zeus; together with the unexpected and misdirected
blessings of Aphrodite, which propelled her to act.

It was Eris's idea all along to sack Troy. She just needed to shift the blame and the responsibility to others so
that the deed could be reasonably re-directed onto someone else and then carried out by mortals.

This deed was blamed on someone else, that someone else was Paris. After taking Helen, (Menelaus' wife), back to Troy, the kettle of contempt boiled over.

Agamemnon, who was the brother-in-law of Menelaus, launched an expedition to reclaim Helen. Over one thousand ships were launched. The siege of Troy began in 1,180 B.C. and lasted for ten years. Somehow the idea of reclaiming Helen and securing the passage that led to the Black Sea was too good to pass by, or pass up.

This idea seeped into the heads of men, like water into a dry dune, and began to manifest itself in armaments like warships, a navy, battle-hardened warriors and a flotilla of equipment and resources that were brought to bear down on Troy. Troy in general and Paris, in particular, did need to be destroyed.

At least that how the Achaeans felt about it; as far as Arjun was concerned. It was Agamemnon who had appointed Arjun as Captain the year before. Now, he was the Captain of the ship named Theseus in memory of his warrior father.

Arjun's father, Theseus, was also a warrior of the seas and of no small reputation amongst the people of Greece. A monument was erected to his memory near the wharf in Kymi, carved out of marble with the head facing east, the right arm wielding a spear and the prow of a Trireme situated beneath his feet. The whole sculpture was situated to appear as if it was bursting out of solid stone on a gathering wave, chiseled with all the care of a great stone mason; each detail was executed with great skill.

For his current assignment, Arjun was also assigned the men and the equipment to carry out this task in the voyage to Troy. He and one hundred other ships were on their way to Troy when this encounter with a sea monster, this unexpected malady occurred.

This assault was planned to be the last thrust in the defeat of Troy. As fate would have it; Arjun's ship and ten other ships got caught-up in a dense fog while in the middle of the Aegean, and then they were attacked by the elements of nature and that awful monster. Arjun wondered if anyone else in his section of ocean survived the sea monster, or was he the only one.

Did anyone else see it? Are there more monsters out there than one? And if he was the only one meant to survive, why?

Why? Why did I merit survival and all my other companions perished? He kept repeating this disastrous ending in his mind over and over again, refusing to be comforted.

Arjun's make-shift raft was taking on a little water now. The sail was soaked again and almost useless. With the wind picking up speed he could not hold it in position any longer. He only hoped that the wind was hurling him in the right direction on the watery path to the island of Skyros.

I need some water, Arjun thought to himself. After the cool of the night pressed in on him, his need for water became direr. His head pounded, his lips were chapped, and his throat was dry. *Could he last until morning? He* wondered. He would have to! The raft kept moving, drifting and that's all he could remember.

Arjun's eyes opened, he found himself face-down in the sand and the shallow tide. The waves were breaking at his feet. Moist black sand caked his mouth and nose. He could taste a few grains of sand in his mouth, they were salty.

He noticed his raft swaying back and forth in the gentle surf at the edge of the pebble-strewn beach.

He had made it! *Made it to where? He* wondered.

Was this Skyros? Still, face down in the sand, his eyes began to focus. Gathering his arms and hands beneath him, he pressed himself into an odd triangular position and then up into a kneeling position. The fresh air almost choked him as he struggled to clear his mouth of the sand and a small piece of sea-weed that clung from the corner of his lip.

The need for water is all he could think of. *Water, I need fresh water!*

Now standing upright, he scanned the beach for any sign of water. There did not seem to be any immediate sign, but over his head to the distance of a few feet, he could just reach ripened fruit hanging from a tree. This was fruit like none other than he had ever tasted!

The fruit was red in color and had a soft yellow center. The soft yellow center was rich with liquid, which streamed down his now thinly bearded chin, as he placed it between upper and lower teeth to scrape out the flesh of the fruit. Arjun fed with haste for several minutes. His eyes began to focus and his mind began to sharpen. He could talk again!

His glance back to the raft revealed how close to sinking he had come. The wooden planks were waterlogged, and the craft did not now even float in the shallows. The shard of sail was still barely attached.

After a few more bites of fruit, he hefted the raft up onto the shore far enough so that the tide would not pull it away. His next thought was a shelter. *Where can I find some shelter to protect myself against the unknowns of this place?*

The morning sun was starting to heat up. Arjun, now somewhat coherent, decided to build a small shelter next to the large boulder outcropping situated just above him on the beach. It would offer some protection from the sun and was surrounded by a small grove of cypress trees to which he added his tattered fragments of sailcloth. *This will have to do for now,* Arjun thought. The island hills rolled on before him. Except for the trees, this place was in every sense of the word: desolate.

With a few more pieces of fruit in his hand, he set out to explore this new place.

CHAPTER THREE

Arjun

Skyros was a bite-size island in the middle of the Aegean Sea. The island had a few fishermen visit from time to time, but there were no apparent permanent residents, he could see that.

Arjun, after walking the shoreline of the island could see that there was only one fresh water source. The spring was located at the base of a small hill near a white marble out-cropping. Water from the crack in the rock provided a refreshing and clear handful with a meager but steady supply.

Water bubbling out of the stone fissure formed a small pool situated in a tiny meadow surrounded by ferns and watercress.

This was the only clean water on the island that Arjun could locate.

The long day alone on the island gave way to a gentle evening and an amazing sunset. He wondered about the Oracle of Selene. *Where was the oracle? Am I on the right island?* He did not know for sure. His wanderings led him to a steep hill surrounded by tall granite cliffs on three sides.

The hike to the top of the hill was a scramble, it was challenging but manageable. Once at the top, the perch afforded a commanding view of the bay in which he was washed up. The groves of wild olive, cypress and oak trees gave way to bare hills and endless views of the sea in all directions. He climbed the hill to its precipice. *There! That's what I'm looking for!*

At the top of the hill, he found a circular granite stone that had all the markings of Selene. The white granite stone was a perfect circle with scalloped edges to simulate moonbeams. The stone was raised in the center and curved downward to give it a convex shape. Embedded in the stone were dozens of star-shaped crystals forming unique arches or curved lines across its surface.

Each crystal seemed to catch the light and send it off in different directions forming the elements of a small rainbow after gathering the evening sunlight. *So this is the oracle,* he thought to himself.

I wonder how it works? Arjun gazed upon the stone as the sun was setting in the western sky. He was treated to the last rays of a glorious sunset. To his left, the moon was rising and so were his hopes of obtaining a message from Selene.

The stone started to glow a brilliant white. The crystals began casting prismatic light forming a sort of electric dome of light over the oracle itself. The ground underneath Arjun trembled.

Arjun crouched a little, and then rested the weight of his body on one bent knee. He looked around to see where he could steady himself from the shifting earth, as a shaft of pure light formed in front of him and seemed to envelop him. In the light, he could see her! The Goddess Selene stood before him. This was no vision, it was real.

Her features were as fair as the moon on a summer evening. She wore a long flowing pure white gown to match her flowing ivory hair. Her eyes flashed of pure white stars, and then they gently cast their gaze upon him.

Selene addressed Arjun:

"I have seen your bravery in battle, and as a sailor. You have the gift of your father Theseus. I know your destiny and your potential; I know how creative you are in solving a problem. I have seen your future. I have seen your past. There is nothing you can hide from my view." This statement did not seem to ruffle Arjun, as he knew he had nothing to hide.

"My son, Arjun, you have proven yourself worthy to be called my Son." Said Selene, as if reading his thoughts, answered a question that had been on his mind since the ship-wreck appearance.

Selene continued: "Therefore, I have decreed before all the Gods, that you are part of my family, my flesh, my bone. And as such, you are now an adopted son of Zeus, and as a son of Zeus and his mistress, you will discover that you are, and have always been, endowed with demi-god like powers.

"If you are wise, you may never be overcome by the influence of magic controlled by Eris and her minions. Beware of the trickery and deceit. Beware of pride. Don't let your pride lead to your undoing.

"The moon will always shine its light upon you. The power of Zeus will be shown in your skill with the sword. I have gifts for you," the goddess stated.

Arjun reached out to receive the gifts: First the Sword of Zeus. It was a beauty! The sword was composed of fine steel and a titanium razor sharp blade with a golden hilt. Inscribed on the handle were the symbols of all the phases of the moon and other intricate markings. The rays of lightning glowed white-hot on the flat rear end of the blade, matching on each side. The blade came to a narrow point that reflected the light from all sources around it.

In the reflection of the blade, Arjun could see glimpses of the future and of the past. He could see the Charybdis the Sea Monster lying on the bottom of the ocean floor. He could see the life of his late mortal father, Theseus.

He could see the marriage of Theseus and Selene, and then fully realized that his biological mother was indeed the Goddess Selene.

In the blade's reflection, he could see a flash of light with a glance of Kiera, and he could see that he was not the only survivor of the beasts' attack; however, he could not identify the men who survived, even though he strained to see the vision.

Flashes of other scenes crossed his blade as well. He placed the sword in his belt and then Selene bestowed upon him another gift. The most elegant steel bow he had ever seen. It was perfectly balanced, and he drew back the string to feel its power.

Selene also gave him twelve silver and golden tipped arrows in a white leather quiver. "These are for your mission." She stated: "Each arrow will be needed if you are to succeed in vanquishing Eris and her minions."

"You will need the help of faithful friends to wield these weapons, however, choose your companions carefully, and beware of treachery."

A passing look of confusion came over him. "My mission?" Arjun queried. "I thought my mission was to vanquish Troy?"

Selena continued. "Your mission is no longer concerned with Troy. I have others that are appointed to that place. Your mission is to enter the Palace of Zurenda, release my people, restore my sanctuary, my temple, my house, and bring Eris to justice for the war that has consumed my people these last ten years."

The Goddess gave him another item.

"I will also give you an additional Olympic sword. The Sword of Ares." She explained with this caution: "You may allow the use of this sword only to that of a true friend."

Arjun looked the sword over in his hands. The sword he now held was as exquisite as the first, and only the markings were slightly different. Arjun's thoughts raced, *how am I going to carry out this mission?* However, it was no use to hide his thoughts from the Goddess.

She knew his thoughts and answered. "My son, you will know what to do and when to do it. The Oracle of Selene has spoken."

Suddenly, the shaft of light disappeared, and the stone's rainbow glow was diminished. Arjun was left to himself to consider and reflect on this visit. When he came to his senses, he could feel the hilt of two swords in his right hand and the bow and the quiver over his left shoulder.

He now realized that he had a mission and it was time to get going. After a little searching along the shoreline, Arjun found an old dingy that had been upended and caught under some roots that were near the shore. He was a little surprised that he had not noticed it before, but relieved none the less.

Getting the boat upright and cleaned out from the weeds, debris and small stinging jellyfish that had attached their soft bodies to the hull; removing them was a bit of a job and became his next task.

After an hour or so, the boat was ready to sail. The small sail was attached to the thin wooden mast that appeared to be serviceable but needed to be tested to be sure.

The other task that needed to be completed was to make some water containers fill them and find some food.

Arjun estimated that this trip across the Aegean Sea could take a few days, maybe a week. He needed to be prepared.

There was enough red clay in the hills above his boat that he could make jars by working the clay in the water in the spring. Arjun took his old sail and gathered clay into the fabric, then soaking the clay, creating a thick paste, and adding some strands of dry grass he began to make some crude jars. This effort yielded several crude jars, and after firing them in his small campfire, they appeared to be good enough and strong enough for holding a few days' worth of water and some food.

Fortunately, there were a few fruit, nut and figs trees on the island and Arjun placed jars full of them into his boat.

Arjun also added some wildflowers and found a beehive in the process. Smoking the bees out of the hive to harvest the honey was not that complicated, but it took a lot of effort. It cost only a few bee stings. It seemed that he was nearly ready to make the trip back to Greece.

His only way to navigate was to follow the sun. He knew that if he headed west, he would hit land, it was just a question of when.

He loaded his gifts from Selene into the craft: Two swords, the bow and the quiver with a dozen arrows. He thought briefly about the arrows. *I wonder how I will end up using these.*

CHAPTER FOUR

Kiera

K iera was a member and the leader of the Kymi Academy of Female Archers. "Ready, aim, release!" Kiera commanded the league of women archers to fire at their targets. Everyone did. The girls were each equipped with a hand-made bow and a few arrows which they brought to the range each week for archery practice.

Targets were set at twenty-five paces away from the firing line. The archery school was half-way up the mountain above the coastal town of Kymi. The commanding view from up there afforded a panoramic view of the Aegean Sea and any approaching ships coming into the harbor at Kymi.

Archery school was not a new invention for the men. The men of Euboea had been doing this for what seemed like centuries. However, with so many of the men out of port, and in various locations between Greece and Asia-Minor including Troy, there was a need for the women of the island to be able to defend each other and themselves if the need should arise.

Kiera was the instructor. A fine archer herself, she could hit a fig with her arrow at one hundred paces.

"Ok, ladies, let's retrieve the arrows and try again." Kiera, acting more like a range master with her commanding alto voice. Six girls all lined up to take another round of shots.

This time, they were shooting at apples for targets at a distance of fifty paces. "Ready, aim, release!" All the arrows went flying to their marks. Only one arrow missed and hit a stone under an apple glancing off the grass below. A second volley of arrows was prepared, drawn-back and sighted. "Ready, aim, release!" Kiera shouted. Arrows again went flying. All the arrows hit their marks that time.

"Great job ladies." Kiera shouted: "Retrieve your arrows." The girls obeyed the command and made ready for a third trial. The third volley was prepared and ready. Each girl had the new target in sight. A fig! This tiny object was sighted at fifty paces. The command to "Release," again came. Arrows flew to new targets with astounding accuracy. Everyone hit their mark.

A cheer when up from the student archers that you could hear across the mountainside. Delighted smiles adorned each face as the girls went to retrieve their arrows for the last time of the day.

"Class dismissed for the day, and excellent shooting ladies!" Kiera complemented their efforts.

Personally, Kiera was pleased with the results. "Class will be held, two days hence," she shouted to the girls as they collected their gear and made their way down the hill and to other daily chores. Kiera had domestic duties as well. She needed to get back to the pier and help process the afternoon catch.

When Kiera was not making war on apples and figs, she helped with the family business and sorted fish on the wharf. This was not her favorite job, especially when there was a weird creature that found its way into the net.

To keep things simple, Kiera wore a white tunic with a white pleated skirt that stopped just above her knees. She always carried her bow and quiver of arrows with her and a small dagger that fit snugly between her loosely fitting white tunic and the leather belt around her waist. The short pleated skirt allowed for freedom of movement and she preferred to wear only ankle high shoes that were very easy to run in. Running from the archery range to the pier took only a few minutes.

Kiera could outrun anyone else in Kymi. For a girl of nineteen, she was turning out to be very beautiful. At least that was the way her father Erastos, saw it. He would brag about his daughter's archery skills to anyone who would listen.

Most everyone, at least everyone in the village could see the truth, however, a father that was very proud of his only and favorite daughter.

CHAPTER FIVE

Kiera

Arjun had known Kiera and her family for years. They had grown up together. Kiera lived all her life on the Island of Euboea, dwelling in the port city of Kymi. Kiera appeared, to all those who only casually knew her, as an ordinary girl.

Kiera's father, Erastos, was a wharf merchant that operated a shop at the local fish market. The market had been a family tradition for generations. Kiera had aspirations to be an archer. Some of the villagers told her she could not do it, but she could do it, and she did it very well. Kiera was also skilled in sail making. With the help of a few other workers, she could produce a sail a day in the shipbuilding effort.

When Kiera and Arjun were younger, they met quite by accident, or was it? Arjun still remembered that day like it was yesterday. He was bringing his boat to the dock and needed some help to secure the moorings. He tossed the coiled rope to the nearest deckhand he could see.

Kiera was not a deckhand; she was returning to her father's fish shop when the coiled rope came flying at her and struck her in the left arm, knocking her to the ground. Arjun, seeing that his aim did more bad than good, managed to jump off his moving boat and land on the dock with a careful leap. He reached down to grab the coiled rope and quickly tied it off to the nearest post. After the boat was secured, he went over to offer assistance to the person that he knocked down.

Arjun, extending a hand to the young maid, pulled Kiera up to her feet. He took Kiera by the right hand and asked if she was all right while pulling her to a stand.

"I'm all right!" Kiera blurted, all the while rubbing her shoulder to work out the sting of the rope's impact. "You need to aim better!" She told Arjun, while her green eyes flashed with a little bit of anger and frustration.

"What if you had hit me in the head?" She queried.

"Sorry." Arjun managed the boyish apology. "Can I help you to your home?" he asked with a tone of inquiry in his voice.

"Very well," Kiera relented, "and you can meet my father too, maybe he will teach you how to toss a rope!" she added with a mischievous smile.

The walk from the pier to Kiera's home was not that far. Kiera was shorter than Arjun by a half a span, but she made up for it with the most golden hair and the greenest eyes which seemed to level the playing field. Kiera led the way as they wove their way to her white-washed home that sat high above the cliffs and had a commanding view of the harbor and their shop on the wharf below.

Kiera's home was small but comfortable, and her father was there to greet her with a tender kiss on the forehead as she came through the door. "Welcome, my favorite daughter." Father hugged Kiera and placed another kiss on her forehead.

Kiera remembered more from that first encounter with Arjun. "And who might this be?" Erastos asked as Arjun made his way into the room.

Kiera replied: "This is Arjun, he is a sailor. He accidentally hit me with a rope while docking his boat, which knocked me down this afternoon and then after helping me up, he offered to walk me home."

A little intrepid, Arjun entered the room and asked if he could remove his gear. "Yes, my boy." Said Erastos. "Make yourself at home, and I will send for some refreshment." One of the servant maids was dispatched at once.

Since that chance meeting years ago, Kiera had grown more beautiful, taller, and stronger.

She was more skilled with the bow than Arjun, and Arjun knew it. While he was in Kymi, they practiced their skills together, shooting at small objects like walnuts and pieces of fruit that would offer archery practice in fine-tuning range, elevation, and even windage if the target was moving like birds on the wing and other small game.

CHAPTER SIX

Lycos

U nbeknownst to Arjun, Lycos was still alive. Lycos was one of the other trireme ship captains involved in the flotilla headed to Troy. Like old friends, Arjun and Lycos spent years sailing together as cohorts and co-captains.

The voyage to Troy was going to be just another routine trip to the sea. Or so they thought. Although the sea monster did not destroy his ship, it was damaged in a manner that was almost as bad.

The trireme that Lycos was in charge of was caught up in a giant waterspout. It was like a tornado over open water. The spout lifted the ship right out of the water and spun it like a top, sending men and equipment flying off into the seawater. Once the waterspout caught hold of the boat's mast, the force of the wind ripped the mast right out of the hull creating a gaping hole right through the middle of the craft.

Unfortunately, this caused more sailors to go flying into the sky and concurrently into the depths. The waterspout also ripped the sail right off the mast. There was nothing the sailors could do in the wake of this destructive force. In addition to that destruction, each side of the ship's hull was torn apart, and the craft began taking on water. After a few tense minutes, Lycos ordered the remaining men to abandon ship.

Another spout was on its way towards them, and it looked like it would finish them off for sure. Lycos and the remaining crew jumped into the turbulent water as a last resort to escape the second spout, now bearing down on them hard.

Dozens of men in the water were trying to hold on to something, anything. Most of the men did not know how to swim and were laden with heavy armor, the weight of which immediately pulled them under, made worse by the gathering undertow and current of a sinking ship.

Lycos and a few others were able to escape the sinking ship and managed to hold on to some half-empty barrels, keeping themselves afloat. This approach was helpful and worked for a little while. Lycos managed to tie himself to a single barrel at the waist with the leather strap from his belt. This maneuver allowed both of his hands the freedom of paddling or plying through the water.

The sun was already heavy in the western sky, and the night was coming on. Lycos realized that he would be alone drifting in the sea, drifting into darkness.

Staying close to the others who managed to escape the ship was no use. A few of the sailors drifted north. Lycos drifted east. The barrels were too hard to control let alone steer. The men drifted in different directions.

Lycos was alone at sea. The water became a little colder as the sun went down. *Where would he end up?* He wondered. He did not relish the thought of getting eaten by a shark or by a sea monster. He dared not make too much noise or vibrations in the water with the worry that this might attract a sea monster or a giant fish.

At least he had his dagger on his belt. He could use that to defend himself if needed.

The night was long, and Lycos dared not sleep on the chance he would miss the opportunity for rescue or worse, fall asleep and never wake up.

Notwithstanding, the gods were with Lycos, (*at least one, he reasoned*). The light of the moon seemed to pull him across the sea to an island that was not that far from his wrecked ship. By midnight, he was on solid ground! And oh! What a great feeling that was! He managed to pull himself through the surf and found a beach where he could rest. His half-full barrel of fresh water was also a blessing. He was able to take a good long drink. And then another. Refreshed he looked for a spot to stay the night. That place came in the form of a small cave, just the right size. Scanning the cave, he quickly determined that there were no unwanted occupants inside either. *Maybe the gods are with me.* He thought to himself.

Lycos was able to rest for the night. The next morning, he found himself looking directly east and into the rising sunrise. This orientation was a helpful reference, and by being a mariner, he was able to get oriented on where he might be.

His stomach was growling. *I need some food*, he thought, *I wonder if I'm on an island or the mainland.* He did not know.

The sunrise was especially welcoming that morning. The rays of suns seemed to strip away any feelings of failure and fear that his ship had been wrecked. But the sun's rays could not strip away the sickening feeling that most, if not all, of his men were likely drowned in the sea.

"Was he alone?" There was only one way to find out. After drinking some more water from the barrel, and finding a few fish in the shallows that he could spear with his dagger, he managed to get a fire started to warm up and dry out, while cooking a hot meal.

He kept his fire small, and he did not want anyone to notice him before he was ready to be seen.

There was too much to do, and too much to think about and consider. He needed time to explore this new place, and time to figure out where he was.

CHAPTER SEVEN

Marcus

arcus was a good sailor. And so were his companions: Jason, Kaleb, and Aedish. Unbeknownst to Lycos, four of his sailors managed a little better than he did after the storm wrecked their ship.

The last time Lycos had seen them was before the storm hit the ship. They had rounded up several barrels while treading water together with some rope and a little sailcloth, they lashed these elements together and formed a sort of tubular raft.

This they managed to climb on to and dry out while the sea current took them on their way to an island that they could barely see in the distance.

Marcus and the men did not know it then, but they were sailing straight to the island of Piperi. Marcus saw land first. "Land Ho!" He shouted to the others. The other three sailors did their best to steer with hands and feet in the water.

All of them engaged in a sort of crude dog-paddling motion toward any land they could reach in hopes of rescue.

Their efforts paid off, at least partially. They arrived on the island before dark and managed to pull the raft up on the shore. The barrels were partially full of wine, olive oil, water and dried apples.

"It was like the gods were watching out for us," said Aedish.

The others agreed, and they went to work making a shelter for the night.

Kaleb was more reserved, and cynical in his opinions. "Our ship is lost!" He said it with a tone of disgust and consternation in his voice. "The other men that were with us are all likely lost at sea, eaten by sharks or drowned."

"And what of our captain? We have not seen Lycos since the start of the storm. Maybe he is lost too." Aedish lamented.

Marcus interrupted: "Help us pull on the rope; we need to get these barrels to higher ground before the tide comes in." Everyone pulled. The barrels were arranged in such a way as to form a modest shelter on the beach. The shards of sailcloth were strung over the barrels to build a small hut or shelter and to offer some protection from the elements. It was time to rest.

The sun had just set, and it looked as though the men were going to be here at least for the night.

The next morning's sunrise was spectacular. Crepuscular rays of golden light penetrated through broken clouds and washed the landscape illuminating the island that lay before them. It was time to explore this new place. Explore they did. The sailors did not realize that they were on the island of Piperi, nor did they care, they just wanted to figure out where they were in relation to the rest of the world and how they could make it back to Athens, back home.

As the men were walking through the windswept forest of oak and wild olive trees, they stumbled upon a trail that looked like it was well used and could provide hope for a rescue. Following the narrow trail for some distance, they took notice of a rock-like structure on the far horizon. It turned out to be a building of some sort. Not a rock as they had supposed.

The trail took them up a small hill and along some very jagged cliffs. Wandering down the countryside, they passed a sizeable cavernous ocean inlet where the waves could be heard crashing on the rocks far below them. The trail continued and began to form into a cobblestone paved surface.

The trail now showed signs of promise, a chariot path and evidence of service animals.

"Horses!" Cried Jason, "a whole herd of them over there," pointing to a distant green meadow without any fences or other restraints.

"Maybe we are on the mainland and not on an island," Marcus said hopefully.

The men came closer to the horses and decided to crouch down behind some bushes. They continued watching from a safe spot, to see if any other people were around.

While they were hiding in the thicket, they noticed several women dressed in battle-gear coming toward the horses and leading them off somewhere to the east.

The women did not look like the ones from Athens. They looked very much disciplined and had the appearance of warriors who were ready to do battle.

"But where, and against who?" Jason whispered.

"What manner of civilization is this?' Marcus whispered back.

"Amazons," Aedish observed. "Let's follow them and see where they go." He suggested.

The men followed the warriors at what they thought was a safe distance to see where the women were going. They were careful to avoid detection. Or so they thought. This idea only worked for a precious few minutes when suddenly they realized that they were being followed and were now trapped by a dozen women warriors on horseback coming up from behind them.

There was no outrunning them, no escape. The men formed a circle back-to-back, and stood their ground without any real weapons to defend themselves, only their wit.

To the Amazons, the men looked tattered and worn out from their ordeal on the ship, surviving the perils of open water, and now this!

One of the women, who appeared as the leader, raised the spear in her right hand over her head as if to stop the others. Horses now encircled the men with finely crafted silver spears pointing at their chests.

"Who are you?" The woman who took a dominant role in the conversation demanded. "What is your business here?" She demanded further. "Speak!" She commanded.

"We are shipwrecked sailors that washed ashore last night." Kaleb blurted. "We were looking for rescue on this island and took hope that we would find that, when we saw the horses." Kaleb offered.

"We did not mean to trespass," Jason added, with a very nervous trembling tone in his already nervous voice.

"Ladies; we have a few more prisoners for the dungeon," said the woman who was clearly in charge. "I am Zedra, Captain of the guard, and these, (pointing to the other women), are my lovely assistants. Bind them!"

CHAPTER EIGHT

Zedra

T he fortress of Zurenda was a short walk away from where the men were captured. It was a dusty march, and the men were deprived of drinking water as they went down the trail at spear point. With hands bound together, and to each other, the men made their way down the gentle hillside and into the fortress.

The hand-hewn rock walls had the appearance of white granite that glistened in the sunlight of late afternoon. As they approached the gate that led into the compound, other women clad in the ordinary dress of the day, not the warrior garb of their captors, stopped and paused to observe the newcomers.

One woman washing laundry in a big pot over an open fire was especially interested in the new guests.

Her face was old and withered, apparently bearing lines from a lifetime of hard work and little reward. Another woman they passed looked at them from the second floor of a small bakery shop. She was beating the dust from a rug outside the window and against a wall of stone.

One younger woman and a few small girls looked up from their work in the vegetable garden as the prisoners passed.

Still, others paused from their duties and took in the view of more men coming down the pathway to, as they supposed, miserable incarceration and eventual death.

Jason noticed that there were not any other men around.

That fact was soon answered by Zedra, even before the question had been asked. "We have no men in this village," she said as the prisoners made their way into the compound and past the outer steel gates. "We do not need them." Zedra further clarified. "All of you will follow Kendra to the dungeon, where you will await your trail." She commanded.

Each man was made to walk through strange grey smoke before entering the dungeon. This choking fog somehow placed a spell on their minds, and it was all but impossible for them to think clearly or rationally after inhaling the substance. It was like each of the men were placed into some dazed state of mind as they entered the stone hallway that led to the dungeon.

The edges of stone step down into the dungeon were covered with some greasy black grime. The stone steps were worn down and almost slick from heavy use or wear. The black grime was everywhere; on the steps, the walls, and the doors.

The odor coming from the palace was at best repulsive. The men were forced down the stairs and pushed through a metal doorway at the bottom. Aedish slipped on the slime and lost his balance in the process. Jason was there to pick him up, but the arm he used to steady his friend was growing weak from the mist.

Once the men were inside the dungeon, the men were repulsed by its lingering and acrid smell, the smell of death. The air was heavy with moisture. A few iron framed beds were visibly chained to the wall. Old straw littered about the floor, and there was only one water source in the room. There was a lead water pipe that ran across a small brass basin and then overflowing, the water spilled on to the floor and ran down a small drain in the corner of the room doubling as a latrine. The only light inside the dungeon was a few tiny windows the size of a man's fist that allowed both air and light into the chamber. The windows were like punched square holes near the ceiling and too high to reach without a ladder or the combined effort of the prisoners.

In reality, there was very little to see anyway, the windows on the exterior wall only permitted a narrow view of the sky or the edge of the ocean in one direction and an occasional shaft of light when the sun was at the other end of the sky.

"Gentlemen, I hope you will enjoy your stay!" Kendra said with a smirk on her face.

The thick iron door behind them was shut, and the men could hear the metal bolts screech into their closed position ending with a final "clank." They were here to stay.

Jason

The compound covered a large area of land. The massive stone exterior walls formed a formidable exterior barrier and outstanding protection. The outer court leads to an enclosed larger courtyard where there was room for raised gardens, fountains, and sculptures. The heroic, but desecrated sculpture of Selene was located inside the Palace's great hall.

The female maidservant quarters and the Amazon guard's quarters were on the left side as you entered the impressively tall iron gates. Rows of dead or dying rose bushes and other like-minded perennials lined the main walk-way covering the plant beddings right up to the chamber doors.

To the right, were grand gathering rooms that had the appearance of temple sanctuaries cluttered with dust and debris.

The walls of the palace were covered with stone - chiseled murals depicting scenes from a by-gone era. An ancient era or period of prosperity for Selene, whose temple this was.

Behind the second set of gates, the wall jutted out enough to accommodate the dungeon stairway and the place where the men were confined.

From those interior openings punching across the top tier of stones in the dungeon, Jason could see everything.

The doors to the palace had the appearance of gold lined with silver, and jet-black hinges and casings. Jason busied himself counting hinges on each massive door before slipping off of Aedish's shoulder, nearly falling to the stone floor.

Jason was relieved that the men caught him as he started to slip. "Well gents," Jason said with a sigh, "we are here to stay. I don't see any way to escape this dungeon, much less make our way to the courtyard and try for the exterior walls."

This news did not detour or discourage Markus. He tried to scramble up the stone wall to the windows to have his own peek of the situation. Aedish steadied his legs while he took a look from the perch above his shoulders.

"It's no use," said Markus, while turning his head over his right shoulder, to address the other men, we are here to stay."

Even as optimistic as Jason was about an escape, his worried voice seemed to choke out these words: "We need to out-smart the guards when they come to open the door. Maybe we can create a distraction so that we can gain some advantage over them and….a….

"And a what?" whispered Aedish, "we have no tools, no weapons, no resources, and we'll be lucky if they decide to feed us before they let us starve to death down here!"

Jason cast his head down with his eyes fixed on the floor. A quick wave of helplessness swept over his face. His tone of voice changed too, and maybe some of his optimism. "Maybe there is a way, but I don't see it right now."

It was getting darker in the dungeon. The sun was going down. The men all realized that this would be their first night in the fortress.

This thought was made worse by the fact that they did not even know where they were. All the men knew was this: They were just a few sailors, prisoners, in a dungeon somewhere in the Aegean Sea....

They realized that they were entrapped by an unfriendly band of women warriors. Amazons! Who apparently hated men.

CHAPTER TEN

Eris

"My beloved daughter." Eris said, "I am pleased with your efforts to capture the men of Athens, the last warriors of the Trojan siege. You will be rewarded once the men are eliminated!" Eris spoke softly over the misty smoke wafting up from the pool of water in the middle of the courtyard.

The pool of water concealed her reflection, but the water started to become disturbed and almost began to boil during the conversation with her daughter. Eris wore a black flowing singular gown that was not entirely transparent, laced with the emblems of her deity. The dress was more like a thin cloud that enveloped her person rather than fabric with point and needlework.

Included in her gown were silvery traces of leaves and branches that were sewn into the seams and were almost too subtle to notice. These objects and a strange assortment of others hung off her shoulders and seemed to float around her terminating just above her slippers.

Her complexion was fair, but her nose seemed a little narrow at the center, and her dark black eyes seemed to glow grey and then red, changing color with the tone of her voice, or with her mood.

The Goddess wore her dark black hair down over her shoulders and nearly to her waist. Thin strands of gold adorned her neck and hung almost to her navel. Silver bracelets or bands were fastened around her upper arms and wrists. Delta shaped earrings of pure silver hung from each lobe.

Each bracelet contained intricate details and images of golden apples in all the stages of the fruit's life; from the trees first blossoms and first budding to a candy red flash across the ripened golden fruit. These flashes seemed to match her mood just like her eyes.

Her ankles were adorned with gold bands just above her golden laced high-heeled slippers.

Only one person dared to look at her with the naked eye. That person was Eris' daughter, Zurenda.

"Zeus must now pay the price of his offensive actions," Eris stated. "We will rise to conquer the world, my daughter." As she now reached out to stroke Zurenda's slender chin and touched it raising her chin to a slightly upward position allowing them to make eye contact.

Now looking straight into Zurenda's eyes, Eris spoke firmly. "We will overcome the oppression of Olympus and the Titans, my daughter. A new order is on the horizon. A new day for the world is ready to burst upon us." Eris firmly stated with conviction and with resolution. "Nothing will stop us!" Eris exclaimed. "I have ordered my creatures of the deep to finish off the rest of the sailors left stranded in the sea. Aeschylus and the other Nereids will do my bidding on the water and you, you, my beloved daughter, will do my bidding upon the land. Soon the world will be ours!"

The delusions continued: "Zeus will soon be relegated to Hades where he belongs! And so will his Mistress Selene! We will topple the statue of Selene and claim this island and this palace for our own. Selene and her righteous ambitions to rebuild this palace will come to naught!" Eris stated as she began to look upward. "All this will be accomplished in good time, my precious daughter."

Zurenda looked down and then to the side, and then up again at her mother. "How can I take on all the men of Athens, and all the gods of Olympus with so few Amazon warriors my Mother?" She questioned. "And what about Selene? Surely she will be crafting a counterplot against us. She will try to stop us!" Zurenda stated frankly.

"I will be there to help you, my daughter. Together we will triumph!"

The water in the pool began to boil again. A grey swirling misty cloud enveloped Eris. Zurenda looked up, and Eris was gone.

She was a little confused but now felt the wiser after the vision. Zurenda walked back through the palace doors. Her guards swung shut the palace doors with a loud clank, then calling to her Captain Zedra. "Bring me a shackled prisoner!" She ordered.

CHAPTER ELEVEN

Arjun

The boat was more like a dingy than the ship Arjun used to prowl the Aegean Sea on his way to Troy. The craft had one seat next to a small mast. The boat was fitted with one rope, that looked like it had seen better days, and it reeked of swamp smell after the water grew foul.

On the bright side, the craft was at least seaworthy. Arjun took it on a few trials out into open water the day before he made up his mind to leave Skyros. All his clay jars fit in the front of the boat leaving him enough room to sit down and guide the craft with a make-shift rudder made from an old piece of drift-wood.

It was time to leave.

The weather appeared calm on the morning of his departure from Skyros. The atmosphere offered just a faint breath of wind from the Southwest. Arjun had lost his compass in the wreck, and so he had to rely on dead-reckoning to set his course. He knew that Greece was to the west, that much was certain. The sun and the stars had already revealed that much information. It had to be there, and there was no other possibility. *Maybe if I'm lucky*, he thought to himself, *I can get close enough to the coast to recognize the harbor at Kymi. If I'm not lucky, I may have to travel on foot to my final destination.* That was a risk he was willing to take.

Arjun had already been on this island for a week. It was time to go. With one last foot on land, Arjun pushed off and took his seat in the boat. The tattered sail was trimmed, and even though it was not a big sail, it was all he had. It would be enough.

The first half-hour on the water was uneventful. Arjun was making good time, and it looked like he would be able to put Skyros in the distance as a dot on the horizon behind him. Soon after this milestone was reached, the sea water began to boil all around him. A thick fog, a steamy mist enveloped him and enclosed his craft, blocking his view from any landmark.

"What is going on?" Arjun shouted to the sky, to no one in particular. No answer was returned. The seawater continued to boil. The seawater was hot to the touch and the boiling action was forming massive bubbles on the surface. *Great, I'll be boiled alive! Lobster style.* He watched as his sail went slack and his modest wake came to a screeching stop.

Arjun knew without a visual point of reference that his boat was not moving forward. *Where will this end?* He thought. Soon the water bubbles started bursting to release hot water and gas on each side of the boat. The floating bubbles would pop over his head releasing water into his craft. "Help!" he shouted! The words were barely forming and barely escaping his chapped lips. "HELP!!!" He shouted louder. It was no use, no one could hear him. "Eris, Poseidon, is this your doing?" He shouted into the thickening fog.

Above him in the mist, he could hear what sounded like ravens flying high overhead, circling for a kill. From the screeching, it sounded like hundreds of them. None of them could be seen; they could only be heard. Shreakish shrills and the sound of beating wings filled the air.

Slimy bubbles kept popping over his boat. Each bubble seemed to have the reflected image of the sea monster he killed only a few days before. The image would stare at him from the surface of the bubble, and then disappear with a "Pop!" Water from within the bubbles and the sticky goo they were made of started accumulating on the deck of the boat.

The floor became sticky and moving his feet about the small craft was getting to be more of a challenge each passing second.

Arjun needed help! Just then an idea popped into his mind. He thought about what Selene had said to him. He thought about his destiny. He thought about Kiera. Maybe this sword can somehow help me. He reached for it.

Carefully, he removed the sword from his cache of supplies, and standing up in the rocking, slime-filled boat, while trying to balance himself as best as he could, he reached the sword heavenward. Holding the sword as high over his head as he possibly could with both hands gripped firmly on the hilt, he shouted to the sky: "BY THE POWER OF ZEUS!" Immediately, a bolt of lightning came out of the sky and connected with his sword. The initial force of the bolt caused his knees to buckle; then the intense pressure of the lightning bolt caused him to drop to one knee.

Gathering all his strength, he then rotated the sword scribing a giant arc in the air above his boat. Dozens of lightning bolts shot out from the tip of the sword in every direction evaporating and incinerating the heavy mist that hung over him. The power of the sword began incinerating the bubbles, the Ravens, and the slime.

Indeed, the seas were illuminated with the flash of a great white light in every direction. Arjun had never seen before, nor had he ever experienced that phenomenon. The malady was over! The seas were calm and clear. The air was fresh and still. Arjun could think again.

Arjun finished kneeling down to rest, and to consider what had just happened. As he sat there, hundreds of incinerated fried and smoking ravens came floating by his boat as far as he could see in every direction. *Undoubtedly this was a surprise that Eris cooked up for me,* he thought, not daring to say the words out loud.

Instead, the words that came out of his mouth were a little awkward but had a familiar tone. "Thanks, Father! Thanks!" Arjun remembered nothing after that. By the next morning, Arjun had arrived in port at Kymi.

CHAPTER TWELVE

Arjun

A rjun was tall for his age. At nineteen, he was thin, healthy and very agile. His blue eyes seemed to penetrate anyone who would look upon him. His flowing blonde hair was restrained only with a thick band of silver around his forehead. Thin-faced and a long, strong nose gave his features a defined warrior look about him.

His heavy leather armor went down with his ship, and a white linen shirt and leggings were all he had to wear.

The trip across the sea did take its toll on his clothes. Rags and tatters were all that was left behind. The sea monster and the rest of his ordeal shredded his shirt.

Arjun was found asleep in his dingy at the Kymi port, bobbing up and down on the surf.

No one could recognize him. No one, except for Kiera, that is. She just happened to be at the dock that morning as Arjun came floating into port. Kiera rushed to him and began without any prompting, to dress his wounds, cuts and scrapes.

Others at the dock soon joined the effort in mopping-up the slime in the bottom of the boat so that it would not capsize at the pier.

Arjun's forehead was covered with sunburned blisters. His lips were parched, cracked and bleeding. His beard was rough and short.

Kiera asked another sailor to bring her a vessel of water. She poured water on Arjun's face and neck to cool and clean him. Next, she used the hem of her skirt to wipe the water away and to dab some more on his blistered fore-head. An old man named James, with a small donkey cart came up to the place where Kiera was. He helped load Arjun into the cart. The watery leg of Arjun's trip was now over.

CHAPTER THIRTEEN

Erastos

The cart was pulled up to Kiera's home. James led the donkey up the pathway with care, so that the cart would not tip over, or otherwise lose its precious cargo of one occupant. When she arrived home, her father, Erastos, and James helped unload Arjun from the cart, Erastos placed him on his own bed to rest.

Several hours passed. Arjun finally re-gained consciousness. After opening his eyes a few times, and wiping out the sand and sleep, Arjun thought he had died and gone to rest in the Elysian Fields. He could see that he was with Kiera and her father again. To Arjun, it felt like home.

Erastos was a kind and gentle man. He was as kind and loving as he was round and plump. His dark brown hair matched his dark brown eyes. Always willing to help a friend would be the way Kiera, his daughter, would describe his gentle qualities.

"Arjun, what brings you back to the village?" Erastos inquired. "We heard the news that the Armada you were in met with disaster on the seas west of Troy. We were worried that you were lost to the whim of Poseidon or Hades."

Arjun explained: "I was shipwrecked by a terrible sea monster and after drifting in the sea for a day or so on a piece of debris I managed to pull from the wreck; it took some intuition, but I decided to sail to the nearest island I could find. That turned out to be Skyros." Kiera and Erastos listened intently to this story.

Arjun continued, "After the incident with the Charybdis, and after a few days recovering on the island, I, by pure accident found a small abandoned skiff and sailed west knowing that I would make landfall somewhere on this coastline."

Erastos interrupted, "There are no such things as accidents! Surely it was the will of the gods that you have come to back to Kymi at this time." He added, "Let me make you some mutton soup."

While Arjun was convalescing, Kiera, always the archer, had noticed the twelve new silver and gold-tipped arrows in Arjun's quiver and asked him for the use of one or two with her practice routine. Arjun shook his head and said: "No," and then told her again. Kiera reached for them anyway. "NO!" He explained to her that the gods had restricted the use of those arrows to be used only as directed by the gods.

"Which gods?" she queried.

"I cannot tell you right now, perhaps later. I'm hungry!" Arjun blurted, as he pulled himself to a sitting position at the edge of his bed.

This comment suddenly changed the subject. Erastos, as if by perfect timing, entered the room with some fresh soup, bread, and olive oil. "Eat this!" Erastos entreated.

The bread was followed up by some figs, and then a piece of pecan pie. Food never tasted so good. Arjun ate one helping, and then another.

After a few more hours of recuperation, Erastos brought some clothing in for Arjun to wear, and after a much-needed bath, he donned the new clothes. Erastos gave him a new white linen tunic and white trousers. He also received new boots and a new leather belt. Arjun felt clean again.

After a little while, Arjun and Kiera set out for a short hike in the hills above her home. While holding hands, their hike took them to the tallest hill overlooking Kymi. It was the perfect place to view the sea, the village, and the sweeping vista. It was a beautiful sight! It was good to be home!

Their wanderings took them to the eastern shoreline of Euboea. They climbed up the steep cliffs and the ravines. Arjun, daring not to leave the gifts from Selene out of his sight, carried his bow, quiver and the two remarkable blades on this excursion.

Kiera was just glad to be outdoors spending time with her best friend. Kiera asked Arjun about the blades and the bow. Again, she only got half an answer. "They are a gift from the gods." Arjun continued. "I have a task to accomplish for Selene."

"Did you see her?" Kiera questioned.

"Yes." This was the only reply that he felt like he could offer.

"Is she pretty?" Kiera probed.

"Yes, she is beautiful but not as beautiful as you." Arjun clarified.

At that response, Arjun pulled Kiera close to his chest wrapping his arms around her slender shoulders. They shared a kiss. Not just a quick 'hello peck,' but a good long 'welcome home and I'm glad you're safe,' kiss.

CHAPTER FOURTEEN

Lycos

L ycos was a tall man, slender for his height and sporting shoulder-length brown hair cut at several odd angles. His hair was cut at an angle that his knife could reach with his left hand up over his head. Needless to say, his hair was a bit choppy above his brown eyes and never symmetrical.

Underneath his silver helmet, the brown mop he called hair, did not matter. Nor did it matter that his clothes were ragged from his shipwreck ordeal on the open sea.

For a young man, the same age as his friend, Arjun, he was resourceful and intelligent.

He never let the odds beat him down, or let discouragement get his goat. His high cheek-bone made him look stronger and feel taller than he was. The physical features helped improve his morale and the morale of others who knew him.

After a quick walk along the shoreline, he realized that he was on an island and it was tiny. The island was about half a parasang in width and three times that in length. No trees grew on this island, only berry bushes and a few thick willows. There was not any small game or wildlife either, not even birds. He was on a desolate rock!

That desolation gave Lycos an idea. He still had the barrel, that rescued him from the sea, and he could make a better raft from the patch of willows that he found nearby. He knew how to make a raft. This knowledge came in his youth as he and Arjun constructed rafts of anything they could get their hands on and test them out in the stream near Kymi.

Sometimes the rafts would sink. Sometimes they would float. It was a trial and error process, but they learned together. Lycos remembered that on one occasion during their youthful play-times, they made a raft that looked like a pirate ship. A ship complete with two levels, a mast and a sail. The pleasant thought made him smile, if only for a moment, until he remembered that the pirate ship they had constructed was made of old discarded boards, a few stolen planks from the lumber yard and unbounded creative willpower. They would ply the banks of the river with playful delight, at least until the assemblage fell apart in the rippling stream and they were forced to abandon ship.

Reality interrupted Lycos' daydream with a thud! He uttered out loud, to no one in particular: "I guess I had better get to work!"

CHAPTER FIFTEEN

Zurenda

In the dungeon of Zurenda, the men all huddled together to keep warm. Each morning, the mist from
the sea would roll in and seemed to penetrate the
walls of this cold, damp place. Waiting for the axe to fall,
or for their fate to happen was not at all the ending the
men were contemplating.

Instead, they were working on an escape plan, but there
were so many challenges and so many unknowns.

"Was the mist coming from an iron vent big enough to
crawl through?" Asked Hadrian, who was already in the

dungeon with a few others before Marcus and his group arrived.

"Could the stones be removed, or is one or two of them loose near the corner where water seems to flow out?" Jason wondered out loud.

"How about the stones on the floor, or under the floor? There is always a secret chamber under the prison's stone-cold floor." Kaleb suggested.

Marcus and the others were willing to try anything to get out. Before they got their chance, the men heard the entrance door bolt slide open.

"Hey, you with the long black beard!" One of the Amazonian guards directed her comments toward Marcus.

Marcus came up to the small iron window in the middle of the wooden door. Marcus had already been shackled in leg chains and handcuffs. Getting to the window in the door took some effort on his part.

"Come with us," was the order from the guards.

The intrepid Marcus, now escorted by two tall guards, treated him with contempt as they dragged him to the open court before Queen, Zurenda herself.

The court had the appearance of a vast vaulted room, gilded arches, Greek columns and stone tracery. The Throne room was about forty cubits square and flooded with natural light from the oval clearstory windows that sat atop the white marble walls.

Just below the arching domes were images of the gods. The room was filled with light. The light was everywhere except on the black stone floor, which billowed the same grey fog that sent swirling eddies of smoke into the corners of the room, and around the columns.

It was like the fog was alive and seemed to have a mind of its own, flowing freely in odd directions. The fog's flow was decidedly unnatural.

From her throne, Queen Zurenda, with the wave of her hand, ordered the guards to bring the prisoner forward.

Marcus, fully chained, was compelled to bow on one knee before the queen's throne.

"What is your name?" She inquired of Marcus. "Marcus!" He answered. "And what is your business in my land?" Zurenda continued.

"With your permission, Oh Queen, I shall tell you in truth. We were on our way to Troy as part of the last flotilla sent from Greece to conquer Troy and spoil the city. Our ship was dashed upon the sea, and all of my men were lost to the deep except these few men that are with me."

"Why were you saved?" Zurenda inquired.

"We know not, except by the will of the gods," said Marcus.

"Which god?" Zurenda pressed.

"Selene, your grace." Marcus answered.

Now leaning forward from her highly decorated throne and chair, Zurenda asked Marcus this question:

"How do you know it was the Goddess Selene?"

Marcus mustered a response: "Her image was etched or carved upon our ship's bow. She is our patron."

The queen stood in front of her throne. Her right index finger pointing toward Marcus and the left fist curled. She demanded answers: "WHERE IS YOUR GODDESS NOW?"

"Has she abandoned you? Has she forgotten you? Is she powerless to save you?"

Finally, in frustration and exasperation, with her pearl white teeth clenched, Zurenda cried: "DO YOU KNOW WHO I AM?"

"No, oh my Queen," Marcus explained as he lay prostrate with his face only a few inches from the floor, "I do not know your name."

"I am Zurenda, the daughter of Eris." Her vivid instruction to Marcus continued. "You will not leave this place! You will not return to your precious Athens."

Zurenda concluded her remarks with this promise: "The only trip you will get is the free passage that goes straight to Hades!"

To her guards, she spoke firmly and calmly: "Send him away!"

Silence came over Markus. He was speechless. There was nothing more to say. He and his brethren were in a den of vipers, sworn and mortal enemies to the Goddess Selene.

This group of Amazons hated men, especially the men of Athens. His mind wanted to focus on an escape, but it was no use. Zurenda's guards were at his side. He was escorted back into the dungeon, through the maze or labyrinth that was somewhere beneath the throne room. The wood and iron door slammed shut behind him. There was no going back.

CHAPTER SIXTEEN

Eris

"**E**ris is an immortal Mud-Cake!" At least she was, according to Selene. The two Goddesses had not been on speaking terms for what seemed like eons. Rather than talk to each other like adults, they used messengers working for Hermes to do their bidding.

The last message Selene sent Eris went something like this: "Why have you kept my sailors captive for so long? Have you no compassion?" Already knowing, full-well, that the answer would be "No."

When Eris received this message, she decided to make it worse for the prisoners and decreed their sustenance be reduced to only bread and water, without any broth. Zurenda was only too happy to comply.

Eris, replying to Selene, again by messenger, told her: "There will be no new ships given to replace the ones which were destroyed." Eris, further explained that, "the intruders, the trespassers, your sailors are scheduled to die for their crimes."

"Of course, that is," Eris reasoned, and almost as an afterthought, "if they do not die of starvation before then!"

Given how frail these mortal men were, she told Selene that Hades would be given notification presently that more souls were on the way!

The Palace of Eris was almost the color of mud. Thick grey mud. Each column in the great hall leading to the Throne room was engulfed or encircled with a thin layer of grey smoke. The walls were made of a thin white layer of smoke and the color or hue of the smoke would change with her mood.

The palace walls were covered with smoky images of destruction and discord the world over. From the jungles of Africa, streaming pictures of Africans fighting between rival tribes to the scenes from wars with a rival state called the Hittites and other scenes from as far away as Asia.

The scenes would change including the most current views of contention in the academically inclined halls of Athens. When her mood would change, the feeling and the atmosphere was always followed by a whiff or puff of blue-grey smoke.

The murals and the scenes of destruction would change from time to time from one distressed place on the planet to another, according to the vapor's whim.

Indeed Eris was the Goddess of discord.

Selene knew well that Eris did not like men, mortal men in general and Athenian men to be specific.

Eris had a plan. "A permanent solution." This project was hatched long ago in the black recesses of her stone cold heart. She was merely going to rid the earth of men in general and anyone who claimed Selene as a patron in particular.

Unfortunately for the Athenian sailors, this plan included Marcus and all the other men rotting away in Zurenda's dungeon.

Eris reasoned that Zeus himself would not even find out about her "plan" until it was too late, and there would be nothing he could do to stop her. He would be power-less, which is right where she wanted him to be.

This action would leave Zeus no choice except to allow the boundaries of Hades to be enlarged, making room for more unfortunate souls, and relinquish some or all of his power to her. The plan was almost perfect, with only one possible flaw: Selene.

Eris continued her string of evil thoughts: *And after I kill all the men in Athens, that favor the mistress of Zeus, he will have no power to stop me from carrying out my plan to the fullest measure.*

Eris' plotting continued, speaking now out loud to her dark enveloping fog, and to no one in particular. "With each mortal male death, I will grow more powerful."

On glancing into the future, Eris predicted that Selene would be a weak goddess, always placing her faith in the kinder virtues of reason, fairness, and forgiveness.

"Well I have news for her; the world is not fair!" Eris uttered! "Life is not fair!"

Eris continued to impart her wisdom to the curling smoke next to her throne. "Experience and treachery will beat youth and ability every time." Eris concluded her ti-rade with these words: "Only a miserable death and an express trip to Hades is fair! Fair by me!"

With the Trojan War wrapping up, it would seem that
Eris was off to an excellent start in removing men from
the planet.

In the short time that Marcus was in the dungeon, there
were three other lost sailors that had joined their ranks in
the dungeon of Zurenda.

The dungeon was running out of room! "Time for
some more executions!" Zurenda told her guards. "Let's
pick the biggest, strongest and bravest man we have in
prison to be the first one eliminated." The guards looked
over the prison roster and decided on a man that seemed
worthy to die in the chamber below the throne room, die
fighting a few young lions, that is. Hadrian was chosen.
The afternoon's entertainment was going to be good!

The guards were summoned to bring forth a prisoner.
It was Hadrian's unlucky day. He was dragged back
through the labyrinth, into the center of what appeared to
be a considerable chamber underground, a few dozen cubits away from the dungeon's door. An Amazon guard
positioned at each side. Once in the room, the guards un-
shackled him and left him standing there in the dark.
Once the guards were safely outside the chamber, the door
was shut behind them, and all sounds went quiet again.

This silence, however, did not last very long. There came a loud creaking noise as Hadrian looked upward to observe the movement of the ceiling in the direction of the sound. The ceiling above him began to separate. First a small crack in the center of the room. Just enough space to let a sliver of light pierce the darkness of the chamber.

The light penetrated the chamber casting a slice of light to the floor upon which he stood. In the light, Hadrian could see shards of bones strewn about the edges of the chamber, and then he noticed that other gated doors were leading into this space. Taking heart, he began to check each one to see if any were loose in hopes of a fighting chance to escape. "Nothing!" He shouted to the empty chamber. His echo: "Nothing, nothing, nothing," reverberated around the room. The crack in the ceiling began to open wider.

Within a few minutes, he could see that the whole ceiling had retracted and women were standing above him in the clearing smoke.

"Release the Lions!" Zurenda called from above the chamber. She was sitting on her throne and had a commanding view into the chamber from the safety of her perch high above.

Another door opened from behind Hadrian. It was a lion. A young female lion! But that was not all. A second door opened and out came a few more lions into the chamber.

This won't end well! Hadrian said to himself, as he looked for a corner in the room to take up a defensive stance with a few large bones in each hand.

As if on cue, all the lions leaped toward Hadrian. A loud blood-curdling human cry went up, followed by the sound of crushing of bones. That was all Zurenda could hear from the viewing deck above.

All went silent. It was over. Zurenda commanded that the floor be shut. "Time for the feast!" She declared, half mocking and half serious. Zurenda, turning her head, cast a last look into the pit as the open floor was closing. The planks of stone that made up the ceiling screeched rock on rock, and then it closed completely, retracting the floor until all the light in the chamber became eliminated. The environment within the chamber retreated into pitch-black darkness, even the sound of lions devouring flesh could not be heard from the palace chamber above.

Marcus and the other men could not hear anything going on in the "chamber," as they called it.

They could only imagine that some foul sporting event was being played out at their expense.

"If we were only able to secure some arms, we could put an end to this," Marcus told the others. "Several men have left our dungeon, never to return since I have been here."

An emaciated and small looking man with a long stringy looking white beard named Gregory came forward from the shadows of the dungeon. He spoke of several men that had been "removed" from the dungeon, even before Marcus and his companions had arrived.

"They are killing them!" He spoke in a raspy whisper. "Seems like one every other day. We have to get out of here," Gregory said. "Who knows, but that you, (pointing to Aedish), could be next!"

CHAPTER SEVENTEEN

Lycos

While Lycos was busy making a raft, he was scanning the horizon too. Always keeping a look-out for passing ships or anything that might get him closer to home.

It was no accident, however, that on the third day of his raft making project he looked up and saw a small boat coming his way. The boat looked like an old fishing boat, a small and little boat that seemed of little or no consequence.

It was, however, a boat, and Lycos needed a boat!

The boat got larger as it came into view and made its way to the shore where Lycos was. Lycos was stunned, it was almost like someone knew he was there and knew what he needed. Lycos imagined that the gods were going to help him this time.

To his joy and surprise, the boat held two persons, only two. Lycos strained his eyes to make out the figures as they were still out in the surf. One of the passengers looked like a woman. How strange, Lycos thought to himself as he strained to see the other person on the boat.

Could it be? No! I don't believe it! *But it is...It's Arjun! But how can this be?* Arjun was in Troy? And who is that girl with him?

Did Arjun desert the Athenian Navy?

Is this a mirage?

Am I going mad?

Lycos was pretty sure he was not going mad. It was indeed Arjun and Kiera. They had come to rescue him!

What a welcome sight! A few minutes later, after a hearty clasp of hands and a long embrace, the three friends were united on the rocky shore of Skantzoura island and catching up on what had happened since the fateful day of the shipwreck.

Lycos said: "How did you know I was here? No one knew that I was here on this rock of an island, except maybe the gods."

Arjun explained: "I saw your reflection in my sword the other night. I could tell that you were on the Island of Skantzoura. I had sailed by here before, and I knew exactly where you would be. I knew that I had to come and get you somehow." Arjun continued. "This small sailboat we borrowed belongs to Kiera's father Erastos. We used it to come for you."

"I'm glad you came!" Lycos exclaimed. "I was about ready to set sail on this, (pointing to his wicker raft), and hope that somehow I could make it to the mainland."

"What about your ship?" Arjun ask.

"It was destroyed in a freak storm about half-way to Troy. There may have been a few survivors, but I have not seen anyone since the shipwreck." Lycos recalled.

Arjun commented: "My ship was wrecked too. Not by the storm, but by a giant sea monster that tore the ship apart. I was the lone survivor and lucky enough to make it to Skyros where I was marooned for many days."

Arjun added: "Finally, after several days, I found an old dingy along the shore in a state of disrepair. I cleaned it, fixed it, and sailed it back to Kymi and to Kiera.

Kiera was glad to see that both of her friends were together again and safe. She spontaneously organized a group hug, and the three embraced for what seemed a long time. It was good to be together, even if they were in the middle of the Aegean Sea, the middle of no-where.

Arjun told Lycos and Kiera that he saw another vision or dream in the blade of his sword the same night that he saw Lycos. Arjun said that there were several sailors, maybe the same ones from Lycos' ship that were washed up on the island of Piperi.

"We must go there now to save them." Arjun declared, with more urgency in his voice than normal. "We must save them from the Lions' den."

Kiera interrupted. "Say what? Lions?" She questioned.

Arjun continued: "We must save them from the evil Amazonian Queen that rules that island." Arjun exclaimed: "We must go there and save them from an evil spell that has somehow gripped that place." Arjun explained: "Selene as my witness, we will go and save them."

Lycos' curiosity piqued over the mysterious blade that his friend had showed him with its strange visions of faraway places and the quiver of arrows which Arjun said couldn't be touched. Lycos had to ask his friend a very practical question: "Arjun, what is up with your obsession with these two blades and these arrows?"

"A gift from the gods," was all that Arjun was willing to offer as an explanation.

Arjun did not understand the full meaning of the blade either, or the arrows for that matter.

What Arjun knew was this: These implements worked together to help find his way home to Kymi and then they worked again to help him find Lycos. Arjun confessed to Kiera and Lycos both, that the swords have some magical ability about them and that he needed to follow the visions upon their surface if he expected any help from Selene.

CHAPTER EIGHTEEN

Selene

S elene was not the only one who knew of the quest, even if this was her idea all along. She somehow needed to keep this information from coming to the attention of Eris for a little while longer if the plan was going to work.

How to keep a lid on it? Selene had an idea. She would create a diversion elsewhere that would draw Zurenda's and Eris' attention from Piperi.

But what? She wondered....

With only a day's worth of sailing away from Piperi, she needed Arjun, Lycos and Kiera to be able to slip into Piperi un-noticed, undetected. Hack their way into the Palace of Zurenda, free the men, and get out without being caught or killed.

Sounds simple? Not really. There was still a sea to cross, no desirable place to hide a ship, and a night rescue was not much safer with the full moon coming into phase within the next day.

"So how do we just hide them in plain sight?" Selene asked, consulting with her courtiers about the problem.

Selene knew that there were a jumble of fishing boats headed that way, maybe Arjun could just join them? Blend in?

The plan was almost too simple, too perfect.

But then, everything I do is perfect. Selene thought to herself.

All these great ideas seemed to flow right into Arjun's head at the exact moment Selene was thinking them. Like their minds were connected with a hard-wire.

And then Selene came up with another brilliant idea! Seemingly too impossible to accomplish! But she would do it! She could do it! She had to do it!

CHAPTER NINETEEN

Arjun

A rjun was learning how to be a Demi-God. He needed practice, lots of practice. The lazy drift over to Piperi did not exactly go as planned.

While learning how to use his new swords, both he and Lycos would spar on deck and practice for hours, with an occasionally unplanned plunge into the sea. Neither of them seemed to mind. Arjun allowed Lycos to use the other sword Selene had given him. The clanking noise of crossed blades attracted the attention of some flying fish, and a few mermaids, but little else. Kiera kept out of the way.

There did not seem to be any spies of Eris or Zurenda lurking about, at least none that could be readily seen.

While below deck, Kiera removed the arrows from the leather quiver and studied them carefully. She noticed that the designs on the shaft of each arrow were different. Kiera found this a strange curiosity. Every arrow appeared to be hand-crafted with raised silver markings that read like instructions on how that particular arrow was intended to be used, and when.

One strange arrow that caught Kiera's attention perhaps more than the others was because it had an image of a sea creature upon the shaft. Another had the picture of a bird of prey. Still, the others had images that changed all the time and did not make any sense at all. One of the arrows seemed to swirl with some strange smoke. *Weird?* She thought. *Maybe the arrows themselves were confused about their targets. Perhaps the images would change later.* She did not know.

Arjun was dead tired. It was late in the afternoon. It was time to lie down and get some rest.

Lycos was at the helm. Kiera was top-side spotting for monsters. The seas were remarkably calm.

Before Arjun lay down, he took one more gaze upon his sword. His sword was shiny but lacked any new images to read or gaze upon. He knew somehow that tomorrow would be a big day. Not sure why, just a feeling. That's the last thing he remembered.

The next morning Arjun woke up feeling good about his decision. He reflected on why Selene had given him two swords in the first place when one would have done the job.

Arjun realized bit by bit that his friends were somehow destined to help him with his mission, even if they had no clue about the purpose or the challenges that lie ahead. He told Lycos that the second sword was his to keep. He may need it shortly. He also informed Kiera that she was to keep charge of the arrows and the bow.

Everyone knew that she was a better archer than he was. He frequently freely admitted that fact, at least to Kiera. She reached for the quiver and the bow as if she was just waiting for Arjun to come to the same conclusion that she had already arrived at days ago.

Sure, she would be happy to wield the bow and the arrows. In handing the weapon to her, Arjun explained to her to pay close attention to the markings or engravings on each arrow; otherwise, it may not hit its mark, or worse, it could be used against her in the process.

Arjun explained that she should only shoot the arrow that must be shot.

"And how am I supposed to know that, sword boy?" Kiera queried, with a wry smile forming on her lips.

"You will know. You will know." Arjun said, "Just trust your instincts."

Breakfast was not that eventful, dried fruit and some bread. "Sea-fare," Arjun told Kiera and Lycos.

Lycos did not seem to mind. He was used to it, he was starving too, and did not matter what kind of food was available. It all tasted good.

While chewing on his dried apple, Arjun told Kiera and Lycos that something big would happen today. He admitted that he did not know just what, but that they should be prepared for anything that the gods or the devils could throw at them.

"We know a few facts," Arjun said lifting his index finger in the air: "Let's review: First: We are on a ship headed to Piperi. Second: We will be approaching it at mid-day, without any cover. Third: We have some evil witch to fight when we get there, and who knows what else? Fourth: Eris may or may not know that we are coming. And fifth: (Holding his thumb in the air), we know that there are some sailors on this Island, maybe in a dungeon or prison or some other dreadful place. Anyone want to add more fun facts?"

Lycos was not the least bit phased by this list. He raised his left eyebrow and muttered "Old hat" while chewing on his last apple slice.

Arjun smiled and then laughed out loud in response to Kiera's gaping mouth. It was show time.

Piperi

P iperi was in sight now. The sun was blazing hot, and Arjun was getting nervous because nothing had happened, and it seemed like nothing was going to happen.

They would be spotted, captured and tortured.

"Great!" Arjun said. "I have led my friends into a trap!"

Lycos kept scanning the shore-line for anyplace that would work for a surprise landing. Only rocky shoals and cliffs could be seen.

"Maybe we are on the wrong side of the Island," Kiera observed. "Let's keep sailing around the east end and see what happens."

Lycos and Arjun both agreed, seeing no better plan at the moment.

The wind was picking up, and the chop on the water was starting to bounce around the little ship. Whitecaps broke over the bow and splashed the deck with seawater and seaweed. Something had to give.

"Something had to happen. Anything, well, almost anything." Lycos stated cautiously.

"We can do without any surprises from Eris." Arjun offered.

"Or anyone else." Added Lycos.

Then, as if by a stroke of good luck, Lycos noticed a small cave at the water line as they rounded the sheer cliffs on the east side of the island.

"Make way for the cave." Arjun declared. "We need to make the cave before anyone notices." He added.

Kiera helped Lycos break-down the sail to make their craft look less noticeable in case anyone happened to be watching…and then the mini-miracle began! The discovery was almost like divine help on tap!

Nothing like anything they had ever expected all of a sudden began to unfold before them. It was the lucky break the team was looking for and needed! This spot gave them the unique opportunity to make landfall at the hidden cave, hide the boat, and figure out what to do next.

CHAPTER TWENTY-ONE

Selene

Selene's other name is "Luna" by the Romans. And Luna had a major surprise for everyone. *This surprise will surely catch Eris and Zurenda off guard.* Selene thought. *No one can even do this spectacle except me. No one is even capable of this stunt except me.* She mused.

While the sun was beating down on Arjun, Kiera, Lycos, and the rest of the world, following its usual pattern for the day, so did Luna, the moon. Luna had only a few hours of lag time. Just at the moment that Arjun, Lycos, and Kiera needed some help, help arrived.

The sky began to darken. Indeed, the whole day turned into night in the blink of an eye. This event shocked everyone! No one understood it. Arjun, Kiera, and Lycos were nervous too; they had never seen this kind of magic displayed before.

"Was it a sign from the gods?" Lycos asked.

"Was it a curse?" Said Kiera.

Whatever it was, it took them off-guard along with everyone else.

Arjun told them both to "relax," he perceived this to be their opportunity to make it inside the cave, secure the boat and rescue the prisoners.

Arjun sensed that Selene had something to do with this darkness and he would thank her personally later if he survived the rescue attempt.

A few seconds more and they would be safely sheltered in the cave. To Arjun's surprise, the cave was fitted with a proper dock, and a tunnel, that led upward into the palace above.

"How perfectly wonderful!" Arjun whispered to the others. "Let's draw weapons now and make our way to the Palace. I'm sure this is the way."

The stone tunnel gave way to stone stairs and then to more stone hewn corridors chiseled from the solid rock.

The tunnel, already lined with torches made the climb easier, and it was clear to see that this was standard access for the people living here.

"Now, where is the dungeon?" Kiera asked, knowing somehow that the answer was up ahead. At the next intersection, they made a left turn and then a sharp one to the right. Her hunch was right!

Arjun called it "womanly intuition," admitting that he did not have any of that stuff!

With weapons drawn, they neutralized three guards that stood watch near the dungeon's entrance, but they weren't there yet.

The Amazon guards were stunned by this sudden change of light to darkness through the tiny portal-shaped skylights above them, coupled with the quick drop in temperature that made them feel extra cold.

Looking upward at the darkened sky above them Arjun measured their progress: "So far, so good."

Lycos said as he readied his blade for the next guard. "I hope this keeps up!"

The dark sky persisted.

The three rescuers advanced further into the labyrinth of tunnels looking for their quarry. Two more guards were taken down, almost without a fight.

"Over here!" Arjun heard men's voices.

"Over here in this cell!" The plea came louder and stronger. They followed the sound.

"Lycos!" One of the men recognized him and shouted from behind the door.

"Lycos, it's you!" Marcus said from behind bars.

"Come and save us!" In an instant, Lycos, Arjun, and Kiera were at the door where the prisoners were being detained.

With his blade, Arjun pointed the tip toward the lock on the door and hacked at the iron lock several times

While cutting, he added these words in a soft whisper, "By the power of Zeus!"

Arjun directed all of his mental energy towards the lock.

The sword shot out sparks of light, a bolt of lightning flowed out of the tip of the sword and into the lock.

The iron lock then glowed red-hot, and in seconds it was sizzling into a dripping pool of metal on the stone floor.

With a well-placed kick, the hasp quickly broke.

"We need to get you guys out of here! NOW!" Arjun shouted as the men scrambled to the doorway. Gregory was still chained to the bed inside the room and could not move. Arjun used his sword again to burn through the chains that held him fast. "The ankle hobbles will have to stay on for now." Arjun commanded Gregory. "Follow me!"

Lycos led the retreat.

Six men followed Lycos as directed and made their way back to the boat without another contest from the guards.

"We must have gotten them all!" Kiera whispered as they loaded the boat with several more men than it was made to hold.

"We need to get out of here!" Lycos commanded, in an earnest whisper.

Everyone boarded the vessel. Even Gregory with his clanking ankle shackles. They shoved off from the cave's dock.

"This is going all too easy," Arjun said. Just as they made their way out of the cave, the full eclipse of pitch-black darkness gave way to bright and full sunlight again. Almost instantly, the sun was at its full strength once again.

"Very strange," Kiera observed, looking over her shoulder to see if anyone was following them.

The rescue was followed up with another question for Arjun. This time Marcus did the asking:

"How did you make your sword become some sort of a blow-torch, back there at the dungeon door?"

"Oh, Um… Well." Sheepishly he tried to answer. "I have this…sort of gift…. I think." Arjun said, stammering for a proper answer, but searching more for a believable explanation.

Marcus could see that Arjun was uncomfortable in answering the question, so he let the matter drop, but that did not end his curiosity about the magic sword.

Kiera was also surprised about this display of power. She asked him privately. Well, as private as you get on a small boat with a bunch of sailors.

Looking at Kiera he frankly stated: "I am a son of Selene."

Kiera also let the matter drop, while she was looking at the sailors behind them in the wake. The crew and sailors were facing a new problem! Just when the boat was clear of the cave, and the sunlight began to shine again; they noticed that they were being followed by not one, but two ships full of Amazon warriors who were closing in on them fast!

"Arjun!" Lycos shouted: "It's time for another one of your miracles!"

CHAPTER TWENTY-TWO

Rescue

Escape! The boat was already sitting low in the water due to its increased burden. The men on board seemed to know instinctively what to do next. Up went the small sail.

"Trim the sail!" Lycos shouted.

There was not a lot of wind. This fact only improved their situation by a few cubits.

"Now what?" Kiera said, with a tone of panic in her voice. "They are gaining on us!"

"We need to get some speed, or we are all doomed to another shipwreck!" Lycos added.

Just then, fire laced arrows started hitting the sea water all around them. The wind and the oars were not enough to move this boat fast enough for an escape.

"Arjun!" Kiera, cried, now in a flat panic.

"What are we going to do now?"

Arjun did the only thing he could think of. He pulled out his sword and raised it in the direction of the oncoming ships.

Arjun shouting the words that worked moments before:

"By the power of Zeus!" Nothing happened!

This miss-fire was not a good time for this problem! With his voice a little deeper, he tried again. "By the power of Zeus!"

Again, nothing! The fiery darts kept coming and kept getting closer to their mark.

The six men they had just rescued took cover below deck and began looking for anything that would float, fearing that the need would arise only too soon.

Lycos had an idea! In a split-second, he raised his sword up to the sky, and with a loud shout he commanded: "BY THE POWER OF ARES!"

Suddenly, lightning came down from the heavens touching the end of his sword, and from there going in a dozen different directions to vaporize the perusing ships. Both ships and their occupants instantly burst into flames. The warriors were jumping into the water to avoid the flames.

Several of the warriors that were already on fire screamed in pain as their hair and clothing burned with scorching heat. Many warriors were like walking fireballs tumbling into the sea while screeching with their last breath.

Both of the chase ships were fully involved with flames. Each of them sunk within minutes. The warriors that survived the sword attack were swimming or scrambling for debris while trying to get back to shore as fast as they could.

The women removed armor, wet clothes, weapons, and anything else they could to prevent being pulled under the waves.

This scene of destruction did not go un-noticed by Zurenda. High from the palace balcony, she watched in horror and surprise as this scene of disaster unfolded upon her faithful warriors. Zurenda was fuming!

Relieved that Lycos' sword worked, however utterly puzzled as to why his sword had not worked, Arjun took a careful look at the two blades.

"Lycos," he asked, "How did you know to invoke the name of Ares?"

Lycos responded only with a shrug of his shoulders.

Both of them critically compared the two swords. They did notice that there was a distinct difference in the markings. The final analysis, however, was inconclusive. Neither of them could tell why one had worked and the other had not.

This difference had not gone unnoticed by Kiera.

"Okay, Arjun and Lycos, 'Sword Boys!' It's time to come clean on these magic swords of yours!

"You can explain it to me," Kiera demanded, while standing between Arjun and Lycos, "and you can explain it to me right now!"

Kiera insisted, furrowing her brow and folding her arms to make the point.

Lycos was the first one to offer an explanation: "When I had the sword in my hand, I felt like saying 'By the Power of Ares,' instead of 'By the Power of Zeus.'" only partially satisfying Kiera's curiosity. Arjun offered this explanation: "I have no idea why my sword didn't work."

CHAPTER TWENTY-THREE

A New Song

There was nothing wrong with the swords. They were both perfectly sound, or so Arjun thought. "The problem was with me," he said loud enough for Lycos to overhear. "When my confidence waned, back there during the chase, and my confidence became supplanted with fear, my sword waned in power." That was the only explanation he could come up with that made any sense.

Deep down, Arjun sensed that he would have to go back to the island and face the Queen. They managed to carry out the rescue without being confronted by her. Maybe he was not ready. Perhaps none of them were. Not yet anyway.

While the three heroes were busy collecting their nerve, and their wits. The men whom they had just rescued began expressing thanks in a most unusual way; they spontaneously started singing a new song!

> *Thanks be to Selene,*
>
> *She has rescued us from death,*
>
> *She has given us new life,*
>
> *She has given us new breath.*
>
> *May her Olympic light yet shine.*
>
> *Oh, may her Olympic light yet shine.*
>
> *And may the one who wields the sword of Zeus,*
>
> *Vanquish foes yet far and wide,*
>
> *The prophecy, the prophecy, the prophecy, to fulfill.*

During the singing, Arjun told Kiera and Lycos that the swords were a gift to him, given by the Goddess Selene, as were the bow and the arrows.

"They were given to me for a specific purpose," Arjun said matter-of-factly. "I will have to go back to Piperi, as soon as we get these men off the boat and in a safe place."

"Well, I'm coming with you!" Kiera blurted.

"And so am I!" Lycos resolutely added.

Arjun was stunned and silenced at this show of loyalty from his friends. "Okay," he said, "we will do this together! But for right now, let's go find some land!"

CHAPTER TWENTY-FOUR

Zurenda

Z urenda exclaimed. "What was the strange darkness? Where did it come from? What manner of
magic is this? Why can't I do this great magic?"
Zurenda had more questions than answers.

"I can't believe that the prisoners and their rescuers got
away! What an undisciplined and undedicated legion of
Amazons!" Zurenda started screaming at Zedra, her Captain of the Guard. "Why did you let them get away?"
Again, raising her voice and screaming at Zedra.

Composing herself, only slightly better than she already had, Zurenda clarified her intent: "Once our surviving warriors have returned from the fire attack, that our 'guests' forced upon us in the sea," she took a long breath, "once they are back to the palace I will feed them to the lions myself!" Zurenda's blood boiled, showing no compassion and no mercy.

Zurenda's complexion changed-up just a little as she made this promise while adding a new threat to her faithful captain. "And you." Zedra. "You will be the first one on the menu!" Zedra was stunned! She suddenly felt betrayed by her Queen! She instinctively reached for her dagger to provide some measure of self-defense. But it was too little too late. Zurenda screeched at her captain!

"Remember what my mother said about the prophecy?" She quizzed Zedra.

"The Warrior from Olympus, the man who can command lightning from a sword, shall be the ruin of my kingdom!" Exasperated, Zurenda turned her back to Zedra and threw her hands high in the air. "Dear Mother Eris, what should I do? Mother! Mother! Mother!"

There was no immediate reply.

CHAPTER TWENTY-FIVE

Council of the Gods

C ouncil of the Gods. Meeting Number: MMLXXI.A.1. c.

Hermes: "With your deities' permission, this meeting is now called to order. Attending are the honorable gods and goddess as follows: Hermes, Zeus, Selene, Eris, Poseidon, Artemis, Ares, and Hades."

Zeus was the first to speak: "The first item on the agenda today is this: Who is the man called Arjun and what is he doing sailing around in the Aegean Sea causing trouble?"

Selene: "Arjun is my son… our son," glancing in the direction of Zeus.

Zeus: "How is it possible that he is my son? I don't even remember him. Is he adopted, or blood-borne? Further, why is he going around invoking 'MY' power and laying waste to every good thing at each port he enters?"

Zeus exaggerated as was his usual style, to make a point.

Selene: "Arjun is my blood borne son. You, my Lord Zeus, are an adopted father to him by virtue of our relationship. He is a Demi-God and as such, is entitled to the gifts, privileges, and responsibilities that any Son of Zeus would deserve." Selene, more than a little ruffled by his question added: "Do you wish me to discuss further, my Lord, the details of this adoption in this public forum?"

"I get your point, Selene, my sweet," Zeus replied, realizing that she was right…again! Turning to Hermes who was taking notes, he remarked "let the record stand."

Poseidon: "I have a question for the Mistress Luna. Why did your son Arjun kill my pet of the deep? Charybdis never did anything to harm him."

Selene: "My son was defending himself and his shipmates. 'YOUR PET?' She questioned. 'More like YOUR MONSTER!' A monster that was trying to kill him!"

Poseidon, with a smirkish smile stated: "Very well, you are no fun at all today!"

Hades: "I think you all are missing the point here! The point of this meeting is that this man, Arjun, is disrupting my alliance with Eris, and I can scarcely get anything else done in a day, except going around cleaning up his messes."

Eris: "Something needs to be done! My Amazonian daughters were deeply humiliated by this up-start of a Demi-God. It should not be so!" She added these words to make her point: "This upstart warrior needs to stick to his own business of killing Trojans and leave the business of…" Eris stopped and caught her breath, not finishing the sentence, especially while in the presence of Zeus.

However, it did not take much imagination for everyone else to figure out what she was going to say next, or rather, what she did not say.

Zeus: "Okay, this 'Son' has obviously learned that he has some demi-god like powers, even though Selene and I have done our best to shelter him all these years by placing him with a mortal family, in a sleepy backwater village of rural Greece." Zeus pressed the question: "Did someone run off and tell him he was a Demi-God? Well?" Zeus now, looking at Selene right in the eyes, only to receive a shrug of her shoulders and distant nonchalant glance back from her.

Selene, responded to the question after several tense seconds, "I confess, I did help my Son recover from a nasty shipwreck brought on by Eris and Poseidon," casting a steely glare in their direction. "I was only trying to help him survive. I may have imparted to him, some 'gifts' at that time to comfort him and encourage him."

Zeus: "Well, it is plainly obvious to me that he has learned a few things about being a demi-god. What about Cassandra's prophecy?

Eris interrupted. "Your Lordship, I perceive that Selene is up to something. I cannot have this boy running around getting in my way. I have important projects that I'm working on that must not be interrupted by an immature boy with an Olympic Sword. You must do something to stop this menace, or I will take matters into my own hands!" With that said, Eris rose up from her chair in an indignant display. Her black and grey clouded covering was barely keeping up with her swift movements. "I shall sow forth more discord if I don't get my way!" Eris threatened.

Zeus added some common sense to the discussion. "We are not here to start a new war," now pointing his right index finger toward Eris. "You have had spilled blood enough with this Trojan War. That war was started by none other than you!" Eris smirked during his lecture. Zeus continued: "How many more mortals must die because of you! You are excused from this meeting!"

"This Council will hear no more of your petitions." With this edict from Zeus, Eris recoiled and then drew her bodily form into a cloud of grey smoke, disappearing in a puff!

Selene: "Let me, your Lordship, train the boy. He needs more time and more training before The Prophecy can come to pass. Surely you have observed his bravery in his daring rescue and subsequent escape from Piperi. In fairness, however, he has only half-finished the job that the Oracle gave him to accomplish. He has two mortal friends that will help him. He just needs some more time."

Zeus: "More time is hereby granted, my love. You have a few months to train the boy. I can offer no more guarantee of power, or promises of protection after that."

"Then the meeting is adjourned?" Hermes asked with some hesitation.

Zeus: "Not yet."

Hades piped up: "I am already processing several new arrivals from the last lion feeding by Zurenda. How much more space should I make for any new arrivals?"

Zeus: "You had better make room for more, many more. This war is not yet over. In the end, you will need to employ extra security over certain individuals, who I don't want ever to get out!"

Hades: "As you wish, my Lord."

Hermes: "That reminds me, topic number two, your Lord, if I may…"

Zeus: "You may proceed."

Hermes: "Artemis has filed a complaint that one of her very best bows and a quiver along with twelve Olympic arrows have gone missing."

Zeus: "That reminds me, I seem to be missing one fine Olympian sword."

Ares piped up: "I'm missing a sword as well. That was one of my finest swords too. I wonder where it has gone?" Ares' golden eyes flashed the color of fire and then cooled to reflect his change in temper.

(Both of the Gods were now looking in Selene's direction).

Zeus: "Selene, what have you to say about these missing articles my dear?" Her sheepish facial expressions betrayed her deed, together with her undeniable look of guilt. Before she could answer, Artemis spoke up.

Artemis: "Your Lordship, I perceive that Selene's son needs these items to accomplish the task that the Oracle of Skyros has given to him. If you, gentlemen, will allow the use of your swords, then I will allow the use of my bow and my arrows." Artemis continued. "At least lend them for a few months, and we shall see what this newly found demi-god can do."

Zeus: "Request granted. I want this mission to succeed."

Hades: "Lord Zeus, so do I." the God interjected, "I have a vested interest in the outcome as you already know."

Hermes: "Any further comments or a new agenda item?"

Ares: "I have always been a big fan of war as you all know, but this mission, if successful, will put me right out of business. What will I do then?"

Zeus: "Ares, there will be more wars in your future as I'm sure you can foresee," commenting on this topic; in what seemed an almost nonchalant way. He began to clean his nails. Zeus looked up and then added: "But this mission for Arjun is about the Trojan War and the sinister and surreptitious goals of Eris and her daughter. We need to wrap it up."

Ares: "Very well, Sire, let this mission succeed, and I will stand-down, and I will not interfere."

Selene: "I just want to thank you all for your support. I know that I may have procured materials in the wrong way, and for that I am sorry; however, I appreciate your forgiveness and your understanding."

Hermes: "Anyone else on this topic? Seeing none, I propose that this meeting be adjourned."

Zeus: "This meeting is hereby adjourned. That will be all. Thank you!"

Selene's facial expressions showed visible signs of relief wash over her face given the outcome of the meeting. She knew that she and Arjun had a few months to get this mission completed. A few months to save the world.

CHAPTER TWENTY-SIX

Selene

"Well, that did not go so bad." Selene said under her breath to comfort herself as she was leaving the chamber and heading back to her quarters.

As she was leaving, Zeus reached out and caught her by the elbow, pulling her close to his chest. Close enough for a hug and a kiss. Then looking into her crystal clear eyes and holding her by the chin in a tender way said, "My dear, make sure that our Son does not fail." Then he added. "We must rid the Olympiads of Eris' menace if there will be any peace restored to mortal men, Athenians, and the House of the Gods!"

"Yes my Lord," Selene said, with a soft and gentle voice, managing a meager smile. "The boy will not fail. Our son will not fail!" She replied in the kindest feminine voice making Zeus lose all concentration. All the pent-up anger or frustration just evaporated away. *Like magic,* she thought, even if the anger and frustration directed at her was well deserved.

After Selene was in the clear, she straight away determined to do the one thing that would help her and her son Arjun to succeed. She walked immediately down the Olympic Palace corridor to the women's chamber to have a heart to heart talk with her best friend....Artemis.

CHAPTER TWENTY-SEVEN

Zurenda

In the Palace of Zurenda, still holding her hands high in the air, The Queen begins to lose hope that her mother Eris will answer her plea. This absence of communication with the deity only hardens her heart and strengthens her resolve. Now, with her fists clenched she orders the execution of her Captain of the Guard, Zedra.

Zedra, feeling shocked and betrayed, made a motion for her dagger, instantly realizing however, that she had already been disarmed by Zurenda's magic; her dagger was already careening through the air and sailing down the corridor well out of her reach.

Zedra then began to tremble and beg the queen for her life. Two guards standing just behind her, on Zurenda's command, bound her feet and then her wrists, making them secure behind her back as the sliding floor beneath her began to open.

Zedra lost her balance during the process. The floor opened wide enough to allow the Captain to fall backward into the pit, hitting her left shoulder on the edge of the stone floor as she fell into the pit. In the process of falling, her thin body rolled a little to the right. This action caused Zedra to fall face first into the lion's pit.

Zurenda ordered the floor closed immediately. Only the muffled cry of the lions and the muffled screams of Zedra could be heard from above the chamber. The floor had already shut tight. It was over. Zedra was dead.

"Send for Kendra!" Zurenda demanded from the two remaining guards attending the queen in the throne room.

The Amazonian guards were dispatched immediately to bring forth the she-warrior.

Presently, Kendra was in the palace throne room standing before Zurenda, she addressed the agile warrior with her kindest voice, while staring into her sky blue eyes, and caressing her noble chin. "Kendra, my faithful and dedicated Amazon. Effective immediately, you have been appointed the new Captain of the Guard." Zurenda explained further: "Your task, whether in life or death, is to capture the man called 'Arjun,' and bring him to me alive that he may be tried for his crimes against our people!"

Kendra was a little surprised at the news, but prepared for this assignment, and was ready, and willing to fulfill the wishes of her Queen.

Kendra took a step back from her Queen and bowed with her right arm swinging across her chest in a sort of circular motion. "It shall be done, my Queen!" Kendra then turned around and left the room.

This new assignment left Kendra to wonder about her predecessor Zedra, but only for a fleeting moment, her only thought from that moment forward was to capture Arjun and bring him to justice. Kendra consulted her guards. "Where should we start looking for this man called Arjun?" She asked.

One of the guards suggested that a place to start looking might be on the island of Euboea. "There you will find him," Aeila said with resolute confidence. "There you will find him!"

CHAPTER TWENTY-EIGHT

Kymi

L and was spotted late on the second day at sea. Everyone was getting a little cramped in the small boat. The drinking water had run out. The men were getting irritated after being crammed in such tight quarters. They tried hard to be grateful recipients of their daring rescue; however, reality was setting in, and everyone was dying to be somewhere else. Lycos kept himself busy by filing the remaining shackles off the men who still had them around their ankles and wrists. This service was productive and appreciated.

Kiera did not like the boat ride either. She was the only woman on the boat, which made the voyage more uncomfortable for her.

The group of refugees finally placed a foothold on friendly soil. Home turf, Kymi.

Being back in Kymi never felt so good! Kiera was the first one off the boat.

Erastos was there to meet them. "My beloved daughter!" Erastos shouted above the noise of the fish market He pushed to the side boxy pouches and other odd shaped containers in his path that were strewn around the pier. "Come and let me embrace you!" The two met and exchanged a warm embrace, followed by a traditional kiss on the forehead for Kiera.

Next, Arjun came into his view. He was busy helping the sailors unload and find some much-needed water, making sure that their need of nourishment was satisfied before his own.

"Arjun!" Erastos belted in his baritone voice. "I'm so glad you have made it back to port, with my daughter and the others!" This declaration was followed by another round of kisses and hugs, in plain sight of all the dock hands sorting their daily catch.

"Have you found a place for your men to rest?" Erastos quizzed Arjun.

"No." Reported Arjun.

"I will feed them all at my home." Erastos insisted.

The men from the boat followed Arjun and Kiera until they had all made their way to the white-washed home perched on a cliff.

Erastos told the men: "Passage will be arranged for each of you to return to your homes in the morning. Tonight we celebrate your return!" He declared. "You are all heroes of Greece! Tonight you are my guests!"

This generous gesture was a help and comfort to Arjun. He chose to sit on the outside balcony and watch the sea. Good food and good drink followed as he sat there with Kiera and Lycos and made plans to return to Piperi.

"I have to go back and face her." Arjun told Lycos and Kiera. "And I don't feel very prepared," he confessed.

"Who am I that I can take on the Daughter of Eris? She has more magic than me. She has more power than all of us put together." Arjun was looking for some confidence, comfort, and team building. Arjun sighed, and his shoulders drooped a little as he contemplated the task that was at hand.

"Okay look here, Sword Boy!" Kiera said without any hesitation and or any reservation. "You're not going to Piperi alone! Lycos and I will help you;" she raised his chin to meet her insistent but comforting eyes.

Lycos piped up. "We can do it together!" He reassured his friend of many years. "We were able to rescue the men with help from the gods, then why not go back and vanquish the daughter of Eris?"

"Sounds simple," Lycos mused. "We just sail back there, storm the palace and vanquish her minions and then defeat her. What could go wrong?" Lycos added with growing confidence.

"And what about these special 'not all the time fully functional' Olympic swords?" Arjun queried. What if they don't work when we need them too like mine did not work on the boat. Then what?"

Kiera was more perceptive than both Arjun and Lycos at the moment. "Don't you guys remember the great darkness that fell on the palace at the instant that we needed to get in and get out? How was that done?" Arjun answered, "By the gods, of course."

"Then let the gods help us out again when we need it the most." Kiera proposed.

"We will get help from the gods." Arjun reassured, "I just don't like the mystery factor in all of this, and I would like to know how the operation will happen before we have to make up stuff by the seat of our pants."

Lycos interjected: "I think that the arrows you gave to Kiera will help us figure this out. They are a gift from the gods, and we have not so much as used any of them yet."

"Yes," Arjun noted, "We have the arrows. We also have the swords. Lycos! Look at your sword right now." Arjun said with a voice full of surprise and wonder. It was glowing white-hot silver, in its sheath and emanating a brilliant white and bluish light."

Lycos did as directed. Arjun observed that the Sword of Ares had a vision upon it. All three of the friends could see the vision on the blade clearly.

It was not a vision that anyone was expecting. The vision was an image of the northern mountains.

"Olympus! Really?" Kiera questioned.

"Why go to Olympus when Piperi is the other way?" Arjun said.

No one knew the answer, at least not yet, but they all understood the message. They must first go to Olympus.

CHAPTER TWENTY-NINE

Kendra

K
endra was no less a warrior than her newly dead
sister in arms, Zedra. However, because of the
spell which Zurenda had cast on her mind, she
was a vassal that would do whatever task that may be
commanded of her. Kendra perhaps did not even realize
that her sister in arms was dead.

The execution and elimination of Zedra was all too
convenient, (at least for Zurenda), and no one knew that
could do anything about it, or had any clue of what was
going on, or the presence of mind to stop Zurenda's bru-

tality – even to her loyal warriors. The guards that were in the room when it happened just did their duties in stoic silence while the fury of a demi-goddess had been unleashed on an unsuspecting mortal.

But none of that mattered to Kendra. She was on a mission. She was going to capture and bring back alive the man called Arjun. What he looked like, she did not know. Where was he? No clue. Only the stubborn will of Eris or Zurenda could guide her to Arjun. It was clear that no one else would.

Kendra was a tall woman, slender from her shoulders to her waist. Her blonde hair was cut just above her waist and braided into a single plait. At the end of the plait was a silver clip, threaded together with a silver pin.

This silver clip managed to hold the braided assemblage together.

All of Zurenda's 'she-warriors' wore the same uniform. Kendra was no different in that regard. She was different when it came to hunting. Kendra could find anything, anyone, and anywhere. She would put a hound dog to shame when it came to tracking prey.

Zurenda knew that attribute and exploited this gift to her advantage. Kendra wore a dark tunic and a multi-sectioned leather skirt that extended from her waist to just above her knees, including high laced shoes and leggings.

In addition to the others, Kendra sported a golden waistband and an assortment of chain mail and straps of leather armor to cover her upper core.

Kendra wore a silver necklace that had the emblem of the Amazon Nation stamped upon it. The Greek letter 'Δ', delta.

The letter was upside down so as to look like an inverted Greek Δ.

This emblem was worn to symbolize the triangular relationship of the Amazonian warrior, Zurenda the demi-goddess, and the Goddess Eris. Although her warriors did not know it, this was the object that Zurenda used to control them and order them about.

But none of this mattered to Kendra; she was on a mission. She was not sent alone, however. Zurenda appointed a dozen other warriors to travel with her.

Zurenda knew that to accomplish this deed would not be an easy task.

CHAPTER THIRTY

Erastos

For the men recuperating at Erastos' home in Kymi, the war was over. News of the fall of Troy and the victory over this foe was bittersweet.

Aedish lamented to his brethren "I wish we could have been there to see it in person."

Jason added his lament: "This would have been my first battle. The sweet taste of victory, but it was not to be."

Even Marcus added some perspective to the conversation: "What's done is done, my brothers." And then with a sigh, and drawing another deep breath, "At least we did our duty to Athens, and to our homeland, Greece. Now it's time to write a new chapter in our lives. As for me, I'm going back home to resume my work as a sculptor."

Aedish was not as prepared to go home. "I wish I had a place to go home to. This mercenary life is the only life I have ever known, one bloody battle after another. I suppose I will make my way to Athens and enlist for the next conflict."

Marcus was almost of the same mindset, however, he wanted to get back in the water and sail his father's merchant ship from Athens to Alexandra. "There is still plenty of trade to do on the water. And now with the threat of Troy over, maybe I can seek my fortune on the waves of the Mediterranean."

Kaleb pipped up: "I wish to go back to the farm, life is simpler there."

Gregory told everyone that his trade was that of a blacksmith. "I'm going back to Athens and start making more implements for war. War is good business," he added with a wry smile.

Jacob surprised everyone when he declared that he was going to set up a shop here in Kymi. "To sell flowers," he offered unapologetically.

Jason told everyone that he wanted to take a journey into the North counties, find a place there where he could start a new life, take a wife and settle down.

Gazing off into the distance as if he was already there, Lycos had other plans. He told the men: "I will help Arjun and Kiera complete a mission and then decide after that what to do with the rest of my life, assuming I survive," adding these last few words for comic relief.

Erastos encouraged: "Have some more food and wine, my brethren. Please help yourselves."

By then the evening was wearing on, and the men were ready for some sleep. Erastos tried to make the men as comfortable as he could, choosing to sleep on his home's roof and giving up his bed for the night so that these heroes of Athens could rest undisturbed in the relative safety of this island port. This place called Kymi.

"Sleep well my brethren." Erastos encouraged, and then oil lamps were blown out.

CHAPTER THIRTY-ONE

Erastos

T he journey to the forest and the mountains of Olympus was going to be several days, if not a week. There were still a lot of obstacles to face, including the channel of water between them and the mainland. Fortunately, getting to the mainland would be possible, as ships and boats were crossing the straights of Euripus all the time. Catching a ride on a merchant's vessel was routine, and maybe the most "normal" activity that they could do while traveling West.

The threesome planned to take less used paths to avoid encounters with Amazons and monsters. This necessitated that they did not take a direct route to Olympus.

Erastos gave them some fatherly advice: "After knowing what you three are up against, I suggest you keep a low profile as you make your way to Olympus. No doubt there are others who may be aware of your mission and may try to stop you if they can."

Erastos continued his caution: "Don't speak to anyone, and try to blend into the background." And then he added: "By the Gods of Olympus, I believe you can do this, but," he added, "you must also believe in yourselves too."

Erastos added one more nugget of wisdom:

"The women warriors known as the Amazons are fierce. They have a feared reputation that spans the known world. Local myth states that they originated in Scythia, but we have heard tales of the warriors infesting the land of the Aegean. Surely this Queen of Piperi you have spoken of is one of them."

Erastos added this final caution: "Be careful and aware, keep each other's backs and never let your guard down."

Erastos gave Kiera an affectionate kiss on the forehead, and they were off.

CHAPTER THIRTY-TWO

Chalcis

While at the harbor of Chalcis making ready to cross the Euripus Straights, Lycos noticed a small group of women, about a dozen or so, that looked a little strange to him. The women were all wearing battle clothes underneath togas, and that seemed out of place for this location.

Women in Greece were not even allowed to go to battle, much less wear the implements of war. The women tried to disguise their battle clothing by posing as merchants and street vendors. The white togas and the clothes of the ordinary folks were somehow not quite right in the mind of Lycos.

"We need to get out of here!" He told Arjun and Kiera. "I think that those ladies over there near the wharf are following us," Lycos added with concern.

"I think you are right, Lycos!" Arjun agreed. "Let's sprint down this dock and get on the boat that is just leaving."

Kiera shouted: "What about the food we were going to buy?"

"Forget it!" Arjun told her. "We need to get out of here now!"

There was no hesitation. After a quick sprint down the dock, and a long leap onto the departing boat, Lycos and Arjun managed to make it into the craft. Kiera's jump was a little short. Splash! Kiera went all the way under the surface of the water. Coming up for air, Arjun extended his arm to pull her to the side of the gunwales.

Spitting and coughing, Kiera was pulled from the water into the ship by Lycos and Arjun. A blanket was handed to her by one of the other passengers on the boat so she could dry off.

No sooner than the three friends managed to make it safely into the craft, the women that Lycos suspected as warriors were standing at the dock. Their togas came flying off, and they started shooting arrows at those in the boat, barely missing their mark, but hitting the water around them instead.

"Whew!" Arjun said with a sigh of relief as they crouched down in the boat. "We were almost captured by the warriors of Zurenda. I'm sure of it." Arjun reasoned. "As Erastos said, we need to blend into the background."

The boat captain turned his head toward Arjun after noticing the attack. "Who are you? And what is your business here?" He demanded.

"We are…we are um.. Pilgrims on our way to Athens." Arjun offered in response.

"Why were the Amazons trying to kill you? You don't look like pilgrims! You look like… like thieves!" The seasoned captain observed.

Arjun ducked his head a little searching for an answer to give the captain and noticed out of the corner of his eye that several arrows were embedded in the gunwale of the boat.

"Pulling one out and observing it, Arjun commented: "This arrow is a gift from Zurenda." He clarified. "Look at this delta symbol on the shaft."

From their position in the stern of the boat, they could see the folks at the pier running around in sheer panic, and scared silence as the warriors of Zurenda took their fury out on the crowd near the dock, for having missed their mark.

The boat captain was not pleased with Arjun's 'pilgrim' answer, but he let it go. They were finally underway. "Pay me three drachmas in gold, and I will forget that you were ever here," the captain ordered.

Lycos handed him a few gold coins. The matter of payment was settled. They were on their way.

CHAPTER THIRTY-THREE

Artemis

Kiera was used to swift traveling. This trip made better because she was with her friends. However, sometimes this became awkward for her and stops took longer than they had planned. The threesome did not know where they were going. The trek to Olympus was going to cover new ground for each of them. They only knew that they were heading "Northish," and that was enough to keep them going.

Kiera was learning to travel light, however, and she was no slouch. She did her best to keep up with the boys as they leaped off the dock on to the mainland and sprinted up the cobblestone streets looking for cover and the opportunity to "blend in," as Erastos had counseled.

After night fell, they came to realize this would be their best time to travel. That opportunity came sooner than planned or even expected. A few horses came into their view. The horses were being stabled in the fields just west of town. This was the transportation opportunity they needed.

Finding the owner nearby, and after doing some haggling, they managed to purchase three horses with the gold drachma pieces Kiera had thought to bring along.

Traveling by horseback gave new meaning to their night flight. Now on a dead run, the threesome headed north to Olympus.

A couple of hours had passed as they rode, and Lycos spotted an old abandon farm barn where it looked safe enough to spend the day resting. The old farm had a few mature apple trees in the side yard next to the pen in the back where the horses could rest and water.

While they were there, resting and watering the horses there was a bizarre sort of knock on the door. Tap. Tap. Tap.

The hair on the back of Arjun's neck stood up straight. His first thought was that the Amazon Warriors had found them. He dared not open the door. Instead, Arjun and Lycos both drew their swords, and Kiera with her bow drawn, crept out the barn door and around the stables to a place where she could get a better view of the front entrance. Arjun and Lycos followed close behind.

From the hedges near the road, they could see that the visitor was a woman wrapped or covered loosely with a grey blanket, but she had the most elegant silver bow.

"She is not an Amazon," Lycos observed. "At least her appearance would suggest otherwise."

"Could it be Artemis?" Arjun whispered to the others with a surprised look on his face, a facial expression that Kiera had not noticed before.

Artemis was using the tip of her bow again to knock on the door. "Tap. Tap. Tap." She tried the door again.

They had to be sure; Arjun was "done" with surprises for the day. He was not ready for another one.

"Who goes there?" Arjun shouted from their vantage point near the barn.

"Arjun! Hurry and let me in!" The woman at the door demanded.

"How do you know my name?" Arjun asked.

"I am here to help you, and your friends," Artemis said in a reassuring voice.

"How shall we know you are a true friend?" Arjun questioned further while lowering his sword just a little.

"I have been sent here by your mother, the Goddess Selene." Artemis clarified. "I am here to help!"

At this news, Arjun's defenses dropped completely. "Very well, you may come in." Arjun relented.

Kiera kept the bow and arrow trained on the unexpected guest until Lycos insisted: "Kiera, lower your weapon, it's okay." Reluctantly, but obediently Kiera did as directed.

The threesome just became a foursome.

Artemis managed while visiting the team, to conceal her immortal brightness from the group so they would not be incinerated in her presence. She kept her countenance as nearly mortal looking as possible.

The rest of the day passed in relative quiet. Introductions were made, friendships forged, and tensions were eased.

In the barn, as night began to approach and the light of the stars seemed to punch burning holes down through a separated plank on the roof, they took more time to introduce themselves and to break bread. There was so much to talk about, and so much to catch up on. However, Artemis was direct and to the point.

"The Goddess Selene has sent me here to help you in your training."

"Training?" Quizzed Arjun.

Before she could get another word out of her mouth, Artemis emphatically added: "But we need to get to a safer place."

"The vision in the blade told us to go to Mount Olympus," Arjun told Artemis.

"I gave you that vision, Arjun. I needed you to get here." Pleased with the result the goddess added: "And now here you are here!" Artemis said, smiling just enough to reveal a perfect set of pearl white teeth, surrounded by an immortally perfect female face and overall complexion.

Toning down on her immortal brightness, Artemis removed her grey hooded blanket to reveal several braided golden ribbons in her electric white hair.

Arjun glanced back down in Kiera's direction as Artemis' person, even toned down, was almost too beautiful to gaze upon so as not be overcome by her immortal beauty.

"We will get you to a safer place." She added. "We must leave at once!"

That's the cue that Lycos needed. Kiera and Arjun decided to share a horse and allow their honored guest to
have one for herself.

With a crack of the whip, they were off. Artemis took
the lead; they were not going to take the main roads, rather
choosing to sprint through the undergrowth of the forest
that led to the western slopes of Olympus.

Kiera enjoyed the ride holding tightly on to Arjun as
they dodged through the forest. It was good for her to be
close to Arjun again.

CHAPTER THIRTY-FOUR

Aeolia

"Aeolia! We have arrived at Mentor Meadows," Artemis announced. The sun was
just breaking over the hills to the east. At
one point the sun seemed to rise right over the top of
Olympus and scattered crepuscular rays all over the valley
in which they were staying. The horses seemed glad to be
here as well and were turned out into the meadow for
feeding.

"This is our training camp!" Artemis announced once
again. The camp was situated within a tall forest of ever-

green trees that had an essence of protection and strength about them. A small stream ran through the middle of this grove and there was a clearing that had just enough room for outdoor training exercises.

"I have commanded the dryads, oreads, hegemone, and the other earth spirits, to protect you while you are here," Artemis reassured. "The imps of Eris will not find you here," she stated confidently.

Arjun, Lycos, and Kiera took a good look around.

"Artemis is right," Arjun said. "We will be safe here."

The accommodations were very "back to nature."

Lycos and Arjun were assigned to a dug-out that looked a lot like a beaver mound in the middle of a small pond nearby. Their home was a residential mound, complete with a human size entry door which had been constructed by the beavers.

"I sure hope the beavers don't mind us moving in with them," Lycos stated.

"They will be happy and delighted for the company," Artemis reassured.

"As for Kiera, we have her assigned to the tree house up there." Artemis directed her attention to the tree house that was above them. Kiera was straining her neck up-ward, to have a look at it.

The tree house was conveniently located above their heads a good fifteen cubits. The deck of the tree house provided a commanding view of the meadow and the forest floor. The tree house had a rope ladder, and it was reasonably easy to climb up in to.

Kiera smiled.

"Kiera will be more comfortable up there." Artemis surmised. "There is a full washroom and a proper bed, fit for a queen."

"Thank you! Thank you!" Kiera gave Artemis a big hug in the process.

Artemis, now clearing her voice, and a little surprised with the unexpected show of affection continued the instructions: "Meals will be served at exactly 8:00 o'clock AM, Noon, and at 6:00 o'clock PM. don't be late!" "And I almost forgot! Allison will be your camp cook. You will meet her at the commissary."

Allison was not a person, but she looked like one. She was more like a tree spirit, a dryad that looked kind of human only when needed. When she was about her duties in the culinary pavilion, she looked more like a willow tree with long branches that were limber and wavy. Her face was muted into the bark of the tree but visible after a thoughtful gaze toward her.

The other satyrs or nature spirits assigned to the camp included fire spirits, and naiads or water spirits as there were several of them. The meadow included earth spirits which were fiercely loyal to Artemis. The camp was crawling with over a dozen varieties of hegemone or plant spirits as well.

"Finally," Artemis said, "Allow me to introduce the training spirits that are assigned to this camp and will be your companions throughout the quest." Artemis went on to explain to the threesome that these four training spirits would prepare the group for the quest against the evil and the treachery which they would have to face when confronting "Her."

"Her?" Arjun knew the answer, but want a better explanation.

"We won't be mentioning any names of the opposition while at the camp," Artemis explained. "The defenses of this camp are only secure to a point. Don't weaken them by vocally naming our foe."

"Understood." Arjun nodded his head in agreement. So did the others.

Artemis continued her introductions:

"First we have Fabian the Centaur. Fabian is in charge of treachery and weapons training.

"Second, please meet Rama the Satyr. Rama is in charge of deceit training in all its forms.

"Third, we have Quin the Faun. Quin is in charge of magic training. For there will be powerful magic to challenge, withstand, and overcome.

"Last but not least, we have Zooey the Hegemone. Zooey will be in charge of Martial Arts training and other odd topics of interest."

"Any questions?" Artemis asked.

"No not for now," Arjun observed.

"I'm good," Lycos commented.

"Sounds great!" Kiera exclaimed.

"Very well." Artemis said, seemingly satisfied with the response. "Make yourselves comfortable in your rooms, catch some rest, and be back in time for breakfast! Your mentors will be waiting."

CHAPTER THIRTY-FIVE

Kendra

Kendra and the girls continued scanning the horizon. "They must be here somewhere!" Kendra
demanded. "Keep looking!" She commanded
her guards. The warrior guards scoured the countryside
from Chalcis to the foothills of Olympus itself.

"They are nowhere to be found." Jayla, one of her
guards, reported.

"Surely they are hidden by some magic," observed Hel-
en.

"Keep looking!" Kendra insisted. "We can't go back to Piperi empty-handed."

Their searching took them almost to the edge of the Aeolian grove that Artemis had so carefully prepared. Even the dryads held their breath on a few occasions as it seemed the warriors of Zurenda would come bursting right into the clearing without any notice whatsoever.

However, true to Artemis' word, the warrior guards did not discover them. Their searching took them off course with a little trickery by Quin. She managed to send them on a long fruitless chase through the eastern forest as far away as Mount Ossa.

"That will keep them busy!" Quin mused. "It will also keep them confused about where the actual camp might be located. They will also be confused about where they have been, for their tracks will be erased as soon as they are made."

To add to the deception, the scenery around the camp kept changing, adding and subtracting layers of foliage to the disguised location.

In truth, the camp was hidden in plain sight. The magic used by Quin kept the trees shifting from place to place, including other subtle way-finding markers that a person would think were fixed and stable, but were not.

Each day the scenery changed around the compound. Each day, there were new trees in place of old ones, new hedges in place of old dead ones, and the stream that ran through the meadow was sometimes broad and deep, while at other times, was an almost non-existent trickle.

"This will keep them guessing," Quin reassured. "They will not find us here."

Kendra, Jayla, Helen and the others were forced, by darkness and unfamiliarity of the area, to make camp at the western base of Mount Olympus and wait for daybreak to resume their search.

CHAPTER THIRTY-SIX

Aeolia

While walking to their quarters, Lycos asked Arjun: "I wonder how this training will be unfolded to us. How will it happen?"

"Don't know for sure," replied Arjun. "All I know is that we need to learn all we can from Artemis and her team of trainers."

The beaver den was a little musty, but the bedrooms were large enough to be comfortable. For Arjun and Lycos, it did not matter; they had slept, (or tried to sleep), in much worse accommodations. This den was a place to get some much-needed rest.

Meanwhile, Kiera was getting acquainted with her new roommates. A pair of electric green hummingbirds had taken up residence on her windowsill. The tree house was complete with a deck that encircled the tree trunk offering a 360° view to the forest. Inside, the tree house offered a cozy bed, washroom, and a small sitting area.

"This is wonderful!" Kiera gave Artemis a big hug in the process of their tour.

"I'm glad you like it," Artemis replied while heading down the rope ladder and half-way to the ground. "Remember, breakfast at 08:00! Don't be late."

All the guests assembled for an early morning breakfast.

Even the three horses Kiera had acquired were present and accounted for. Each of the various nature and earth spirits were present.

Artemis began by leading the group in an invocation:

Oh Great Spirit
We hear the wind
We hear the brook
We listen to your leaves
We need your strength
We need your wisdom

Make us wise

Make us ready

Prepare our hearts

Prepare our souls

Prepare us against the day of trouble

Prepare our minds for peace

Arjun found that invocation was "a little weird" as it seemed that Artemis was just praying to herself. He was polite, however, and kept his mouth shut at the thought, and did not mention it.

After the invocation, Allison came forward with her limbs and began serving the meal. She used her willow-like branches, protruding out of the top of her head, to distribute food to everyone sitting around the table. The branches were like limber arms that would gently set a plate of food before each guest. From the outdoor commissary, she could swing her trunk from the cooking area to the serving area and then to the table in smooth motions that seemed so well orchestrated there was never a mid-air collision of plates, cups or tasty seconds.

While everyone at the table was eating, the horses ate oats in harness sacks which they enjoyed very much.

Each cup was filled with an all-natural tea which tasted like peppermint. Allison delivered the drink the same way the plates had been distributed.

Allison was terrific; she could serve and pour as effortlessly as a willow tree responding to the breeze of a crystal clear morning.

Breakfast consisted of sweet flour cakes dipped in natural honey, applesauce, a serving of free-range scrambled eggs and a fresh slab of broiled fish.

"This is all so wonderful!" Said Kiera. "Thank you, thank you so much!" She gratefully added.

Everyone agreed.

Even the nature spirits that did not talk much would show their appreciation in unique ways. The horses, however, did not mind thanking Allison with a vigorous whinny followed by some playful prancing in the meadow.

At the conclusion of the meal, Artemis spoke again: "Time for your training."

Fabian was the first on the agenda.

CHAPTER THIRTY-SEVEN

Mentors

"Gentlemen, if I could have your undivided attention," shouted Fabian. "Okay, Lycos, draw your sword!" For the next full hour, Fabian trained with Lycos on the art of Olympic swordsmanship, blades crossed, clashed and scraped with the occasional stream of white-hot lightning scattering across the meadow. Usually harmless, the lightning would sometimes scatter nipping the tail of a forest spirit with surprise.

Next, Fabian introduced high-jumping forward flips and back-flips into the exercise routine. Seeing a centaur do a back-flip was impressive, almost artful!

Next, Fabian engaged Arjun and Lycos at the same time, with a sword in each hand. Fabian stopped the training only when Lycos looked utterly worn out.

"Next!" Fabian shouted in Arjun's direction. One-on-one training for Arjun was a little different as his skill with the sword was very much established. Arjun was already handy with a sword and this one in particular.

Fabian was acutely aware of the power of Arjun's sword, and knew from whence it came. He also knew that this sword could lay-waste any object or group of objects that the holder would like to vaporize. However, the sword needed some fine tuning. The sword sometimes had a mind of its own and would work or not work depending on the gravity of the situation.

Like when it did not work in the boat. Arjun remembered. Fabian asked to see the sword. Arjun presented the weapon to him carefully by offering the golden hilt and handle to his trainer.

Fabian received and studied the weapon carefully. "Arjun, here is your problem." Fabian explained: "The golden hilt is missing a stamp or a marker."

This news caused Lycos, Arjun, and Fabian to again examine the hilt. The emblem of Zeus, a raised letter "Z" was only found on one side of the blade.

"It should be on both sides of the hilt, right at the crossing of the hilt with the blade," Fabian explained.

To make his point Fabian called their attention to Lycos' sword. "Look at the sword that Lycos has; it has the emblem of Ares, a raised "A" on both sides. We need to get your sword repaired immediately, but an Olympic black-smith must do this repair with the right tools."

"We will send for him at once," Fabian reassured.

"The sword of Ares, the one used by Lycos has the Olympic stamp on both sides as expected for this Olympic blade. The stamp is the key to its power." Fabian explained. "When the stamp or emblem is not facing the sky or in the direction of Mount Olympus, the power of the sword is greatly reduced... and greatly diminished."

Arjun then realized that must have been his problem when he was in the boat; the emblem must have been facing the water, (Poseidon vs. Zeus), instead of the sky.

"No wonder it did not work in the boat!" He explained to Lycos and Fabian.

Fabian continued his morning training instructions: "Now I want each of you to face and confront each other.

Complete the rest of the morning sharpening your skills in hand-to-hand combat. You may use your Olympic swords or other spears and knives. Use whatever you can get your hands on. Just don't hurt each other for the sake of all the gods."

Fabian was a centaur. Half human, half horse, utterly loyal to Artemis and Selene. He made a great addition to the other earth spirits at camp. He wanted the same result as Selene and Artemis. As a centaur, Fabian could understand and communicate with Kiera's horses and did not mind grazing with them in the meadow.

Within the Olympic hour, an Olympic Black-Smith had arrived. He had a knapsack of tools slung over his left shoulder; otherwise, he was wearing only a white toga and sandals.

He introduced himself as "Steve" short for Stephanus, we supposed. He handed Arjun his business card. He made no delay and went straight to work on Zeus' defective sword. After about an hour of working in the fire over at Allison's kitchen, Steve was getting a little gritty during the process. He returned to the group sporting a small smudge of black soot on his tip of his nose, which he quickly rubbed off with his white sleeve. Kiera thought that was funny and smiled then giggled at the little man.

Steve then presented the polished Olympic sword back to Arjun. The emblems of Zeus were embedded on both sides of the hilt. "Why don't you try it out?" Steve suggested.

Arjun took the sword and pointed it in the direction of a big boulder that was situated just behind Steve and a little to the left. "By the power of Zeus!" Arjun exclaimed as he pointed the sword towards the unlucky rock. Suddenly, a white-hot bolt of lightning shot out of the end of the sword vaporizing the rock into a cloud of dust.

"Yep, it works!" Steve approved with a nonchalant tone of voice. He gathered up his tools, and tossed them in his knapsack and loaded them up over his shoulder.

Steve then vanished into thin air.

Arjun was grateful to have a fully functioning sword again. He knelt down on one knee and said a little prayer: "Thanks, Father!"

While this was all happening, Artemis was training Kiera on the use of her bow. It was like two school girls out on a picnic. They were having such a great time together.

After an hour of shooting targets in the forest, and targets like full-blooming flowers, fish in the stream, and other objects, Kiera's curiosity piqued. She mustered the courage to ask Artemis what the purpose was of the twelve arrows in her quiver. Kiera was already aware that she was not yet allowed to touch or use them in any way.

Kiera commented to Artemis: "I am running out of my arrows and I would like to use the silver and gold tipped ones."

"My dear," Artemis said, addressing Kiera, "they are intended for 'Her' and 'Her' minions."

Artemis explained further: "The only thing that can kill a demi-goddess is three Olympic arrows through the heart." Not one. Not two. Not four. It has to be three."

Artemis enhanced the explanation. "Kiera, she said, the only other possibilities are two Olympic arrows and one Olympic sword, or conversely, two Olympic swords and one Olympic arrow. There is no other way to kill a demi-god."

Artemis continued, "The Swords of Olympus that Arjun and Lycos carry will help a lot in the mission that lies before you. However, my dear, your task is to help Arjun defeat the demi-goddess."

"No one else can do it, not even Arjun unless that sword he wields is helped along by these arrows." The goddess explained.

Kiera thought about that statement for a few minutes. Suddenly feeling overwhelmed, and letting the fear of failure creep into her thoughts, she now realized why she was brought along on this mission with Arjun.

"I guess I do have an important role to play in this mission." Kiera surmised.

"Yes you do my dear," Artemis said with growing confidence in her new apprentice.

However, Artemis' confidence in her ability was quickly replaced by the overwhelming fear of failure. This message seized her breast and jammed her thoughts. Slowly, Kiera began to realize fully, perhaps for the first time, that if she did not fulfill this mission, she and her friends might end up dying in the attempt.

"Am I here to save the lives of Arjun and Lycos?" Kiera questioned Artemis.

"That statement is a partially correct assumption, my dear." Artemis replied. "You are an exceptional archer; we are here to prepare you for success, not for failure."

Artemis finished with these reassuring words: "By the Goddess Selene, who sent you here, you will succeed... you must succeed!"

Kiera had a new question for Artemis. 'Tell me about the markings on these Olympic arrows. What do they mean? And why do they change?"

"They are instructions from the gods, not just Selene and me, mind you. Any god can communicate with you by the markings on the arrows. Think of it this way, Kiera. Lycos and Arjun have seen visions on the flat blade of their swords."

Kiera interrupted. "So have I, but I was unsure of the meaning."

"Consider this," Artemis continued. "When your arrows are glowing white hot inside your quiver, take the glowing one out and look at it. Look for the message on the shaft. If more than one arrow is glowing, take out all the illuminated ones. You will see that the gods know what they are doing in helping you to succeed. Trust in your abilities. Trust in your abilities." Artemis repeated her last sentence for emphasis and then suddenly changed the subject.

"Let's go visit the naiads. I haven't seen those little cuties all day."

CHAPTER THIRTY-EIGHT

Kendra

After camping for a few days on the western slopes of Olympus, Kendra and the girls decided to climb up on to the cliffs and have a look around. From their vantage point above the trees, she could still see nothing.

"Where could they have gone?" She wondered. Below her was a sea of green forests and rolling hills, some steep hills and cliffs with a few granite ridges, and a lot of trees.

"I can see no smoke from a fire," Jayla reported.

"They must be out there somewhere." Kendra insisted. "We need to find a pool of water."

Not far from their camp was a small brook that gushed out of the side of a cliff. The clear water formed a small pool that caught the reflected light of the sun at evening.

Kendra commented to Jayla, "maybe the pool can tell us something." The reflection on the water was perfect. Kendra chanted a few words in Greek and mentioned the name of Zurenda in the mantra.

Suddenly, as if by some strange magic, the reflection of Zurenda was revealed. A vapor of smoke surrounded her image. Grey smoke seemed to pour out of the pool and creep around the base of the pool clinging to their feet.

Without missing a beat, Kendra asked the image where they should go to intercept the men of Selene that had escaped Piperi?

Zurenda began to speak: "Stay where you are, you are closer to them than you think."

Just then, the moon began to rise, and the wind came up troubling the water, erasing the image, the smoke, and the conversation. The vision was over.

"We stay put!" Kendra declared. "We will sit, and we will wait!"

CHAPTER THIRTY-NINE

Zurenda

Zurenda was having the same worried thoughts as her Captain, Kendra. "Why have they been gone so long?" She would shout at the water within palace pool. "I want the pleasure of killing Arjun myself!" A very un-lady like Zurenda screamed like a child, into the waters of the pool. Clenching her fist and shaking it wildly, she complained to the air in the empty throne room, the cobwebs in the empty hall, and any empty warrior hearts that would listen to her ramblings.

The water in the palace pool began to boil and then started to produce grey smoke as it had done in the past. Suddenly, Eris appeared out of the mist.

"My daughter," she said, "You will yet have your desires realized. Kendra and your other faithful warriors are on Arjun's trail. It won't be long before they are discovered. He cannot hide forever."

Zurenda, managing a little self-composure asked a simple question: "Where are they now?"

"My beloved daughter," Eris answered empathetically. "I'm sure they are hiding in the forests of Olympus. They are somewhere around the plains of Aeolia."

The Goddess added: "I am also pretty sure that Selene is in league with Artemis and while I can't quite put my finger on it, they will not be there for long."

"Very well, we watch, and wait!" Zurenda stated, showing a sharp tone of disappointment in her voice.

The vision in the Palace pool closed, and the pool of water returned to its natural state.

Zurenda did something that was entirely consistent with her character. She stormed down the great hall and compelled one of her servants to paint the statue of Selene with black tar. "There, that should insult the former queen of this palace!" She fumed.

CHAPTER FORTY

Wilderness Queen

The next day it was Rama's turn to conduct the training. She was highly skilled in the art of deceit. Rama was a satyr and a shapeshifter. She stood about three cubits tall when she was standing up on her hind legs. As a master in the art of deceit, Rama showed up to breakfast as a fish which immediately drew a recoiled response from Kiera.

"Who invited this fish to sit next to me?" Kiera demanded. "The thing is flipping water all over me; it's so wet and so slimy!" She added while rolling her eyes.

Artemis just laughed. "Relax Kiera, that's just Rama in one of her disguises."

In the blink of an eye, the Rama that everyone knew appeared and the fish disappeared.

"It's still weird having breakfast with a goat!" Kiera added.

"I'm not a goat!" Rama retorted, "I am a Satyr."

Kiera conceded with a puff of air to correct a lock of hair hanging in her eyes, adding a "whatever," to the conversation.

"Well, everyone, that is the first lesson of the day." Rama tutored. "Never assume the person sitting next to you is who you think they are. They could be someone or something entirely different."

Arjun and Lycos were too busy eating to comment. They just watched in muted surprise as Rama then turned herself into a long black snake, and then into a brown bear, a purple beaver and last of all an Amazon warrior. Doing this made the hair on even Artemis' neck stand up. Weapons were quickly drawn and then put away just as quick as Rama turned herself back into a satyr a few seconds later.

Rama's deceit training continued for several hours. The horses did not mind; they just stayed in the meadow eating grass and enjoying an intelligent conversation with Fabian.

Quin taught a class in the afternoon about the magic arts. "Some folks call them the art of deception, but I like to think of it as the art of manipulation." Quin said to the group. "All we do is move or relocate one thing from here and move it to there, and confuse the audience in the process."

Arjun piped up: "The camp we are in, for example, the scenery keeps changing to confuse our pursuers."

"Exactly!" Quin agreed.

Quin told the group that she was the adopted little sister of Circe, "which you may find to be a strange match," she confessed. However, she had learned all her skills from her sister Circe while growing up on Olympus.

Quin, seeing the puzzlement in Kiera's eyes, clarified further. "Well, that's not entirely true." She clarified. "I had to get adopted first, and that's a whole other story.

"After we became sisters, we practiced our magic on horses and cows. When that magic worked, we tried our skills out on larger objects. It was fun!" Quin smiled sheepishly, "At least until our parents figured out that we moved our home to a different town. They were not happy about that," Quin added retrospectively.

"One day, I changed Circe into a python. Nobody knew she was a snake except me, leastwise until the dog went missing! And I liked that dog too! Oh, well! Live and learn." She added with a smile. "Circe did not eat for a month after that!"

"So why do you folks think I'm telling you all this?" Quin quizzed.

Kiera had the answer. "When we are in 'Her' Palace, we can expect that there will be magic poured out upon all who enter."

"Correct Kiera!" Quin praised. "We know that she is capable of changing forms from anything horrid you can imagine into a beautiful woman in the blink of an eye." Quin also explained, "We also know that her mother possesses these same attributes."

"You should be very aware of your circumstances at all times." Quin cautioned. "For example: Shifting walls, fire out of nowhere and all sorts of monsters."

Arjun thought about the labyrinth beneath the palace floor.

"Beware of mortals that suddenly change into animal shapes." For some reason, Lycos thought about horses. Quin continued: "Suddenly appearing strange looking animals that seem out of place."

Kiera thought about the acrid stench that seemed to hang in the air down in that labyrinth.

Lycos thought about the dungeon that Hadrian and the others had been held in - it smelled terrible!

"I try to keep my lessons upbeat and positive!" Quin reassured. "So let's talk about the fun we can have with magic too."

"The only magic I want to do right now," Arjun commented, "is to make my dinner plate disappear."

Lycos smiled.

Kiera giggled.

It was time for a break.

During the afternoon, Fabian took the opportunity to do some more treachery training.

He began: "Treachery is an act of treason or betrayal. Treachery is also a violation of allegiance or faith." He explained. "Our enemy is well versed in the art of treason." Fabian cautioned. "Do not let it happen to you! Do not underestimate her power! Do not let her magic cause you to be pitted against each other."

Arjun interjected. "I can see that our foe might use this to gain advantaged over the team."

Artemis joined the conversation, looking at Lycos and Kiera. "We cannot let her divide us through jealousy, deceit, treason or any other evil act. We must all be united, or we will all fail."

Everyone agreed by nodding their heads. Artemis continued: "You have to check each other in your quest. Do not let the slightest jealousies come between you. They only lead to treachery and betrayal."

"Here is a good example of betrayal that you all know and understand:

Look what happened to begin the Trojan War. It all started with a little jealousy between the gods, and then turned into kidnapping, lies, deceit and then all-out war." Artemis summarized: "Don't let it happen to you!"

The rest of the afternoon, training and practice with swordplay and archery went for hours. It was a good afternoon at camp. Kiera enjoyed watching the naiads frolic in the stream. Lycos was busy crossing swords with Fabian. Arjun was busy working with Rama.

The beavers were busy helping Allison get the evening meal ready. It was going to be good!

The scenery shifted again around the camp.

From Kendra's quarters, she could still not tell where the Olympian rogues were hiding. But they had to be out there somewhere! All her warriors were on the lookout for anything that moved.

"Report anything that is remotely out of place," Kendra ordered.

That night as Arjun was sleeping he kept having reoccurring dreams about 'Her.' Very vivid dreams too. He would see 'Her' appear in a vapor of smoke. She was incredibility beautiful to behold. He went to raise his sword, prepared to strike.

His strike was foiled. A second blow was foiled, and then a third. Try as he might, he could never get a clean opening to parry.

He invoked the power of Zeus. Nothing worked!

Waking up in a cold sweat, he quickly reached for his sword and shouted for Lycos. Lycos was asleep, he hardly budged. *It was a bad dream,* Arjun told himself. *Just a dream!*

Sleep did not come easily that night or several nights that followed.

For three nights straight he had the same dream. He finally told Kiera and Lycos about them during a morning training break.

"Maybe you're just nervous." Kiera tried to comfort him, and brush it off; blaming the strange tasting tea they had for dinner the night before.

Overhearing the conversation, Artemis chimed in: "Arjun, it's not nerves. You will have to face her soon enough, come out to the meadow."

"Let's get ready for the next stage of training." Artemis' big surprise was combining all the mentors at once!

Lycos looked at Arjun. "Oh boy," he said. "This is going to be good!"

"Before the festivities begin today, I would like to have Kiera come over here and sit down cross-legged on the grass in front of me," encouraged Artemis.

Kiera did as directed. Once comfortable in the tall grass and swooshing her skirt out a little to keep a tiny black ant off her right leg, Artemis did something that surprised everyone.

"Today in the presence of all the forest spirits, I officially crown you, Kiera, the 'Queen of the Wilderness!'" She said smiling. As if on cue, Rama brought over a small woven crown made of mulberry leaves and placed it lightly upon Kiera's head. Kiera was very shocked, surprised and amazed. Her mind flashed to the thought that this was some kind of a joke. But this was no joke, "Now behold your Wilderness Queen." Rama announced to the whole group assembled to witness this event.

Even Allison was excited and shot her limbs skyward in celebration. Lycos, Arjun, and the others looked on with a warm sense of approval. Kiera, now a little overwhelmed at the gesture, and shocked herself, asked Rama and Artemis if this was a joke or part of the deceit training.

"No my dear," Artemis reassured. "Your skill with the bow has earned you this title. From now on you will be known to the forest creatures and nature spirits, as the Wilderness Queen, and they will willingly obey you."

Still cross-legged on the grass, Kiera was left to wonder if this meant that she was now a demi-god or had demi-god like powers. She did not feel any different, except maybe feeling a little stupid for not asking Artemis the question before the day's training session was over.

Out in the field, Fabian engaged the men in the standard hand-to-hand combat, swordplay, fencing, and a few unexpected tumbles.

Meanwhile, Rama appeared as her normal self, a satyr, then a mouse, followed by a raven and then finally a stag.

"A stag?" Kiera questioned.

The stag started talking: "Grunt, snort."

Ok, Kiera, reasoned, *maybe it is a real stag and not a deception.* Her hunch was right, the stag was real, but the animal was placed there by deception.

The tree behind Kiera started talking too.

"You see my dear," said the tree. "You can never be sure of what is in front of you or behind you."

Rama clarified: "I'm in the tree right now, but I placed the stag there by magic. Take a shot at the deer with your arrows," the tree directed.

Kiera obeyed and aimed at the stag. Sling! Out went an arrow, hitting the stag squarely in the neck. To Kiera's surprise, the stag immediately disappeared.

"How?...What?" Acting surprised but catching on quickly.

"Deception," Rama noted, now her voice was coming from a toadstool mound, and no longer from the tree.

Just then, Fabian came over to engage Kiera with his sword. She sprang into the air and leaped clear of the centaur only to land flat-footed on the top of Quin's shoulders. "Or are you someone or something else?" Kiera questioned. She leaped off of Quin doing a backflip and landing on the earth with a steady stance.

Quin suddenly took on the image of her worst foe. It was Zurenda standing right in front of Kiera!

Without missing a beat, Kiera reached for not one, but three silver arrows from her quiver, placing them in the bow and drawing back ready to fire. This motion was all made in a split-second. Just as she launched the arrows, the image of Zurenda changed. It became a sack of oats. The arrows pierced it cleanly.

"Good girl!" Rama complemented as Kiera took a second to think about what she had just done.

Arjun and Lycos came running over to join the group after they saw the arrows fly.

"Why were you shooting the silver arrows into a sack of oats?" Lycos asked.

"I saw her image in the sack of oats, and my instinct took over," Kiera explained.

Lycos and Arjun both realized right then and there that Kiera was ready for this mission. Were they? Lycos wondered. *Not yet*, he thought. Just then oats spilled out of the sack and on to the ground prompting dozens of little yellow songbirds to dive-bomb the training area and begin feeding from the spilled grain in chirping delight.

Kiera retrieved the silver arrows and placed them carefully back in the quiver. For her, she knew the exercise was over.

Zooey was a trainer that always packed two very thin swords around on her belt. They crossed at her waistline and were held there by a black belt. As a trainer, Zooey wore a long white robe, when she was not pre-occupied as a hegemone.

In real life, Zooey was a small fig tree. Her leaves were soft and short. Aside from her lighter than green color, she was the brains behind the shifting scenery that the camp had enjoyed up till now.

Zooey could change shapes at will, however as a trainer, she preferred the 'ninja look' and wore it well. Lycos and Arjun were getting used to the forest coming alive by this pint-sized individual in their training exercise, but did not expect the tree next to the brook to become a trainer.

Without any warning, Zooey faced the pair with both swords blazing. Her ninja style had her jumping over the men with ease. Landing behind them and then quickly preparing for the next sortie.

Swords now drawn, Lycos and Arjun realized that they had to work together to tackle this foe. Zooey came charging towards both of the men with her swords blazing. Quickly reacting, Lycos and Arjun both positioned their swords to take down the aggressor.

"Stop!" Artemis commanded, just as Arjun was prepared to swing aggressively into the attack. Zooey, leaped again into the air doing a full circle before coming down on the pair, cutting a tiny lock of hair from each men's head.

"Why did you make us stop?" Asked Arjun.

"Patience my boy!" Artemis reassured. You were both going to take out Zooey for real that time. I could not let that happen."

Lycos looked surprised and only said: "Oh! I was expecting a mist, or a ghost or perhaps a tree."

Zooey showed some relief on her face, but she told the boys that "if they worked together, they could overcome any foe, including the dark queen of Piperi."

It was time for the evening meal. The group was ready for a break.

Zooey turned back into a tree. Quin turned into a faun, Rama turned back into a satyr and Fabian did not need to turn back into anything.

"Centaurs don't do that silly stuff," Fabian told the group. "We're always Centaurs, and we like it that way. We never change!"

The fair weather they had enjoyed at camp turned off stormy and cold. Grey storm clouds were pressing in on

Olympus. Soon the rain began and seemed to encompass the meadow and the forest around it.

"Guys it looks like we had all better take cover," Artemis suggested. After a few minutes of intense rain, the clouds and the weather produced a little lightning, enough to see across the camp in the ensuing fog.

"It might be magic," warned Quin. "Weather like this is not seasonal or timely, remember what I taught you."

The storm turned out to be a real storm, not deception or another illusion. Lightning flashed striking the hill nearest the camp, and thunder clapped overhead. The rain continued right up until sunset.

The forest spirits all retreated to their homes in the woods. The horses found shelter under a new grove of pine trees that Zooey had just placed there.

"Thank you Zooey, how wonderfully convenient this shelter is," Fabian commented.

Dinner was served indoors, up in the tree house. From the exterior deck of the tree house, Kiera could see the sun setting in the west just under a bank of storm clouds. She also caught a glimpse of a bright flash of light on the hills east of their location.

I wonder what that flash was? Perhaps it was a distant strike of lightning? Maybe it was Rama playing another trick on them? Or just perhaps it was the flash of a blade or spear in the evening sun-light. Perhaps a campfire, but whose? Could it be something worse? She thought to herself. *I'd better tell the others!*

CHAPTER FORTY-ONE

Discovered!

D inner with everyone up in the tree house proba-
bly gave away their location. The tree house was
just high enough in the air that the magical
shield generated by Quin may not have been enough to
conceal all of them at the same time.

"We have found them!" Jayla reported to Kendra.
"They are just below us in the forest meadow, I don't
know how we could have missed them before, as it seems
like we have combed that section of forest multiple times,"
Jayla reported.

"Let's mount the horses and go cut them down!" Kendra demanded.

Within minutes, the Amazonian Warriors were crashing through the camp, swords, and spears blazing.

Artemis' little group had no choice but to stand up and fight; the surprise attack by the Amazons was so sudden there was no time to escape. Swords clashed, arrows flew, a thundering herd of horses trampled down the meadow, the culinary, and set fire to Allison. She screamed in horror as the flames licked at her trunk, but there was nothing she could do about it except stand there and take it. With some quick thinking from Artemis and a quick flick of her wrist, the Goddess caused the nearby stream to douse Allison and put the fire out.

"You folks remember what we have taught you!" Artemis shouted over the confusion of the battle.

"Take defensive positions!" Commanded Rama.

The entire group was involved in the fray.

Lycos was crossing swords with Jayla. Arjun was crossing swords with Kendra. Fabian was crossing swords with Helen.

Artemis and Kiera were shooting arrows at some of the others on horseback from the eastern deck of the treehouse.

The whole camp was in commotion.

Rama, Quin, and Zooey were taking on different bodily forms to help stop the attack.

Newly doused, Allison would take any foe within reach of her limber branches and wrap them up into a suffocating and fatally tight squeeze.

Without warning, Rama turned into a giant solid round stone and began rolling around crushing a few Amazons in the process.

Quin turned herself into an oversized hawk and conducted nose-dives on the remaining warriors, by pulling out their hair, scraping their flesh, and using her talons to pick warriors up and then violently drop them to the ground.

All this action helped. The team managed to make Kendra and her Amazons un-nerved enough through these unusual tactics combined with loud piercing screeches from any of the earth spirits that could make a noise.

Zooey just stood there and remained as a fig tree which everyone, including Allison, thought was strange. The benefit of the 'Zooey Tree' however, was soon apparent.

She started tripping warriors with her roots; she would snatch the warriors with a well-placed root and then drag them across the field, tossing them back and forth between the bank and the stream and between the thick grove of trees again and again.

It did not take long until the horses were all scattered, including Kiera's.

Silence fell over the forest meadow. All the warriors of Zurenda had been killed. All of them that is, except for one.

The injuries sustained by the team were a few sword scrapes to arms and legs. Arjun and Lycos were both pretty scrapped up, but nothing was broken or badly bleeding.

Kiera and Artemis were seemingly untouched from the battle, still enjoying the relative protection and advantage that tree house afforded.

Fabian sustained an injury with an arrow to the left hindquarters. However, the shaft was not deeply embedded, and Quin was able to remove it and stop the bleeding.

Kiera, now inspecting for damage, noticed that during Arjun's sword fight with Kendra, Arjun sustained a small sword cut to his right cheek. The cut burned more than it bled, as small drops of blood were weeping slowly down his cheek.

Arjun told Kiera: "This injury only strengthens my resolve to end the conflict." A few more spins with the sword and he managed to overcome Kendra. Tripping, she fell backward into Zooey, impaling herself on Zooey's swords in the process. Kendra's sword flew out of her hand and went up over her head, and beyond her reach.

At that moment, Kendra was the only surviving warrior. She was pretty cut up, especially on her right arm just above the elbow; and across her torso from being impaled. She was barely breathing but coherent enough to talk when the team got near her to check for signs of life.

Kiera helped Lycos dab her forehead with a damp cloth, Artemis lead the interrogation.

"Who are you, and why were you trying to kill us?" Artemis demanded.

She replied in a whisper: "My name is Kendra. I am the Captain of the Guard for her Majesty."

The questions continued.

"How many Amazons were with you?" Artemis pressed.

Kendra winced in pain. "Twelve," Kendra replied.

At that news, Lycos quickly turned and checked the field to make sure that no one had escaped into the forest. No one had. They were all dead, and accounted for.

"What business do you have here in the wilderness?" Artemis continued her questions.

Kendra responded by taking a gasp of air. "We were sent here to kill you, all of you, except one."

"Who? Who were you commanded to spare?" Artemis demanded.

By this time, Zooey changed herself from a fig tree into a large sword packing frog who hopped into the stream to clean herself.

Kendra's eyes were glazing over. She had a small line of blood coming from the corner of her mouth, and trickling down her cheek. Coughing a few times her eyes rolled back in pain.

Again, Artemis asked the question. "Who were you commanded to spare?" Through more coughing, Kendra answered in an earnest whisper: "The man who wields the sword of Zeus."

Arjun's blood ran cold! He vividly realized, and was sickened with the thought, that all this carnage was because of him. They were only after him!

Artemis asked another question, even though she knew the answer.

"Why the Sword of Zeus, what is your business with that?"

Kendra, now almost gone, cracked her eyes and said with a final raspy cough: "Because of the prophecy, the proph... the proph..."

One last gasp for air and she was gone.

"This fight is over," Artemis announced as she laid Kendra down on the bed of grass beneath her head.

Arjun made this declaration: "We have to go to the Palace of Zurenda." Then making eye contact with Artemis, Arjun rephrased the thought with an almost distant stare: "I have to go to the Palace of Zurenda."

Artemis looked at Arjun right in the eye: "Arjun, you will not be going to face Zurenda alone. We, all of us, will go with you to defeat her."

CHAPTER FORTY-TWO

Artemis

The time for preparation had passed. Artemis directed the forest spirits to bury the dead. Almost like magic, the forest came alive with activity. The soil, trees, plants and other earth spirits took the dead and gently covered them with earth, vegetation and interred some of them under the stream.

It took only moments to return the forest and the meadow to its original state before the fighting began. Artemis complemented the dryads, hegemone, and oreads for their quick and efficient work. Kendra's body was buried in the narrow space between the stream and the cooking hearth. Before the day was out, her grave was carpeted with a variety of wildflowers of every description.

Artemis then called an impromptu meeting with the team. She motioned with her arms for everyone to come close: Whispering "Come around close everyone, we have to leave this place, and leave right now! We cannot trust that these warriors will keep silent in their graves. Their path to the underworld will be slow and treacherous; they will look for opportunities to delay their journey and final arrival in Tartarus. We cannot risk them overhearing our plans as we move to a new location. Gather your things and let's be off."

Fabian, now limping from the fight but still able to walk, presently arrived with all the horses.

"Here are your steeds," Fabian announced. Arjun was especially glad to see the animals. His first thought was freedom. His second thought was for that of his newly anointed Wilderness Queen, Kiera.

"Come here my honored queen!" Arjun said with a bit of a wry smile. Arjun reached out to Kiera, and they both stumbled to the horses.

Arjun's last comment was this: "What are we going to do with all these extra horses?"

Fabian replied before the question was formally articulated: "We will bring the horses with us," he said, "they may be useful in bartering for a boat."

It did not take long for Artemis, Arjun, Lycos, and Kiera to ready the horses to leave.

Fabian was invited to join them as well as Rama, Quin, and Zooey; each took a horse and led a few extras for the next leg of their journey. Even Fabian led a few extra horses on the trek outward.

Artemis gave the command: "Ride!" and they were off.

CHAPTER FORTY-THREE

Council of the Gods

Council of the Gods. Meeting Number: MMLXXI.A.1. d.

Hermes: "This meeting is now called to order."

Attending are as follows: Hermes, Zeus, Selene, Ares, Poseidon, and Hades.

Zeus brought the first agenda item to the table: "Where is Artemis!" He demanded. "I need her at this meeting!"

His hands were now pounding on the table for instant results, and for dramatic effect.

Selene: "My Lord, she is busy helping our son."

Hades: "You think that going around killing all of Zurenda's warriors is helping your son?"

Selene: "I know that they got into a scrape with Zurenda's Amazons. However," Selene cleared her voice, "that's hardly a reason to be upset."

Hades: "I am going to have to put up a new neon 'No Vacancy' sign if this killing continues. By all the gods! Selene, can't you control this young upstart of a Demi-God?"

Selene: "Do you all need to be reminded of his mission?" Selene entreated. "He is just getting started, and he will be cleaning out the House of Discontent soon enough." She concluded and sat down in a bit of a huff.

Zeus: "Well, it just does not look good for Artemis and this up-start demi-god to go around killing all the women in Greece. Am I just to sit here waiting for the complaints to start rolling in from lesser gods the world over?"

The frustration finally got the best of him, and Zeus blurted: "I just want this mission completed! I don't need any more blood spilled on our western slopes, and I certainly want the end result to be realized." Further, he added. "Your time is running out, we have lost precious time already!" In a huff, Zeus got up from his throne and left the chamber.

Zeus's Brother Poseidon sat there and said nothing. He was content to remain quiet. He already had a few plans of his own.

Hermes: "Any other agenda items?" His golden eyes perked open and smiling.

Selene: "I have one more, your Lordship. I would like the record to show that I wanted to officially thank each of you for your continued support of this mission."

Hermes: "Noted, anything else?" He asked.

Selene: "No, no that's all."

Hermes: "Then the meeting is adjourned."

With that Selene got up and left the chamber, leaving Hermes, Hades and Poseidon alone in the room.

Poseidon then spoke candidly: "I will personally see to it that this young apprentice does not make it back to the shores of Piperi."

Hades: "I will make room for one more occupant, your Lordship."

The gods stood up from their several thrones and exited the chamber.

Hermes thought about what was said by Poseidon after the official meeting had ended. After he had time to process the sediment he said to no one in particular, "I need to get a message to Artemis, and quick!"

Artemis was not that easy to find. She was hiding in the woods with Arjun and company as they continued to flee from the Aeolian Meadows. Their flight took them deep into the backwoods and hills and valleys of the country to their south. Traveling with over a dozen skittish horses tends to slow one down.

CHAPTER FORTY-FOUR

Zurenda

Bad news travels fast. Zurenda learned of the defeat of Kendra and her warriors by way of Hades. The message that came from the pool in her palace was not the news she had expected.

"I can't believe that twelve of my Amazon warriors and my Captain of the Guard are dead!" Zurenda lamented, with a half-baked mixture of surprise and grief.

"Yes, my Lady, all twelve and their leader. They checked in with my welcome staff this morning and have already been sent on to Cerberus for their labor assignments."

Zurenda asked a follow-up question while the image in the pool was crystal clear. "And what about Arjun and his friends?" She ventured.

Hades replied: "None of them were killed in the battle. And now they are coming after you, with great fervor my dear."

"Excellent!" She said clasping her hands together. "I will be waiting for them!" adding: "I will be ready!"

The message closed. The water in the pool became cloudy again.

Just as Zurenda was ready to leave the Palace room the water in the courtyard pool began to boil again. The familiar grey smoke began circling out of the water and took the form of Eris.

"My dear Zurenda," Eris said in a consoling voice. "I am aware of the carnage that befell your warriors." She said with empathy for the fallen. "However, Arjun and his friends are on the way to visit you with the same level of destruction. You will need a new army to greet them. Be ready!" The vision faded and the waters were becalmed once again.

Zurenda wasted no time; she called for all the Amazon warriors in the compound to come to the palace hall. Within minutes, about thirty warriors were present and stood at attention in the hall, ready to receive orders.

Zurenda addressed the ladies: "We have a new challenge to meet," she said to the assembled group. "Our foe is well organized. They are experts with the implements of war. We can only defeat them through the use of treachery, dark magic and excellent skill with the bow and the sword."

Zurenda continued: "We are not expecting an army with banners." Instead, she said, "we should expect the unexpected: A few men and women, and a few odd-looking animals, and maybe a lesser god. That's about it. We need to train for this and, the training needs to start now."

Zurenda motioned towards Talia, gesturing her to come over and stand beside her. Obedient to a fault, Talia did as directed.

"Kendra has fallen!" Zurenda announced. "Talia will be your new Captain of the Guard. She will choose from your ranks division leaders."

Talia stepped forward. "I choose Ada, Coreen, and Mara as division leaders." Talia continued. "Each of you ladies will fall in behind them. Ada will be in charge of the perimeter defenses. Coreen will be in charge of the prisoners in the dungeon." Concluding, Talia stated: "Mara will be in charge of the dark magic, and I, I will be in charge of the treachery."

Zurenda added her approval to the new Captain's directions: "Excellent choices! Now to your station's ladies, we should expect our visitors in a week or two. We don't know how they will arrive, but we will be ready! We must be ready!"

Zurenda concluded her remarks to the assembled warriors: "We need to feed some lions!"

CHAPTER FORTY-FIVE

Warrior from

Olympus

With a new dose of confidence from Artemis' comments, Arjun felt like they were prepared to meet Zurenda. Thinking back on the rescue operation they did on Piperi gave him some good insight into the physical layout of the palace, but as Quin had cautioned, the labyrinth under the palace could move and change forms without warning. He kept going through the check-list in his mind.

Olympian swords, check.

Olympian bow and silver arrows, check.

Training, check.

Forest spirits and trusted friends, check.

Goddess of the Woodland, check.

Horses, and spare horses. Check and check.

Arjun asked himself these and other question over and over again: *I wonder how many more prisoners Zurenda has captured while we have been away at Olympus. A few? Dozens? And what about the lions? I wonder if there is a way to eliminate them before we have to face them.*

For this and many other worries, Arjun would not be comforted. In his dreams, he kept seeing Zurenda and swinging his sword, but nothing would ever happen. *Is she a ghost?* Wonder kept him worried and alert.

Artemis stopped the group long enough to rest, as well as to provide some water and grazing for the horses. By watching Arjun, she could read his thoughts. She kept quiet; however, she knew that Arjun had to think this out in his way and in his own time.

Lycos announced to the group that they were somewhere south of Olympus, and perhaps had another day's travel to meet the seashore.

Meanwhile, Artemis was cupping a drink of water with her hand from a nearby stream. While doing so, she saw the stern reflection of Zeus in the water. In her mind, she could hear his words: "Come to Olympus at once!"

Artemis knew that this stop might be her last with the team. She told everyone that she had just received an urgent message from Zeus and needed to return to Olympus at once to answer his call. Currently, the group consisted of Arjun, Lycos, and Kiera, together with Fabian, Rama, Quin, and Zooey.

Artemis called the group together for a final huddle.

"My friends," she said warmly. "You must travel the rest of the way to Piperi without my assistance. However, you are well prepared for the journey, and the task at hand."

Tears welled up in Kiera's eyes. "I feel like I'm losing a friend," she said. "Now my dear," giving Kiera a long embrace and placing her hands on Kiera's chin and cheek. "You are all in good company. I perceive that you will all eventually succeed in your mission. You may face setbacks, but ultimately you will succeed."

Then turning her head, with her eyes fixed on Arjun, she finished her statement with a confident declaration: "You will all be led by 'The Warrior from Olympus!' Arjun, the Demi-God! You will be in good hands." Finishing this thought and adding some reassurance, she stated: "I will try to meet you at Piperi."

After that announcement, Artemis mounted her horse and rode off into the northern wilderness.

Arjun had been told by his mother before that he was a demi-god. But this time the words coming from the Goddess Artemis reinforced that sentiment and started to sink deeper into his heart. This new title was repeated by Kiera, and then by Lycos: "Arjun, the Demi-God -The Warrior from Olympus."

Arjun did not feel any different about himself or his life in general. He was still a young man. He knew he had his faults. He knew he was not perfect. He knew that he could be killed. He was, after all, not immortal, nor was he invincible. The cut on his cheek from Kendra taught him that. He could still bleed the same as other mortal men, but he was encouraged by the fact that they won the fight with Kendra and her warriors.

Arjun reflected upon the whole outcome of the contest in the woods with Kendra. *Was it a miracle, a twist of fate, or the will of the gods?*

CHAPTER FORTY-SIX

Lycos

For some reason, Lycos made an excellent navigator and scout. After Artemis left the group and headed for Olympus, Lycos took over the role as the company scout. The way was not complicated; however, there was plenty of path wayfinding which Lycos seemed to have the knack.

After several hours the group stopped to rest for the night. Lycos and Arjun both unsheathed their swords and laid them on a fallen log to study them carefully for any messages or visions that the gods might have for them.

After gazing upon them for a while, Kiera interrupted with a surprise. "Okay, Sword Boys. Supper!"

As if by some magic, Kiera and the other girls had whipped up a pot of soup. The meal consisted of freshly boiled vegetables, mushrooms, honey and some flatbread on the side.

"This meal hits the spot!" Complemented Arjun. "Much better than grass," added Fabian.

The rest of the group chuckled, but no one complained about the meal tonight. It seemed that everything was going to be alright. Quin took the precaution to place a spell on the camp so that no one could detect them while they slept in the forest.

Just before drifting off, Arjun and Lycos looked at their swords again in the reflected campfire light. No new message from the gods could be discerned.

CHAPTER FORTY-SEVEN

Rama

Rama was not that comfortable traveling by horseback, preferring to walk on her own hind feet. As a satyr, she did know a little about how to handle a horse, but only at a beginner's level. That, however, did not stop her from trying. "The hardest part is getting on." Rama declared. Fabian smiled and then laughed out loud as he watched the spectacle, so did the others.

Rama did not have any fears. She could tackle anything. No challenge was too big for her short frame. Satyrs were a little creepier than fauns, as a general rule, but she did not let that stigma overshadow her efforts or her resolve.

Rama let them always see her sweet side. The deceit training that she was so well known for started in an improbable place.

Rama explained: "Apate was one day walking through the forest wearing a magical girdle. After a long walk, she stopped to rest on a patch of moss. I happened by and noticed the golden girdle and was so captivated by it that I took (snatched) it while she was sleeping and placed it on my back. I did not realize it then, but after that experience, I became more and more deceitful in almost every aspect of my life.

I felt sorry for stealing the girdle from Apate, and I finally, reluctantly, returned it. The ability to use deceit in a training situation, and in real life, never seemed to wear off, however."

Zooey already knew the answer to this question, but she asked it anyway for the sake of Arjun. "How long have you been doing deceit training Rama?"

Rama replied: "A least a two hundred years… or so it seems."

Lycos asked a new question: "When or where did you gain the ability to be a shapeshifter?"

"Oh, it's a long story," Rama replied. "I was at one time walking along the shores of the Ionian Sea, and perchance was bemused by a strange creature that lay at the edge of the sea. Curiosity took over, and I approached the beast. Upon closer examination, I realized that this thing looked like an octopus out of the water, stranded on the sand. I went to see if I could pull it back into the sea and by so doing, would save its life."

Rama continued her story. "The beast started to talk to me. He introduced himself as Proteus, a lesser sea god.

"Surprised, I offered to pull him back into the water, if that's what he needed. Proteus thanked me for the offer and promised me that if I did do this service, he would bestow a gift upon me of great value.

"I then wrapped my horns around one of his tentacles and pulled him back into the water and to safety.

"True to his word, once he became stabilized in the water, he extended one tentacle out toward me. It held a single golden seashell. I accepted the offer, not thinking about the magnitude of the gift and went my way."

Rama concluded. "Months later, I found myself in the forest and suddenly became very hungry, I opened the shell hoping to find a morsel of food or something inside.

Instead, I found a black pearl. I placed it under my tongue for a while and my need for water was satisfied, the next morning I found that I had accidentally swallowed it. The next night I found myself dreaming about being a lion. The next morning I discovered that I was a lion. I tried thinking about other shapes, bears, fish, humans, and found that I could assume any of those body shapes as well. I came to realize that the shell that held a black pearl, when placed under the tongue, or swallowed allowed any who did so to become a shapeshifter. I also came to realize that whenever I removed a black pearl from the seashell, another one was formed or created in its place." Rama continued. "So now, fast-forward a couple of centuries, and I meet up with Quin and Zooey. I gave them each a new pearl from the shell to swallow. Subsequently, they have both obtained the same gift that I have. We are all shapeshifters."

Rama replaced the golden seashell into her black leather pouch. The conversation had changed again.

After several minutes Kiera asked Rama a follow-up question. "Does the black pearl have any other magical properties?"

Rama responded. "Legend states that the pearl in the golden seashell possesses healing or health and wellness properties, even though I have never had the need to try it. What I can tell you is that since this gift has come into my hands, I have never been physically sick for any reason. I think that Quin and Zooey can attest to that fact as well."

Kiera wondered about the gift. "Rama, does this gift have a positive affect on humans?"

"Don't know," Rama replied.

The conversation then turned its attention on Quin.

CHAPTER FORTY-EIGHT

Quin

Quin's preferred alternate form is that of a human, even though she is a faun. Her parents, however, were descended from a herd of grazers living on the northern slopes of Olympus. Quin came to be a magician after some heavy-duty training from her adopted sister, Circe, whom she met quite by accident.

"Tell us about your training with Circe." Fabian asked Quin to explain.

"The first time I met Circe, she was on the path that led to the top of Olympus. I was grazing on the path, and there was a spot so narrow that only one person could pass. Circe demanded that I move for her, but I was stubborn and did not want to give up my patch of grass."

Quin continued. "Circe started in on one of her spells to place a curse upon me, to turn me into something horrible. But I was too quick for her and charged at her bumping her off the path and down onto a ledge. Stranded on the ledge below me, Circe realized she was trapped. Without my help, she could not make it up to the path and would remain there until the snows came. She would have died there on the jagged slopes of Olympus.

Now begging me for help, Circe offered that if I would help rescue her, she would bestow upon me some useful magic. I agreed. I suggested that she toss me up her scarf and I would wrap it around my horns and pull her up to the safety of the trail. She agreed. After she was safely back on the trail, she completed her end of the bargain and surprised me with a gift. Not only did she bestow on me magical powers, by wrapping my head with her scarf three times and chanting some words, which I did not understand, but she also adopted me right then and there, as her little sister in magic. It was a good day for me."

"Wow, what an experience!" Lycos offered. Everyone agreed. "So what is the extent of your powers?" Lycos asked as a follow-up.

"Well, I can use magic to form illusions, and I can use potions of all kinds," Quin informed the group. "I can also cast useful spells, and I'm learning about the other magic skills that I possess all the time, I feel like I'm learning a new one each day." Quin finished. Everyone was amazed.

When Quin met Rama in the forests of Olympus, they became fast friends. Quin received the gift of shapeshifting by swallowing a new pearl from Rama's shell. They have worked together on projects with Artemis ever since.

CHAPTER FORTY-NINE

Zooey

When Zooey wasn't busy being a fig tree or some other strange creation of her imagination she was just plain Zooey.

Zooey was a hegemone that enjoyed resting on the hillsides, meadows, and other well-watered places. At camp, she took the form of watercress next to the stream. The gurgling brook helped to calm her nerves, especially after the fight with Kendra and her Amazons.

Her favorite form was that of a small fig tree, her original form. When an animal or human would come by to pluck or eat the fruit, she would giggle or laugh out loud as the plucking was ticklish and always made her smile.

"You should try it sometime. It tickles!" Zooey encouraged the group, now huddled around the campfire. "The fig tree form is the best!" She added with girlish delight.

"What do you do about dead branches?" Questioned Lycos. "Oh, I just pluck them off or let the wind do it for me. Think of the pruning as cutting your hair. It doesn't hurt, and it feels great after it's done."

Arjun asked: "How did you become a trainer for Artemis?"

"Oh, well." Zooey continued, "Artemis was sitting under my branches one day and started plucking figs. I started laughing, and she realized that I was a hegemone and not just an ordinary tree. Artemis recruited me right on the spot to be a trainer for her."

"With some tutelage from Rama and Quin, I became a trainer and I also became a shapeshifter in the same way they did. It is great fun to take on other forms." Zooey continued. "I have taken the form of humans too, but I don't like it as much as the other creatures I see in the forest; or fantastic creatures you can only imagine."

"Interesting," Arjun observed. "Can you take the form of a ship or some other object?" Arjun questioned further.

"Oh, maybe, but I never tried those shapes before," she said.

"Are you afraid of open water?" Arjun continued his probing questions.

Zooey replied: "Don't know, I've never been to the open sea."

Arjun kept these thoughts in the back of his mind. And then added with a smile: "Zooey, we may have to find out."

Kiera asked a question: "So how did you learn about Martial Arts?"

Zooey replied: "Well, that's a long story." Their campfire was burning down to a bed of embers at this point. Zooey continued, "I started out as a hegemone in a land far to the east of this place. That's when I was a seedling. The people of that place were practicing Martial Arts in front of me in the temple courtyard every day. I picked up those skills by watching the others."

Zooey reflected. "After that, I was uprooted, placed in a small pot, and sent west to Greece by camel caravan. That's how I ended up in the forest of Aeolia. Somehow, my bedding pot fell off a wagon or cart and got pressed or planted in the soil somewhere near this very path that we are on. This all seemed to happen quite by accident or by animals, I don't exactly remember."

Zooey concluded. "I then grew into a small fig tree. Many years passed before I met Artemis and the rest of the story you have already heard."

"That's such an interesting story," Kiera commented. "I'm so glad you are our trainer and part of our group." Kiera then reached out with both hands to tickle the hegemone. Zooey recoiled with giggles and laughter. This reaction put a smile on everyone's face.

Kiera finish her play with Zooey by giving her a well-deserved hug.

CHAPTER FIFTY

Artemis

A rtemis made her way back to the Temple complex at the top of Olympus. Zeus was there at the gate impatiently waiting.

"Where have you been?" Zeus demanded.

"I have been helping your son, and his companions prepare for the encounter they will have with Zurenda, my Lord."

"Good!" affirmed Zeus. "They will need all the help they can get, and not many days hence," he added.

"Your son, Arjun, has grown strong, wise and confident, my Lord, Zeus. His skill with the Olympic Sword, your sword, is very impressive. His display of strength was demonstrated well in the last encounter with Zurenda's warriors." Artemis said approvingly and with a voice of encouragement.

Zeus replied: "Do you think he is ready?"

Artemis: "Yes, my Lord, he is ready, he just may not realize it yet."

"Well, maybe we better test his confidence out a time or two more before he has to face that epic challenge."

Zeus added. "Artemis, you must be exhausted from your trek through the forest. Please come, and have some wine, food, and refreshment.

"Thank you, my Lord." And with that Artemis entered the great hall and found an abundant table of food waiting for her.

Artemis had an enormous appetite; she started to dig in.

A few hours later Selene came into the room where Artemis lay reclined on a white sofa munching on the last clump of red grapes.

"How is my son?" Selene asked intently.

Artemis relayed the same information to her as she had given to Zeus. Between nibbles of grapes, she said: "The stage is set, Zurenda will fall! And when that deed is done, you will have to contend with Eris yourself. Well, maybe not all by yourself." Artemis said retrospectively, popping in a few more grapes and tilting her head toward the cornucopia.

"You may get the help you need or seek from someone completely unexpected." She finished speaking and kept gazing up at the rolling clouds. The grapes were gone, and so was the wine. Selene was still not entirely comforted by this news, but she was encouraged a little by it.

"How can you just sit there eating grapes while my son and his friends are out in the rain, getting soaked, and looking for a message from Olympus? Can't you do something, anything?" Selene pressed.

"My Queen," Artemis looked in Selene's direction, "I'm already doing something about it. My absence at their camp is allowing your son to think things through on his own, and then make some good decisions."

Still not fully comforted with this reassurance, "I need to communicate with my son," Selene said, as she left the great hall and headed for the courtyard pool.

CHAPTER FIFTY-ONE

Forest Camp

The Forest Camp was soggy in the morning! The rain had been coming down for hours. Everyone was soaked. Everything was soaked! The fire would not stay lit due to the intense fog, rain, and moisture. It seemed that smoking embers were all Lycos could coax out of the pit.

Each tree was dripping like a shower stall. Even Zooey, who claimed to like the moisture, said she already had "enough!"

Lycos smiled, so did Fabian.

The rain continued coming down. The brook that Zooey nestled in began to overflow its banks. Water spilled everywhere making its way into the center of camp.

"It's time to move to higher ground or find a raft!" Said Rama, half joking and half serious.

Everyone agreed. Quin chanted a few words removing the protective magic bubble above the camp.

After mounting the horses, the group made their way to a small clearing that led to a decent trail and then finally to a hilltop where they hoped to have a look around.

From the top of the mountain, they could see several more hills and valleys in the distance. They could see the serpentine River Pineios in the distance, every mountain beyond the river was covered with dense clouds, and more rain was falling.

"This rain is so unusual," said Fabian, as he ducked his head under a nearby tree trying to find a little shelter. Fabian invited the horses to join him under the natural canopy; the horses complied and they circled under the driest spot they could find. It was dryer than standing out in the open rain, if only by degrees.

"The horses are restless," Lycos claimed, looking a little worried and glancing towards Arjun who was busy studying his sword.

Kiera had already found a dry spot between a pair of large marble rocks protruding out of the ground like spears from Hades that did not quite make it out of the earth.

The stones tipped in a southward direction just enough to form a narrow but dry alcove under them.

Rama and Quin, now in their natural form, snuggled close together with Kiera, and the three of them managed to avoid the rain that was dripping off the rock and on to the ground in front of them.

One persistent drip seemed to have a mind of its own. It kept dripping on Rama's nose no matter how hard she pressed against the rock to avoid it.

"Face it!" Quin said to Rama, "you're a satyr; you were born to get wet." Rama smiled just a little. The rain kept coming down.

Arjun was not paying any attention to the rain. Instead, his thoughts were focused on the sword, Zurenda, and what lay before them. He kept searching the reflective edge of his sword for any messages from Selene, or a sign from anyone else. *Why did Artemis run off and abandon us?* This thought kept gripping his mind.

After several attempts with the sword, Arjun cast his eyes towards the east and toward Piperi. Just at that moment, the clouds began to break and allowed a single shaft of light to penetrate through the fog to rest on a spot of high ground just to the south of their position only a few hundred cubits away.

Arjun instinctively started running through the forest to locate it. Ducking limbs, branches and jumping over underbrush, Arjun found a path that entailed a few switchbacks and zig-zags up a small hill; he could see the shaft of sunlight illuminating a spot on the hillside before him.

Was it a sign, a message from the Gods?

Whatever it was, it gave him hope!

Panting, Lycos and Kiera caught up with him, and the three of them gazed upon the ground where the illuminating beam of sunlight hit the earth. It was a sign!

There, in the tall grass before them was another round stone just like the one he saw on Skyros.

As they approached, the stone began to glow white-hot, and a rainbow began to form over its surface.

The words of the Goddess Selene could be heard like a clap of thunder.

"My son Arjun and your trusted companions, you must go at once to Piperi. Zurenda and her Amazons have desecrated my Temple and sanctuary; they shall now fall by the sword for their disrespect and blaspheme.

Cerberus

"Attention, attention to new arrivals," came the call over the loudspeaker. "You ladies get in line! Single file!" Cerberus ordered. No, demanded! "We were expecting other souls today, so you have surprised us all with your arrival."

The "ladies" were none other than Kendra and her warriors. Getting down into the underworld took some time. More time than they had supposed. The path from beneath the Olympic forests was full of obstacles, small streams, and jagged rocks. The ladies soon realized that their souls still had a bodily form, and therefore could move about this place as mortals, perhaps easier, and more comfortably. They noted one small exception: The warriors had the un-human ability to pass through solid rock and other obstructions that would normally stop a mortal.

Cerberus turned his back to the group for a moment and then shuffled through some papers on his credenza. "Ah! Here we are," pulling out a folder from the bottom of the stack marked "URGENT!" Cerberus, then looked up, his eyes peering over his small rounded glasses, perched upon the end of his nose and said: "Ladies, there has been some mistake: You're not supposed to be here!"

"Now, what to do? What to do?" He quizzed himself aloud as more new arrivals lined up behind the Amazons, adding to his workload.

"I'm sorry, but we have no assignment for you at this time." After a brief pause and pointing to some benches on the other side of the room. Cerberus simply stated: "You will have to wait."

Kendra's displeasure was evident. She glared at the gatekeeper, in a way that only she could.

Trying to be polite, Cerberus said, with a tone of consternation. "Ladies, please have a seat on that bench over there, while I sort this out."

Reluctantly, Kendra, Jayla, and the others did as directed; the seat was scorching hot, even for a spirit.

What else could they do? By some magic exercised against them in the forest, their mortal bodies had already been consumed by the Olympic forest.

There was no other place to go.

There was no going back.

While they sat there waiting, Kendra realized that there was something that they could do. After some whispering amongst themselves while Cerberus was busy processing the other arrivals - and not looking in their direction, they decided to make a break for it and head down a hallway that had to lead somewhere, anywhere.

Without weapons, they all felt a little "underdressed," but it did not matter, no one else had weapons either. Nobody, except Cerberus, that is. He was armed with a single spear. The shaft was about four cubits long and had a blackened red tip that emitted a small stream of reddish grey smoke while it sat there in the background behind Cerberus' desk.

The spear was leaning against the wall next to the entrance gates. The gates marked the official entrance into the underworld. They were anything but pearly.

Through the gates, the new arrivals could see the cavernous hall that stretched out to the right and the left and beyond as far as eye could the see. Belches and plumes of fire came from the floor of the hall and seemed to be random in location and frequency. Puddles of hot liquid lava formed small rivers of red that crisscrossed the space. Steam poured out of unlikely places, hissing and belching as it released pressure.

After several minutes of walking down the hallway, their exit suddenly became a stone path, followed by a dirt path. Collectively, it felt like an eternity to cross.

Kendra and her warriors found themselves coming upon a small fountain of fresh water just to the left of the dusty red path. This feature seemed strange, but maybe it was the source or a tributary of the River Styx? No one knew for sure; no one had been there before; however, the water looked inviting and felt colder than the surrounding landscape.

Jayla took a drink. The water entered her mouth but immediately spilled onto the red dirt beneath her feet, not quenching her thirst.

The scenery had changed. The hallway they followed gave way to a scene of robust reds, and greyish blacks. Polydora observed, "this is no place like home."

A wobbly red glow was coming toward them and heading down the path. The Amazons all quickly moved out of the way to avoid the oncoming light. To their surprise and amazement, the light grew bigger, closer, brighter. Finally, in the dim light of Hades own realm, they could see what looked like a skeleton riding on some contraption.

The machine under this skeleton had two wheels spaced about three cubits apart, a seat for the rider above them and a pair of bars that allowed the rider to control the direction of the front wheel.

"I have never, in all my days, seen anything like this before!" Said Jayla.

The bicycle was complete with two holding baskets saddled over the rear wheel. The driver of this vehicle was named Joshua; he had a name tag stuck to one of his exposed ribs. He worked for Cerberus.

Joshua's punishment for the rest of eternity was to carry out the task of a delivery boy, assigned to deliver work packets for incoming new arrivals.

Joshua pedaled his bike right past Kendra and the girls. Seemingly, the only flesh left on his bones were two loose fitting eyeballs connected to his skull with only the optical nerve. The eyeballs bounced in and out of his head with each bump on the path. The cyclist took no notice of them as he passed by.

"Quick!" Kendra ordered. "Let's run down this path. It has to lead somewhere." The girls all followed their leader. The walls pressed into the path. It was getting tighter, narrower.

"What will we do if we get stuck?" One of the girls asked, with a tone of worry in her voice.

"We will make it," Jayla reassured. "Just keep going, remember that new ability we have to pass through stone?" Jayla reminded them.

Cerberus finally got the rest of the souls processed and off to their assignments. He then remembered that he needed to get Kendra and her warriors assigned for their upcoming eternity. He looked over his tall black granite reception desk and to the bench where he ordered them to wait. They were gone!

Cerberus panicked, realizing that were souls running around in Hades without a work permit; he did the only thing he could think of. He hit the red panic button under his desk. Suddenly, dozens of red strobe lights began to flash, sirens blared. Everyone was placed on high alert!

Cerberus turned himself from a bumbling old desk clerk into his true form, a ravenous three-headed dog. The surprise change in appearance sent shockwaves of terror throughout the waiting area and the queueing line. His action terrified all the guests who were waiting to check-in. The disappearance of the Amazons, however, had not gone unnoticed by the underworld lord himself. Lord Hades.

Cerberus continued his rampage as a three-headed dog for several minutes. Upon finding no one to bite, he quenched his thirst by lapping water from the nearby puddle. After several minutes he morphed back into an old bumbling desk clerk, went back to business as usual. The Amazons had given him the slip.

CHAPTER FIFTY-THREE

Foes

The rain was coming down in Zurenda's world too. The palace in Piperi was experiencing sheets of rain buffeting the walls and roofs of the fortress. The only dry place to be was inside and under a roof. Before the storm started, Zurenda's Amazonian guards kept collecting more prisoners. They just kept coming. Since the last escape attempt, her prisoners numbered twelve souls in the dungeon.

Talia and the rest of the warriors had been busy. The poor souls came from a variety of miss-haps at sea. The changing sea currents seemed to wash them up on the shores of Piperi with regularity. The merchant ship with the last group of three sailors swamped in heavy seas as the storm that everyone was under created havoc for mariners as well as the people on land.

Zurenda was pleased with the results. The souls that Talia and her warriors were coming home with were adding up. The one prisoner Zurenda wanted, however, had not yet arrived. She knew that Arjun was somewhere between the western flank of Olympus and the sea, but where?

In the back of her mind, she just wanted to *get this over with, lock up Arjun in her dungeon and then feed him to the lions on her timetable, not his.*

But that was not to be. *Patience my dear.* These words kept coming to her mind as a hollow echo or chant. The message was of course from Eris.

Zurenda knew about her fatal weakness. She knew that even as a demi-goddess, all it would take to kill her was three Olympic Silver Arrows plunged into her heart. What she did not realize, and therefore could not account for, was the fact that Kiera, (whom she had not met and did not know), was also aware of this deep, dark little secret. At this point, Arjun did not even know or understand this element of weakness in the Queen.

Zurenda also knew that Arjun had a weakness. Even though he was a demi-god, he spent most of his life living as a mortal man, without that knowledge. At least that is the way she heard it from Eris. As such, he was subject to the weaknesses of the flesh. All she had to do was distract him from his focus, and he could be killed. She could use her beauty and good looks to place him off-guard. Then, toss him into the lion's den and have him eaten for lunch! Demi-God down! This evil thought put a nasty smile on her face. She felt she was ready for Selene's son. Now more than ever.

Arjun knew only this about Zurenda: She was a child of Eris and a demi-goddess in her own right. Beyond that, he did not understand the dynamics of her family life or lack thereof.

He also knew that she had magical ability of some sort and would use that against him. That's why he had Rama, Quin, and Zooey in tow. Artemis said that they would be there to help him. "What else do we need?" He told Lycos and Kiera that night over dinner.

Arjun had no idea about Zurenda's weakness associated with the arrows. Kiera kept that secret from him, thinking that his not knowing would somehow help him in the long run.

Arjun's plan all along was going to be simple: Use his sword, cut his way into the palace, cut Zurenda down, the same way he did with Kendra and her warriors in the forest, restore the palace to its original lunar glory, and finally, re-seat his Mother on her rightful throne.

Simple, right? What else is there to know? Lycos was there to help, and so too was Kiera.

How easy does it get? Arjun reasoned.

CHAPTER FIFTY-FOUR

Hadrian and Zedra

adrian was a big man. For an Aegean sailor, he stood head and shoulders above his shipmates. Zedra was as tall and slender as Hadrian was round.

In Hadrian's mind, they were both victims of Zurenda's brutality. The Queen had betrayed each of them.

Hadrian understood his punishment; He was in the wrong place at the wrong time. Zedra was not as forgiving. She felt that Zurenda used her to make an example to the others.

Regardless, of the personal circumstances, they both found themselves on the journey to Hades together. During their decent, they became friends for different reasons. Zedra needed a big man to help her down the pathway. It was becoming too hot and arduous for her to bear. Hadrian needed companionship, and Zedra seemed to offer that without even trying.

The couple managed to get to the bottom of the footpath that led to Hades. The trail leveled out and became somewhat straight - comparatively.

When at the bottom, the path made a right turn and began to follow the banks of the river Styx. The path meandered along its shores and they were making good time.

Hadrian began to speak: "I wonder what is going on with Arjun and the rest of the folks up top?" He said in his monotone voice.

Zedra answered with this comment: "I suppose that Zurenda is preparing for a mini-war with Arjun and that they have enlisted all of the women they can find."

Hadrian interjected: "Where do all those women come from?" Adding the rhetorical question: "Do they grow them somewhere on the mainland?"

Zedra clarified his apparent confusion: "When I joined the warriors, the Amazons of Zurenda, I was a young girl in a nearby village tending a pot of soup in my house when there came a knock at the door. Our door was not opened but kicked down, to reveal a pair of Zurenda's warriors standing right there in the doorway. After looking me over for fitness, they took me hostage and insisted, (at spear point), that I come with them.

"I told them that I was the only maid in the home and that my parents would be returning any minute from the market. It did not matter. They forced me onto the back of a horse, binding my hands to the saddle, and carried me away to the pier.

"There I was placed on a ship, and sent with several others, to Piperi. Once at Piperi, Zurenda herself pulled me from the line of recruits and placed this delta-shaped necklace over my head until it rested on my neck.

"From that moment until the lions killed me, I could not remember my past. My whole childhood was erased from my mind. I cared not for the future either. My only desire was to serve Zurenda at any cost, even if that price was my life. I still can't believe that the Queen betrayed me after I had given my all to her cause."

Hadrian replied: "I had heard stories like that, but I did not believe any of them were true."

Zedra responded. "They are true, all true."

Zedra, now continuing in that singular thought said: "So now look at me! I'm down here in Hades realm, walking along this god-forsaken path with a dead man when I could have remained a maid in my father's home and had a life, and a family, a future in the tranquil villages of Greece."

Zedra shed a single tear, and then another. "It was all because of that stupid triangle necklace. I regret the day that Zurenda placed that emblem on my neck. Otherwise, none of this would have ever happened." Zedra lamented, and cried some more.

Hadrian tried to comfort her, as best a dead man can. He placed his arm around her shoulder as they walked the path together.

After a while, the path opened up into a high vaulted room or space. More souls were seen coming into this hall from all directions. Everyone gathered to one place. They could see the front desk into the gates of Hades, the gates of the underworld. A crusty old guy named Cerberus manned the front counter.

Hadrian and Zedra both patiently stood in line for their assignments.

After standing in line for what seemed an eternity, they were both called to the front desk.

Cerberus asked for their names, and then shuffled through his papers. "Ah, yes, here we are."

Hadrian, here is your assignment." Hadrian opened the packet. He read the assignment: "You are to join Arjun's forces and vanquish Zurenda." Surprised and a little stunned, Hadrian's eyes grew wide open with the thoughts of this new assignment.

"Okay, Miss, here is your assignment:" Zedra opened the packet. She read the following: "You are assigned to join the forces of the demi-god Arjun and lay waste to his opposition."

Zedra was stunned. She said, "I have the same assignment as Hadrian."

"Can we do it together?" She asked Cerberus. He looked at her over the top of his glasses, almost peering down on her head. "Do it any way you like," Cerberus replied, "you will both be issued a sword at the armory over there."

Cerberus pointed to a nearby cave with massive black bars over the entrance. A neon light flashed sporadically over the entrance and no one around seemed to mind.

Once at the cave's door, Joshua was there to meet them. His bike was leaning up against the open leaf of the cave door, and he was resting his arms on the make-shift wooden counter inside the entrance.

"Excuse me sir," Hadrian interrupted Joshua's reading of the Hades Times, latest edition.

"We are here to collect our weapons for our new assignment."

Acting a little put-out, Joshua got up from his chair and went to the back room. He came back to the counter with two Olympic blades. Both swords were a little dusty, but each one was remarkably exquisite and beautifully balanced.

"Please sign here!" Joshua instructed. Zedra and Hadrian both placed their "X" on the roster. "Do you swear upon the River Styx to return the weapons when you have completed your assignment?" Yes! Yes! They both agreed. "Should you fail to return the swords, Hades will repossess and own your everlasting soul for eternity!" Joshua emphasized. And with that, the transaction was done.

Zedra had a follow-up question: "What sort of ability do these swords have that a mortal sword does not?" Joshua, with his fleshless hands clutching on to the cave bars, formulated a response, but first, he had to stick his left eye-ball back into its socket and adjust his sagging low-er jaw so he could concentrate. He did not even blink.

"The swords you now have were both forged from the gold and silver mines under the Mountain of the Gods, Olympus." Joshua whispered. "That is to say, that they were both made with the skill and care of a certified Olympian black-smith." Placing his boney right hand next to his jaw-bone mouth, he whispered these words: "You will find that these weapons are capable of diving asunder rock and earth, bone and marrow, flesh and spirit, god and demi-god. In fact, there is almost nothing they cannot slice through, kill or separate!"

Hadrian and Zedra thought about these instructions. Zedra exclaimed. "This truly is a gift from the gods."

Joshua corrected her statement. "This is not a gift; this is a loan from the Under Lord. The swords belong to him. You will be expected to take care of them and return them in good condition, or the reaper will exercise the terms of the contract you just signed."

"One more thing you should know, my young friends," Joshua advised. "If you need directions on your journey, just look at the flat side of the blade for a reflection or a vision. It may be useful in showing you the way."

Joshua's left eyeball fell out again. He turned to search for it on the floor of the cave. "There it is!" He said with some delight. "Now, I just need to find my optic nerve."

Hadrian and Zedra took Joshua's lapse of concentration as their cue to leave. Once, Joshua, had his left eye re-installed, and he could focus again, the visitors were gone.

Joshua, seeing that the couple had left, returned to his old dusty worn-out chair behind the counter. It had been a full day's work for him. Joshua said these words to the swarm of roaches crawling by as he sat down. "I sure hope they return those swords, or they will end up looking like me, the keeper of the swords in the House of Hades."

What Joshua did not say out loud, was that as a mortal man, he had made the mistake of betraying the trust of the gods. His life ended abruptly in a battle with Hercules, and his bones were boiled clean before his soul ever left the mortal realm. Mercifully, he was allowed to retain both of his eyes. He would forever be a skeleton in the service of Cerberus and Hades.

CHAPTER FIFTY-FIVE

Forest Camp

The rain finally stopped. The clouds were giving way to sunshine once again. Everything was soaked, however. Arjun was the only one who did not mind. Once the sun's beams were penetrating all the way to the forest floor, Kiera, Arjun, and Lycos made their way back to the camp. They found the rest of the group wringing out supplies and getting the horses into the sun to dry off as well.

Kiera let the warmth of the sun beat down on her face and arms for what seemed like an hour. The sun's rays were like taking a warm bath in the meadow, completely contrasting with the soggy days that now were hopefully fading into the past. Rama, Quin, and Fabian were getting ready to strike camp. Kiera gathered up her wet things and took care to pack the bow and the quiver of silver arrows in a place that could be easily retrieved. The leather quiver was soaked, but the arrows did not seem to mind the rain.

Fabian was the first to speak: "Master Arjun, we need to get going, as our path may already be hedged up."

Fabian explained. "While you three were at the peak communing with the gods, we here at camp became aware that our location was no longer a secret."

Before Arjun could respond, Kiera interjected and asked what they had observed to come to this conclusion.

"My Queen," Fabian continued, "we have reason to believe that the trees around us are not friendly to our cause."

Zooey supported that claim by adding in her high squeaky voice: "These trees are not natural to this place. They keep dropping big giant limbs down upon our camp, narrowly missing us." Zooey observed: "I think they are trying to kill us. I have been suspicious of them since we arrived at this place." Zooey continued: "Since the south wind has come up after the storm lifted, the trees have been talking about killing us!"

Quin added her observations. "The only reason that these trees have not already killed us already was due, in part, to the magic shield that I placed over us when we got here. But my powers," she confessed, "are still not perfected, and this cursed south wind will only hasten their work if we don't get out of here!"

Just then, the ground beneath them began to pitch and heave up and down. Rocks were cracking under their feet and all around them. Tree roots started lurching out of the ground taking a few horses by surprise. The roots came shooting out of the earth whipping the horses around in the air like rag dolls.

After giving them a good shake, the trees flung horses against the rocks, killing two of them and wounding others. The roots, like they had a mind of their own, would then go after another victim.

Seeing this unnatural display, the remaining horses began pulling at their lead ropes wildly and rearing up with fright. One of the roots grabbed Fabian and flung him high into the air. Lycos, thinking quickly, pulled out his sword, and springing up into the air in a forward roll, cut the root on the rebound, slicing it off in mid-air. Fabian came sliding into to the camp with all fours out in front of him to break his fall, dirt flying everywhere.

Fabian, not seriously injured, just shaken up after this incident and was ready to leave.

This event brought with it more tension and excitement than Arjun needed. "Let's be off to Piperi," he said.

And with that, the group packed up, mounted up, and made ready to go. Two horses down.

CHAPTER FIFTY-SIX

Zurenda

Z urenda's hate of men did not come overnight. It was a learned behavior, an acquired taste. She never knew her mortal Father. Eris was the only mother that she knew. Once she was born, the only mother that ever cared for her was Eris.

Eris was no friend of men in general anyway. She despised Zeus and his harem. She despised the other gods of Olympus as well, because she never got her way.

Eris was secretly jealous that she was not counted 'worthy' to be one of Zeus' mistresses. She was jealous of Selene, and all that the lunar goddess represented.

Selene managed to attract Zeus' attention and affection in ways she could not. "Life is not fair!" She would lament to the mirror in her palace chamber. Seeing her pitiful reflection in the mirror without a man in the frame caused her more feelings of regret and contempt. Her natural reaction was to dash the mirror to pieces with her blade.

Each time she would look in a mirror, the sting of regret would overflow, and the mirror became the unlucky object of her contempt, the receiver of her unruly outpouring of passion.

Indeed, when she walked past any mirror anywhere in the palace, the mirror would instantly shatter into a thousand pieces. Needless to say, the palace did not have very many operational mirrors. That did not seem to change life as Eris knew it, but it did make her feel better.

Zurenda acquired this dislike for men through her mother, but her hatred of men took jealousy and contempt to a whole new level. In Zurenda's mind, it was only fair to torture any and all men that fell under her power. They were all part of the 'problem.'

It did not matter who they were or where they were from. True, she was especially pleased to torture the men of Greece and the men of Athens in particular because they somehow reflected the arrogance of the king. "The King on top of the Mountain." In her mind, however, all men needed to pay for the injustice that was done to her mother by Zeus. All men were equally guilty in her eyes.

If the fates were to have been obeyed by the gods, Eris would have married Zeus, thus, she (Zurenda), by rights should have become the 'Daughter of Zeus' and not the daughter of some forgotten earthly king that would never be man enough to claim her as his own. In the eyes of her mother, the Goddess Eris, her crowning achievement, therefore, would be to capture torture and kill a son of Zeus! Just one son would be enough! How immensely satisfying that would be! And what an appropriate sacrifice that would be to offer her mother!

Zurenda further reasoned that if she were able to do this great deed, the injustice that was done to her mother, by Zeus, would somehow be made right.

There would be nothing that Zeus could do to change the outcome. Eris' revenge against Zeus would be complete. The prophecy of Cassandra would fail! Zeus would be humiliated and embarrassed for eternity. The thought made the deed seem even more delicious and appealing.

Zurenda never knew her father. Eris did not speak of him. However, she knew the truth about her lineage, the fact that her father was none other than King Agamemnon.

Zurenda would have liked to have learned more about her father, but Eris never discussed it with her.

Agamemnon never came around. He was always too busy carrying out the will of lesser gods in the Greek fight against Troy. It did not matter anyway. Maybe her father would come home someday, she thought, but those dreams were shattered too when she learned that his real wife, Clytemnestra murdered him in his own house, as an act of jealousy and revenge.

Zurenda had another reason to hate the Olympians. Eris told her that Artemis wanted Agamemnon to sacrifice her, (Zurenda), the firstborn daughter on the doorsteps of Artemis' Temple in Euboea in return for the goddess' assistance to the King in the sacking of Troy.

Even the Goddess of contempt, Eris would not stand by and have her only daughter, Zurenda, sacrificed for the sake of the war.

As an infant, Eris quickly whisked Zurenda away to the island of Piperi for safe keeping, away from Agamemnon and away from Artemis. It was ironic that the palace in Piperi was none-other than Selene's Palace, Selene's own Temple and sanctuary.

But Eris did not care. After Selene's servants were killed or driven out, the palace was deserted. It became the perfect place to hide her little girl from the rest of the world.

Artemis, furious at this show of defiance ordered that Zurenda's half-sister Iphigenia be sacrificed in her stead.

The King, Agamemnon, carried out the deed himself much to the dismay of his wife, Clytemnestra. To make matters worse, Artemis had already aligned herself with Selene. Zurenda's young life became a string of broken hearts and failed expectations. Zurenda was reared in an empty palace with no family, except for occasional appearances from her mother, Eris.

Zurenda was allowed to interact only with other women. That was all that Eris would allow. This course eventually spawned a Queen-Warrior relationship with any women that would happen by her kingdom. Zurenda turned to dark magic, sorcery, and witchcraft to fill up the blank spaces of her miserable life. Tyranny was only a few steps away, and the transition was to her, perfectly normal.

In her youth, Zurenda experimented with shapeshifting magic and found that she could strike terror in every heart by assuming the body of a Chimera. This shape alone would put the scare into anyone who ventured across her palace threshold.

Time passed. She grew older, shapeshifting wasn't as fun anymore. She became content with her human form, although she always retained the ability to shapeshift if the need to do it should arise in the future.

Zurenda's world, for a time, was almost peaceful. That peace came to an abrupt end when Cassandra had to open her big mouth and publish the "Prophecy." After that, her world would never be the same. The innocence of youth was over. There was no going back.

CHAPTER FIFTY-SEVEN

Agamemnon

eing compelled to sacrifice a daughter was one
thing, but willingly doing it was entirely another.
Agamemnon as a King was very effective in leading the charge against Troy. This skill was a perfect fit for
Eris who needed a leader to follow her every whim. What
Eris did not take into account was the dubious character of
the man she would fall in love with, the man she would
have a child with. As a goddess, Eris should have been
above the works of mortal flesh. Instead, she wallowed in
the mire of human frailties and made a bad problem worse.

Agamemnon was disciplined for war, but not disciplined when it came to love. His mortal wife Clytemnestra became suspicious of his conquests when she discovered several mistresses through serendipitous means.

Agamemnon's chief mistress was none-other than the Goddess Eris.

"How was this possible?" Clytemnestra tortured herself for an answer that would make sense. No response or explanation ever did.

Finally, in an act of frustration and revenge, Clytemnestra put an end to Agamemnon's extra-marital activities with a long silver dagger thrust through his cheating heart.

There would be no new King of Greece!

The only consolation Clytemnestra could take was that she still had four children to call her own. Maybe one would rise to be the new King or Queen of Greece.

And what would become of Zurenda? She did not care. "Let her rot on Piperi." Clytemnestra declared.

A daughter lost.

CHAPTER FIFTY-EIGHT

Kiera

K iera had a hard time leaving two dead horses at the forest camp, unburied, un-memorialized, forgotten. She asked Quin if there was something she could do to send the animals to a better place. Could she do some chant to memorialize their service?

The trees were still acting like they were going to try and kill the rest of them if they could get their roots on them.

So, to console her as they were leaving camp, Quin from a distance stood up erect on her hind legs while on the back of her horse she uttered these words in Latin:

"Pax Si vis pacem, para bellum."

The rough English translation is this:

"Peace be to you if you want peace, otherwise, prepare for war."

This thoughtful sediment, accompanied by the haunting tones of an Aulos played by Lycos, seemed to soothe Kiera and also Zooey, both of whom shed a few tears while they were leaving camp and heading down the mud-soaked path.

They knew they had to go. It was the best Quin could do under the circumstances.

Kiera's mind was always thinking about the future. She knew that she was skilled with the bow and as such was trusted with Artemis' bow and quiver, but she had not looked at the markings on the arrows of late.

She had never shot one of the silver and gold tipped ones. She realized that she needed practice, and needed it soon.

The rest of the trip from the forest camp down to the Port of Pagasae was uneventful. *Thanks be to the gods,* was her primary thought. She was glad to be with Arjun, Lycos and the rest of the team. She did not mind that Zooey kept changing shapes throughout the journey to the port. She found it entertaining.

At one point Zooey was her usual self as a fig tree, and then she would change to a human, making herself look like a Greek chef, complete with a floppy hat. After that Zooey transformed into a jungle ape for a while climbing on every tree, she could get her hands and feet on. Kiera wondered if she was ever bored with being a tree.

Kiera very much liked being human. She could not imagine that she could take any other form. She missed Artemis. Thoughts about what Artemis had said about Zurenda kept wandering through her mind. She wondered about the title that Artemis had given her in the meadows. "Queen of the Wilderness." *Was it given just for fun, just to pass the time? Was it real? What did it mean?*

Kiera's thoughts went fast-forward to the trials that they may have to face at the port. The last time they were at a port she missed the boat and took a cold plunge into the sea. She would not make that mistake again! Kiera worried about Arjun's encounter with Zurenda.

Will he be strong enough to face her?

Will he be strong enough to fight her?

Will her magic trap him?

Will we survive?

How will I have to deal one-on-one with Zurenda?

Her thoughts drifted another direction to a happier place.

What about me and Arjun?

Would we have a future together?

Could we ever be more than friends?

Where could we live in safety? Kymi or elsewhere?

Kiera thought about the kiss on her forehead by her Father as they left Kymi. Would she ever see him again?

These thoughts and others kept running through her mind, again and again on the bumpy path to the port. Finally the emotions surfaced and welled-up within her eyes. She wept a few tears, and then several more.

CHAPTER FIFTY-NINE

Cassandra

O n the pathway to the coast, the conversation about the 'Cassandra Prophecy' came up between Rama and Fabian. "What business does this false prophetess have to do with us?" Blurted Fabian, while scratching at the loose mud and earth beneath his hoof along the trail they were following.

Rama replied: "She has everything to do with us. Her predictions of the fall of Troy were all true, even though no one believed her." Rama continued, "We know that she also predicted that the man who would wield an

Olympic sword would be the downfall of Eris and her minions. That means that Arjun, (or someone else like him), will be required to fulfill the prophecy."

"Reason stands that someone who is a demi-god or someone who has been endowed with demi-god like powers will be required to do the deed. This task would have to be accomplished by someone who had the support of the gods, both in Olympus and in the Underworld."

Overhearing this conversation, Kiera kept quiet and continued to listen.

Rama continued: "What we do know is that Cassandra was murdered right after she made this prediction." Rama recounted. "Her insane babblings were discounted by the people as nonsense, fanatical, and preposterous. Any clarification to the prophecy will have to come from the man who bestowed on her the gift in the first place, Apollo himself."

Quin interrupted Rama with this question: "Does Eris know about the prophecy?"

Rama answered, "Yes, she knows. She knows only too well! That is why the warriors of Zurenda hunted down Arjun and the others at the Straits of Euripus, in the forest of Aeolia, and now it looks like they are trying to find us again."

Quin added more clarity to the conversation: "I now understand why Kendra's last breath was about the prophecy. They just want us dead!" Quin finished this thought with a gulp.

Rama continued, "By killing Arjun, the odds of another demi-god coming forth are greatly reduced. The odds of Zurenda accomplishing her mother's vision of world domination are greatly increased."

Fabian interjected: "Rama wasn't there more to this prophecy? If I recall, there was something in there about how the sword and the bow, the raven and the beast, the mighty gods of the sky above and the earth beneath would combine forces somehow to create peace and extinguish war?"

Rama replied: "Sadly, this was the part of Cassandra's ramblings that no one could understand; thus, many people dismissing the whole prediction as utter nonsense."

The pathway they were on was getting wider; it had turned into a road. Arjun piped up: "We need to keep moving, we will be in the Port of Pagasae by morning."

CHAPTER SIXTY

Port Pagasae

P ort Pagasae was a bustling port for being so far off the beaten path from Athens. The buildings were a collection of rag-tag wooden structures that offered just enough protection to ward off the elements, but left occupants wanting for additional creature-comforts.

The port merchants were busy bartering in the town square and along the dock. There was some bartering for Arjun to do as well. He had thirteen horses in hand, and he was in the market for a boat.

Rama, Quin, and Zooey all took the human form of merchants and peasants to keep attention on their group at a minimum. Arjun did not want any surprises and did not want to draw any unwanted attention.

Arjun and Lycos walked through the narrow lanes of the village toward the pier. Awkwardly maneuvering through the town with so many horses, but they seemed to manage it.

Arjun asked an old man near the entrance to the dock if he knew of any boats that may be for sale. He did not.

However; he directed the group to another gathering of merchants a city block or so further down the road.

The man on the street thought it odd that there was a Centaur in the group, but did not pay it any mind.

After a few minutes, Arjun approached another merchant with the same question. Raising his eyebrows at the sight of a somewhat strange group of travelers, and looking over the excellent team of horses through his unpatched right eye, he motioned for them to come closer.

The gentleman's name was Semon, or at least that was how he pronounced it. His smile revealed a few missing teeth, including the front two. His appearance was that of a fisherman. But he made Quin nervous.

He was sunbaked, wrinkled, bent over with age and adorned with tattered and worn-out clothing. Even the hat he was wearing was old.

Arjun began the conversation: "We would like to purchase a boat or barter passage on a boat, and we are prepared to pay with these fine horses."

Semon regarded the horses and inspected the steeds and mares while the question at hand floated around in the air.

"Where did you get such fine horses?" He asked.

Arjun replied: "They belong to us and are ours and ours alone to trade." Arjun stated this without really answering Semon's question directly. After all, Arjun reasoned, it was none of his concern.

"Sell the horses in the town square," Semon advised with a strange flash of evil in his eye. "Bring me back the gold, and we will talk."

Taking the horses back to the town square was a bit of a trick. By now, the crowds were pressing in on the group, and they became more of a curiosity than Arjun wanted to be.

"Who has over a dozen horses at any one time?" Questioned one of the nearby merchants selling dried fish.

"I'll bet they are stolen," cried another person from the market across the street.

This kind of attention was not helping their cause.

Finally, Lycos got upon a rickety wooden platform near the town square. "Who will purchase these fine horses?" He cried to the gathering crowd.

A man dressed in white and red robes came forward from the back of the crowd.

"How much you want for 'em?" The man, known only as Boaz, asked.

"The price is one golden drachma for each horse." Lycos clarified.

Just then, an old lady came forward. She was bent over with age and shuffled to the front of the crowd. She had long stringy grey hair. Her facial features personified the definition of old. From her raspy and shrillish voice came the call: "I will offer you two," holding up two fingers as high as she could reach, "two golden drachmas for each horse."

This comment got everyone's attention. There was an old woman, wrapped in an old tattered dress and a long grey shawl offering double the asking price for the horses. Lycos addressed her: "Going once," no other offers were forthcoming, not even a counter offer from the old man named Boaz. "Going twice? Going three times? Then, the horses are sold!" Lycos announced, "To the little old lady, over there, wearing a grey shawl."

After the sale was completed, Arjun announced to the crowd that he was in the market for a boat. Any seaworthy vessel would do. Again the old lady offered this information: "There is an old ship in the third slip off the main pier. You can have the vessel for twenty drachmae."

Arjun and the others followed the lady to the pier and considered her offer. Zooey's ankle length dress kept getting stepped on by Rama, half tripping her in the process.

The horses were entrusted to a young man at the town square, who took them to the town stables.

Arjun and Lycos considered the vessel in the water. It was half-submerged! Not only was the craft half-sunk, but it was also apparent that the boat was not even close to being sea-worthy.

"Ma'am, we'll have to pass," said Arjun. "We need a boat that will get us to Piperi and back." Without even thinking, their destination slipped right out of his mouth. "I mean Athens." Arjun stammered and tried to recover his words in a quick clarification.

"Arjun, why do you need to travel to Piperi?" Inquired the woman and as she did so, she shifted her hunched shoulders, to a more comfortable posture.

Arjun, surprised she knew his name, added these questioning words: "I perceive that you are in league with the gods?"

The woman had not yet given her name.

"Let me show you what I can do," said the old woman. She then reached out her old arthritic hands, and mumbling some words in Greek that Arjun did not understand; she began to signal to the vessel.

From the edge of the dock, she chanted that Arjun and his friends needed to go to Piperi.

"How did she know my name?" Arjun whispered to Kiera while furrowing his brow.

"Don't know," she whispered in reply.

The old woman broke the suspense that seemed to hang in the air. With her right hand she gestured by raising the boat out of the water, tipping it from port side to starboard side and while draining it out, mid-air, she then, with her left hand, made a fist and flung her fingers outward as if to command the craft to be made whole.

This gesture, along with others, started the wind swirling around the boat, stripping the old paint, repairing the planks and repainting the hull. She commanded the heat from the sun focus on drying out the interior. All this was accomplished in a sort of a mist or a fog, and no passersby would have been able to notice anything strange happening at the pier.

No one that is, except Semon. To prove to Arjun that the boat was sea-worthy, she set her hands down against her legs; the ship followed this motion and splashed down again into the slip. Water went everywhere. Zooey and Rama, who were standing nearest to the dock, got soaked from head to toe. The dresses they wore in disguise became soaked and looked dreadful from a close viewing distance. Quin remained dry and untouched by the deluge.

The old fishing boat, presented before them, was completely restored and sound in every detail. There was plenty of room for more than seven passengers fitted with a galley and brand new coat of paint covering the hull and the interior.

"By all the gods, who is your patron?" Lycos asked the old woman.

"I have found favor with a few of the gods," she replied, "and they have bestowed on me the gift of restoration that you see before you."

Curiosity finally got the best of Arjun. He asked her directly: "What is your name my lady?"

The old woman replied. "My name is Salacia. I am a goddess of the sea. You need to get your group on board and be off to Piperi!"

Arjun offered to give her back the drachma that he had just obtained in selling the horses for the purchase of the boat.

"Keep them." Salacia offered as her hands pressed the coins back into Arjun's cupping palm. "I have no use for gold."

And with that statement to the young warrior Arjun, Salacia vanished before his eyes.

CHAPTER SIXTY-ONE

Sea Spray

L eaving the harbor at Pagasae was easy, way too easy. Arjun reflected on the miracle that unfolded before their eyes of how they managed to obtain a good boat in such a short time frame. With all his friends aboard, it looked like it would be smooth sailing all the way to Piperi. He knew they lost a lot of time in the woods during the storm, and hoped to make up for lost time on the water. He felt like he was back in his element, it was good to be back on the sea.

According to the time frame that Selene gave him, they had less than a week to accomplish this mission.

And then what? He asked himself. No immediate answer swirled into his confused head.

The sea water in the Bay of Pagasae was remarkably calm. Not so much as a small chop or wave. The wind was in their favor too, blowing gently straight out of the Northwest.

Rama and Fabian helped trim the sail. Zooey decided to turn herself back into a tree for the trip. "As a human, I'm already getting seasick," she said.

Quin took a position with all fours firmly fixed on the bow. "I want to feel the sea-spray on my face, for the first time," she said.

Lycos added with a smile: "We should be able to make the Island of Piperi within two days; there will be plenty of sea-spray to go around."

Quin noticed some new markings on the bow while leaning over the front deck to maximize her sea spray. The refurbished boat they were on had a new name engraved on each side of the prow. Letters printed in Greek read:

"Ο Πολεμιστής από τον Ὄλυμπο"

The title, translated into English, read:

"Warrior from Olympus."

CHAPTER SIXTY-TWO

Kendra

While she did not realize it at the time, Kendra was leading her warriors right back to the island of Piperi. The journey underground was slower, trickier, and harder, but they were heading in the right direction.

The path they were on kept flooding with red-hot lava from time to time and getting past the flows of molten rock took time and planning.

On their journey, they passed the Elysian Fields. The fields were very lush with green grass, trees, fresh water coming from the headwaters of the Mnemosyne streams, and plenty of light. The scene was so inviting that going forward to another destination seemed crazy and unnatural.

As they crossed the fields, they could hear children laughing; see couples sitting together beneath large shade trees in what looked like a lazy afternoon setting.

The glow of the sun, or an orb that looked like the sun, felt warm and inviting. The more they all gazed at the place, the less they wanted to leave.

"No ladies," Kendra interrupted, "We need to keep going east. I don't know why, but we just have to keep going." Streaks of disappointment covered each face. However, if Kendra's girls were anything, they were disciplined. "Remember, we were sworn to help Zurenda in life or death."

"All right," said Jayla, as she consented to Kendra's dominant will. "We'll keep on going."

The path they were on led back into the steamy black and red metamorphic rocks from which the Elysian Fields were formed. The cracks between the rock layers were thin, but the women managed to fit through anyway.

They were on a mission.

CHAPTER SIXTY-THREE

Hadrian and Zedra

adrian was well suited as a delivery boy. He did not mind that Zedra managed to piggy-back over his shoulders when she was tired from traveling, and her feet were killing her from the long walk.

Both of their swords clanked together when they came to a narrow spot, but they managed to squeeze through anyway.

Hadrian and Zedra, though they did not know it, were on a different but parallel path to Kendra, eventually leading to Piperi. It was just a matter of time before they all would arrive there.

At one point they came to a dead-end.

"What do we do now?" Hadrian asked.

"Let's look at the blade," Zedra suggested, "Like Joshua said, maybe there is some vision or clue on the blade."

They both looked, and were stunned and amazed! "The reflection on the blade tells us that we should be heading right through that stone wall up ahead," said Zedra.

"Impossible!" Retorted Hadrian!

"Try hacking at the wall with your blade and see what happens," suggested Zedra.

Hadrian drew the sword way over his head, with both hands firmly on the hilt; he aimed at the wall and then delivered a blow to the solid rock in front of him. Sparks and dust flew in every direction. After the dust settled, they both looked on with amazement at the results. The blackish rock in front of them for a goodly distance was gone.

Vaporized.

Disintegrated.

"Joshua was right," Hadrian confirmed. "These Olympic swords are very useful in making a new path where there was none before."

The duo's rock hacking continued for a while. It seemed like forever, but they were making progress.

After a few more swings at the stone, the path opened up again, and they were able to get back to a reasonable walking pace. Zedra was learning that these swords were indeed a gift from the gods.

Before long, they found a small stream that was spraying a fine mist of cool water over the trail through the cracks in the stone. "Let's sit down and rest awhile," suggested Zedra.

Hadrian, always the ambitious one offered to carry Zedra on his shoulders for a spell as they made their way up the small stream. The stream led them upwards and eastward into the fractured bedrock.

After what seemed a long time, as there were no clocks to measure time, nor sunlight to gauge the length of the day, the two friends sat for a while and considered what had happened to them over the course of a day.

They both knew that they were dead. Zurenda's Lions made that point clear enough. They were traveling through Hades, and it seemed like it would never end. They were both given a task to complete before they could enjoy the Elysian Fields, and this job had something to do with a man named Arjun, whom Zedra had never met, and

Hadrian could barely remember as a shipmate on one of his Trireme.

For Hadrian, this quest was entirely out of his comfort zone. Here he was, a newly deceased man running around with an Amazon Warrior assigned to help some man that he hardly knew in life and would likely never know in death. In the back of his mind, he worried that sometime in the future; he would have to face the God Hades and explain himself. He knew he was not ready for that! The thought of facing the gods made Hadrian very nervous.

Zedra did not have a mental concept of what "meeting the gods," could mean. The only god that she ever learned about as a young girl was the Goddess Eris. "Were there good gods and evil ones?" The thought never crossed her mind.

What Zedra did think about was getting back out into the sunlight, feeling the fresh air, and enjoying the sea.

CHAPTER SIXTY-FOUR

Semon

Semon saw everything. He saw the old fishing boat exhumed, as it were, from the bottom of the port. He saw what Salacia had done for Arjun and his team. He was watching as the mist rolled in to conceal the magic and the wonder of saving an old boat that was undoubtedly swamped and rotting in the sea water. He saw the old ship turned into a like-new vessel.

Salacia may have been aware of Semon's prying eyes, but it did not seem to matter to her, she was busy helping

Arjun, and for what possible gain? Maybe she owed Selene a favor. Maybe Selene was beholden to her.

For Arjun and his rag-tag band of misfits, it did not matter. This boat was their ticket to Piperi. Without a vessel, the journey would be impossible.

"My Lord." Semon addressed his master, Poseidon, in the still backwater reflection of the pool near the pier. The flotsam had cleared away just enough to allow a reflection in the filthy tide. "The man Arjun, whom thou swore in thy wrath should not make it alive to Piperi, is already underway in a vessel that Salacia prepared."

"That's very interesting my young apprentice," Poseidon replied. "Thank you, Semon, for the information. I will take over from here. You shall be rewarded handsomely for your trouble."

Poseidon did take over. He ordered up a menu full of meaningful disasters. Semon went back to his task as a street vendor. To the west, storm clouds were building, and it looked like rain.

CHAPTER SIXTY-FIVE

Artemis

A rtemis knew in her heart that the mounting challenge to Zurenda's reign was coming to a head. Everything was in motion for a showdown in a couple of days at the Palace of Zurenda.

"The Palace of Zurenda will fall!" Artemis exclaimed with jubilation. "I will, at last, enjoy the firstborn sacrifice owed to me by Agamemnon, which sacrifice has eluded me these many years. All I need to do is make sure that Poseidon does not interfere, and the victory will be mine!" She knew that this victory would not be hers alone.

I will share this triumph over Zurenda with my friend Selene. The victory over the discord of Eris and her minions shall taste so sweet, and I can almost taste it now!

As she finished dressing, she placed a quiver of silver arrows over her shoulder, with the Olympic bow in her right hand. Artemis was ready.

Hermes reported the news about Salacia's good deed to Selene, who was at that very minute, donning on the implements of war. "Good," Selene stated. "Salacia owed me this favor, after what I did for her in the last battle of Athens."

Selene's battle head-dress was a golden crown that fit snugly around the top of her head from ear to ear. She also wore long golden decorated bracelets on each forearm. Her white flowing dress was girded about with a Golden Girdle. The girdle was similar in quality to the one that Rama stole from Apate while she was sleeping. Nevertheless, this emblem of power was a treasured gift presented to her by a lesser god. To this girdle, was attached her Olympic sword, with the sheath strapped over her left shoulder.

She felt like she was ready for any surprise that might befall her son.

Artemis and Selene were both decorated with the implements of war. They felt ready to take on anything that the other gods might try to do to stop them. In the Olympic chambers on high, the goddesses honed their skills with courtiers. Skills of swordsmanship, archery and a various assortment of other implements of war.

CHAPTER SIXTY-SIX

Eris

"My dear Zurenda." Eris addressed her daughter from the reflection of the Palace pool. "The time is now for you and your warriors to be ready for the assault on the palace by the Demi-God, Arjun," Eris emphasized his title to make sure she was listening.

"The man Arjun is on the sea with his rag-tag forces heading your way. They will try everything to stop you. Be Prepared! Other gods, not friendly to me, are at this time mounting an attack from Olympus," she informed her daughter. "We must be prepared for an assault from any of the four cardinal directions. Be not fearful, my daughter. We will prevail."

This announcement was just the news that Zurenda had prepared for. She had amassed scores of Amazon Warriors to aid her cause. Each warrior wore the controlling delta amulet around her neck; some of the warriors had the emblem inscribed on their armor, weapons, and clothing.

In Zurenda's mind, each warrior was battle hardened and ready for war. Each captain was at the ready.

Eris continued her instruction: "Our opponents will try to use magic, so be prepared for that possibility with your own brand of magic. The foe will try to enter at night under cover of darkness, so be ready with bonfires and other lights to keep them out. Their puny and weak force will be no match for you and your disciplined warriors, my beloved daughter." Eris encouraged.

Eris gave some concluding council: "Prepare the last few prisoners for their termination. We don't want to have the assailers enjoy any spoils of war peradventure they should prevail." As Eris finished speaking her reflection vanished into the black water of the palace pool.

CHAPTER SIXTY-SEVEN

Arjun

A rjun felt a little tense as they made their way out of the harbor. The sun was shining, and the seas were calm. *Everything seemed perfect, what could go wrong?* He thought.

We have a well-trained crew,

We have a like-new boat,

Zurenda could not be as battle-hardened as I. She has been locked up in that dingy palace for years, her whole life in fact.

Arjun gained control of his thoughts, "FOCUS!" He said to himself, loud enough for everyone to hear. His thoughts then continued to drift. *I'm sure she is mounting some kind of patrol on the only possible quasi-land route that could even be attempted. Even then, our way will not be secure; the islands break down in to small clumps of rock as you travel from the mainland. She may not realize that we are entering by sea, and at night. The cover of darkness will afford the perfect disguise.*

Arjun looked at the flat side of his blade. "No warning signs here." From the helm of the boat, he looked over at Kiera; she was enjoying the sea breeze with Quin and watching the Oceanids or sea nymphs enjoy other like-minded spirits in the water. Several of the sea nymphs broke the surface of the water and then dived deeper, bursting out of the surface again celebrating the sheer joy of being alive.

The Oceanids enjoyed riding the wake made by the boat and found that it was especially entertaining.

Lycos was catching a much-needed rest in the galley below deck.

Fabian was near the helm next to Arjun helping him navigate through the harbor.

Rama was leaning against Zooey in the center of the boat, sleeping.

The day looked to be picture perfect.

CHAPTER SIXTY-EIGHT

Monsters

Just as the sun was setting, the troubles began. Suddenly, the boat made a long scraping sound like it had just hit a reef. The ship slowed and then came to a dead stop. Even the gentle Northwest wind was not helping. The wind was still piling up behind the sail, and under its pressure, the boat started to list to port.

Arjun instinctively knew something was up; something was wrong!

He and Kiera both peered over the gunwales to see what was going on. The darkening skies of evening were not helping. While gazing over the port side, long black tentacles began coming out of the water.

"SEA MONSTER!" Shouted Kiera, forming the words just a split-second before Arjun did.

"SEA MONSTER!" They both shouted. Everyone jumped up and took arms in preparation for an attack. Lycos was still groggy and half-asleep as he came stumbling up from the galley, wiping the sleep out of his eyes, and to see what was going on.

More tentacles came from below the boat. Instinctively, Lycos started hacking them off with his sword. Giant squid-like tentacles writhed off the boat's deck. Fabian was slicing away at the tentacles that were coming up over the stern.

Rama, Quin and Zooey, after a huddle followed by a quick decision, all took the same form: They turned themselves into fishing nets and jumped overboard to try and stop whatever was attacking them.

After the girls jumped overboard, the air grew silent and still. "What is going on with the girls?" Questioned Kiera.

Moments passed. Seconds seemed like hours.

Lycos and Fabian quickly threw the cut up tentacles overboard into the darkening surf. Squid blood and ink was everywhere on deck.

The scene looked like a massacre.

After several tense minutes the seawater broke, and up came the girls flying into the air, displaying a very tightly wrapped up sea-monster. Their nets shot straight out of the water leaving a column of water billowing up into the air. Once clear of the ocean's surface, the three shot back down into the water again.

They repeated this action several times.

With each pass, their choking squeeze and grip on the monster grew stronger, tighter.

The giant squid grew weaker and weaker until on the last pass; the squid lie silent across the top of the water next to the boat.

"That should about do it," Zooey told everyone, as she turned herself into a human next to the boat.

Rama and Quin unraveled themselves from the monster, as its big saucer-like eyes clouded over with the look of death. Rama and Quin then readied themselves to release the beast into the brine and watch it sink to the bottom.

"The beast is lifeless and dead," confirmed Rama.

Once that was done they all enjoyed a good breather resting in the sea, and then tried to understand why this attack happened in the first place.

"Poseidon," Arjun observed. "This was a gift from Poseidon. We must be moving on. We have lost an hour fighting this thing; we may lose another day on our attack at Piperi if we keep getting interrupted."

And then with a moment of intellectual clarity, Arjun added: "I'll bet that's what they want! Zurenda is trying to buy time. She is not yet prepared to meet us!"

Zooey turned herself into a dolphin, and after eating a little fresh squid sushi, she swam back over to the boat.

Quin and Rama both copied the dolphin form.

After a brief frolic in the water around the boat, and checking for other monsters, the girls then turned themselves back into their normal forms and Fabian helped each shapeshifter back on deck adding these words of praise: "Thank you ladies for your quick action today. You saved us again."

CHAPTER SIXTY-NINE

Kiera

K iera gave each of the girls a big hug as they re-
entered the boat, handing them each a towel to
dry off as they stood on the deck. Twilight was
over, and the stars were starting to shine. The brewing
cloud bank that was on the western horizon had dissipated
with the setting sun.

The evening skies were still clear, and the milky-way
could be seen from one horizon to the other, but they had
lost valuable time dealing with the giant squid. Kiera had
kept the bow and arrows below deck up to this point, but

she suddenly got the urge to put the bow over her shoulder and keep the quiver of arrows close at hand.

Arjun looked at the flat side of his blade. "More trouble on the way." He told the group as they attempted to clean the deck and tidy up. The squid managed to spray ink all over the deck, and some of the slime drained into the galley. Mopping the deck was in order for all hands.

After an hour of cleaning, Lycos spotted flashing yellow lights in the deep. This made everyone nervous; because these signs were all too close a reminder of the beast that Arjun had to face during his journey to Troy.

"Man the harpoons!" Kiera cried out. "We have company!"

Again, the group scrambled to defensive positions, mustering their collective strength in preparing for another unwanted attack.

By then, the evening had fallen, and the dark skies did not help with visibility. This time, Kiera and Lycos had the harpoons aimed and at the ready. The wrought iron shafts of the harpoons were black and almost blended in with the night. The only light they had were the stars, opting to keep the deck lanterns out to camouflage their size and their shape. This strategy worked right up until the beast came bursting out of the water and tried to do a backflip onto the deck of the boat. The creature looked like a giant yellow eel with glowing tentacles and a razor-sharp set of dorsal fins.

This creature was nothing like the last one that Arjun had to face, however, when it hit the deck of the boat, the destruction started. Each gunwale began to crack from the beam to the main deck. The eel sawed its way off the ship, snapping its gleaming, razor-sharp teeth in every direction. After it slithered off the boat and back into the water, the eel made ready for the second run at her. This time Kiera and Lycos were ready.

"Shoot the harpoons!" Cried Arjun, who was currently at the helm trying to prevent the boat from becoming parallel with the increasingly tall waves. Both harpoons went flying. Both weapons hit their mark but bounced right off the monster without taking effect.

Fabian and Rama helped pull the harpoons back into the boat using their roped tether.

"Kiera, look at your arrows!" Arjun shouted from near the stern towards her.

Kiera looked at her quiver and saw that one silver arrow was glowing white hot. She removed it from the quiver and placed it in her bow.

"SHOOT!" Arjun cried. Kiera took careful aim and just when the beast was about to break the surface of the water, she let the arrow fly. The arrow flew to its mark like a streak of white lightning! It cut through the air with deadly accuracy. The arrow hit its mark, right between the eel's eyes! A shock-wave of light went out from the head of the eel and arched under and over the water; Kiera was more than just amazed. She was stunned at the raw power that lay in her quiver. Her facial expressions said it all.

"I had no idea that this arrow was so powerful," Kiera exclaimed. Kiera, while considering what had just happened, found that her arrow exploded when it made contact with the beast. A split-second later, however, the crew discovered that the eel, well, what was left of it, had impacted the boat.

In spite of that information, the boat took a direct broadside hit, aft of center with the serrated dorsal fin. The whole vessel shook back and forth and then started to list to the starboard side.

"We've been hit!" Lycos confirmed what everyone had feared.

"She's taking on water!" Fabian shouted from the galley.

Soon everything was getting wet.

"How bad is the leak?" Zooey questioned.

Rama and Quin busied themselves in taking down the sail.

Fabian reported from below deck: "The leak was not too bad, a few broken planks, but still the water was coming in."

"We need to make a quick repair!" Commanded Arjun. "What can be done to stop the leak?" He queried.

Just then, Rama had an idea. "I know, I can change myself into a shape of thick black pitch, and that should hold us until we get to a port." Seeing no better idea, Arjun suggested that the change be done immediately. Quin went with Rama below deck and placed her pitch-like body across the breach. She stuck like glue! The water quit spraying in from between the planks.

Meanwhile, Zooey turned herself into a long flexible tubular pipe. A straw! She started siphoning the water out of the hull and managed to get all of it out of the galley within a few minutes.

That was a good thing, as Quin was already up to her hooves in water before 'Zooey the bilge-pump' started working.

After the siphoning was done, Zooey let out a most unladylike belch. "BUUURRRRRP!!!" Her noise surprised everyone. Zooey tried to recover by covering the end of the straw with her hand. A little shade of embarrassment turned her face red, and everyone laughed. Including Zooey!

It looked like the worst was over.

.

CHAPTER SEVENTY

Lycos

L ycos knew something about fixing boats. His years on the sea had taught him that. He knew that Rama's fix for the leak was not going to be permanent or practical. Besides, they needed all the fighting power the team could muster if they were attacked again.

He rummaged around in the galley for anything that he could find that would stop the leak and free up Rama, who would be needed again if they received another attack.

"Lycos." Quin addressed him. "I know that my magic is not that effective when it comes to liquid water-related issues," Quin confessed.

"What about solids, Quin?" Lycos replied while feverishly opening every locker in the boat looking for a bucket of pitch or extra planks, skins, or both. Anything!

"I'm good at controlling solids." Quin offered.

"How about ice?" Lycos' mind was racing one thousand miles an hour. "Can you control ice?"

Quin replied: "It's solid, I suppose I could try."

Lycos interrupted, "Try now! Right here in this bucket of water. Can you make it turn to ice?"

Quin's confidence rose to the occasion, stretching out her right hoof, she intoned the water to become ice. BOOM! A frozen bucket of ice was suddenly sitting before them.

"Good." Lycos encouraged. "Now try your magic on the residual water at the bottom of the boat." Quin did her incantation again. It worked! The water at the bottom of the boat instantly turned to ice.

"Good girl! Now let's try it on the leak." After removing Rama from the breach, and allowing her a few seconds to turn back into a satyr, the sea water again started pouring in from between the bilge planks.

Quin focused, now more than ever, chanted an incantation at the stream of water spraying in. Instantly, the water turned to ice. Rock hard, rock-solid ice! The leak was stopped.

The entire starboard side of the galley was covered in a thick layer of ice that was gathering frost.

"There, that should hold for several hours, if not longer," Lycos said approvingly.

Quin smiled with satisfaction at her accomplishment. The sheet of ice did hold, and the crew was able to rally back on deck and get back to the business of making landfall at Piperi.

By this time, hours had passed, and the Milky Way was burning brightly across the western canopy of the heavens. An occasional shooting star would light up the sky and reflect its trajectory off the sea's surface around the boat.

Orion was rising in the east, and that was a very good sign. It looked like it would finally be a quiet night on the Aegean.

CHAPTER SEVENTY-ONE

Amazons

Squeezing past narrow spots on the path to Piperi was becoming commonplace. Kendra's Amazons found themselves becoming more slender when needed and plumper when there was room between the rocks to allow for it.

The path they were on suddenly turned upward and it looked like there might be a light at the end of this pathway. The girls kept going upward. The path was strewn with a variety of boulders, all sizes. Crawling over them required the combined effort of Amazons helping each other.

Pushing. Pulling. Climbing.

About halfway up the path, they found a place to take a break.

"We rest here," Kendra instructed. The light high above them was ever so faint, but it was light! "We will have to climb toward the next light," she added leaning against the side of a big boulder.

Kendra's thoughts turned into words as the group rested, Kendra spoke. "The Fields of Elysian sure sounded inviting. We could have stopped there and rested for eternity. Why are we doing this? We have punished ourselves enough!" Then, Kendra answered her own question. "The only reason that makes sense is this: Zurenda somehow still needs our help, the kind of help that only we can give."

Reason would suggest that there was no other point to their suffering.

The black rocks they were resting on began steaming again. Beads of sweat dripped down every face.

"We must help Zurenda. We must help Zurenda." Kendra repeated. "Nothing else makes sense. Nothing else mattered."

"But how do we help?" asked Derinoe. That thought was quite puzzling to her and the others.

Kendra answered succinctly. "We will find a way to help our master, our Queen. By all the gods, we will find a way to help her."

"We are spirits right now. We know we were killed in the battle at Aeolia. We do have movement, but we're not that handy with mortal implements, like swords and spears."

"UNLESS!" Bremusa piped up! "Unless…. we can get our hands on an Olympic sword. Then maybe we would be able to do something more."

Bremusa knew that she had no such weapon. She did not even know where to obtain one, or if they even existed. Talk of magic swords filled the villages with folktales that spanned over past centuries in the homeland of Greece.

Kendra reminded the women that they had already been the victims of an Olympic sword. "Remember the swords wielded by Arjun, Lycos, and Artemis? They were Olympic swords. We are no match for them."

The rest was over, Kendra and her girls kept climbing toward the light.

CHAPTER SEVENTY-TWO

Hadrian and Zedra

B y now, Hadrian and Zedra had both gotten to know each other pretty well. Hadrian was claustrophobic. He did not like the narrow passages that led up or down, or anywhere else. He preferred to have a wide-open chasm to hike or climb up. This unwitting behavior might have a dual purpose that had not even crossed his mind yet, nor would it. Not until the very moment he needed it.

Being eaten alive by a pride of lions was not exactly the idyllic death that either one of them had hoped for, or even dreamed of. The horrifying act of having your flesh torn from off of your bones, while yet alive was still fresh on each of their minds.

Hadrian kept blasting away at the solid rock, with his sword, forming a big tunnel as he went.

"More room, less claustrophobic," he said. The closer they made it to the surface, the more shaking could be felt in the surrounding countryside.

They were heading to Piperi. They just did not know it yet. Zedra was worried that they might break through the bottom of the ocean floor and get flooded. She feared that they would be washed away, all the way back to Hades.

This was not a reassuring thought either, but she kept quiet and let Hadrian do all the hard work with his Olympic sword.

Getting washed back to Hades was a real possibility, especially when Hadrian could catch a glance of the inferno pit from time to time as they scaled their way up the chasm.

The Olympic swords they carried were forged in the same place all Olympic swords are created, deep in the bowels of Mount Olympus. The swords they were using did not bear the mark of Zeus or Ares. They bore the mark of Hades, and they were razor sharp!

CHAPTER SEVENTY-THREE

Artemis and Selene

The Olympic Goddesses were both in rare form. Artemis and Selene both decided to ride together in the beautifully decorated silver, and gold lined chariot from Olympus to observe the new battlegrounds at Piperi.

Zeus suggested that they both be there, first: to keep their word, and second: to make sure that nothing could go wrong. However, everyone in Olympus knew that this stage of the battle was really up to the mortals and the

demi-gods at this phase of the conflict. The mortals needed to, as they say: "Sink or Swim."

Their beautifully decorated chariot was pulled by two
sparkling white Pegasi named Crystal and Starlight. The
Goddesses held an excellent position high above Piperi, in
the cumulus clouds, to conceal their presence within the
mist.

Selene was more nervous than Artemis. "What if things
go wrong?" She worried.

"Then it will be up to the gods to decide the fate of
men." Artemis reminded her.

"What about the fate of my son, if this all goes south?"
Selene choked back tears at the thought of losing Arjun to
Hades, or Tartarus.

"He'll be alright," Artemis reassured. "I have faith in
your son. He will be a great Warrior from Olympus! Perhaps the prophecy will be fulfilled right before our very
eyes."

CHAPTER SEVENTY-FOUR

Eris

If you could find a black cloud in the sky, all alone and surrounded by white fluffy ones, that would be the cloud for Eris to hide within. And so it was that she was there, high over Piperi, disappearing into the black mist called the palace chamber.

Eris was so obsessed with the success of this fight that she would not have missed it for the world, literally.

In fact, if the fate of the Aegean world did depend on the outcome of this fight, Eris was 'all-in!'

Eris concealed the essence of her influence in the cavities of the black walls of the palace's great hall.

Her presence there was being felt everywhere throughout the fortress. Zurenda felt at home with this choking oppression. To her, it was just another day.

Over the past few weeks, Zurenda had managed to slaughter dozens of unfortunate men who were unlucky enough to wash up on her shores. For them, there was no escape. The Lions were already getting fat.

But even Zurenda realized that she needed to starve them back for a few days so that they would be hungry enough to eat Arjun and his friends when she coaxed the intruders into the pit. It was just a matter of time. Arjun and his band of misfits should be arriving any hour now.

Eris took the precaution to communicate with Poseidon. She requested that he serve up some aquatic surprises for the arriving guests. Poseidon told her of the two sea creatures that had attacked their puny ship.

"There are more attacks to come," he reassured Eris. "There are a few more monsters for them to face before they make it to Piperi, my dear."

"Good!" Quipped Eris. "Maybe they will be ready to die, happy to die when they get here. All the easier for us."

CHAPTER SEVENTY-FIVE

Peremptoriness

K iera woke up early. The mist of the morning fog was almost too thick to breathe. A white cloud that lay across the ocean grew thicker and thicker with each passing minute.

"Hey, guys!" Kiera shouted! "Get up! I think we have a problem."

Once everyone, except Zooey, was on their feet and hooves, they looked together at the oncoming fog. Zooey was sound asleep, not wanting to budge when Quin tried to wake her.

"Looks like more fun and games from Poseidon," said Quin.

"Quick, check the ice!" Arjun instructed.

Lycos was the first one to respond. He hopped down into the galley. "The ice is okay!" he reported. Adding, "and it seems to be holding up well."

The mist continued to thicken. Soon Arjun could not see the bow of the boat, much less anything else. He instinctively reached for his sword just in case he should need it. Lycos was doing the same thing, almost at the same time.

Fabian was on the lookout, searching for anything he could see. "Maybe it's just a fog bank," he observed.

Rama cautioned, "I think this fog is filled with deceit and confusion. I can sense it and the fog is also laced with fear."

No sooner had she uttered these words than the fog took on a life of its own. Swirling tentacles of white mist, like long sinuous fingers, began to grip the boat and pull it under, like a giant hand that was gripping the craft and making ready to drag the ship beneath the waves.

Lycos raised his sword to the sky. Invoking the power of Ares, he commanded the fog to release its grip on the ship. This action helped stop the fog for a few tense seconds. A moment later, the mist was gripping the boat again with a new-found fury.

Kiera responded: "We have two colors of fog now. One white and one blue! We have doubled the trouble!"

Rama and Quin peered over the gunwales into the deep.

"This thing is not coming from the water," Quin observed. "It is coming from the sky."

Everyone looked up. A swirling colossal sized white and blue cloud was looming high in the sky above them, very unnatural indeed.

At the water's surface, Arjun could see daylight, but this monster was doing its best at concealing any sunlight. The beast had no form, except what the wind would give it. The creature was wrapped up in clouds, with a hundred white cloud-like tendrils, the monster could change shape at any moment.

There was no head, no tail, and no middle. The creature was all around them, and not anywhere in specific.

Rama was the only one who could fight this beast. She soon realized that this was no ordinary foe, and went to work. Rushing into the galley, she looked for a simple mirror, anything that would reflect an image. Finding nothing, she told Arjun and Lycos to stand together in the middle of the boat.

"Men, I need both of you to stand shoulder to shoulder and hold your blades up with their flat edges side by side."

Lycos was confused, but Arjun understood. "Place our blades side by side. Like this," Arjun encouraged.

"Now, I will stand in front of you and gaze into the reflection of the combined swords." As Rama did so, her gaze into the blades only took a split-second's worth of observation to see the full shape and head of the beast that they faced.

The monster was massive; it appeared to be some three hundred cubits in height and about two hundred cubits in width. At the head, the monster had two small red eyes, no nose, and no mouth. The arms and legs, and the hands and feet were the white and dark blue cloudy tendrils that they first observed.

Rama spoke to the beast in the mirrored reflection of the swords. "Why are you here trying to kill us?"

The beast recoiled a little considering her question. Communication with this.... thing was done between the blade and Rama, through thoughts more than words, it was a communication of the mind.

"I have been sent here by the queen to destroy you." The beast clarified his intentions. "Queen Zurenda has commanded that you shall never make it to the shore at Piperi."

Rama related the message to the crew.

The conversation continued. "What is your name?" Rama asked politely.

"My name is Peremptoriness."

Rama realized at that moment that they were not fighting a thing or an object, they were fighting an idea.

"Tell me, Peremptoriness, from whence comes the source of your power?" Rama inquired further.

"My power is my own," said Peremptoriness.

Rama continued the conversation while peering into the blades' reflection. Rama's deception ability kicked into overdrive. "Do you realize that there are others with more power that you?" She claimed with a bit of irony in her voice.

"That is impossible," disputed the Titan Peremptoriness. "No one is more powerful than the purity of the word."

Rama was gaining an advantage, now leading the conversation to a specific direction she added: "There are other Oligarchs that have more power than you, my good fellow."

With this news, a jealous Peremptoriness began to pound the sea with his newly formed fists, water splashing everywhere. "Impossible! I won't hear this talk! The Queen told me I have all power."

Rama reasoned with him, "Well, my dear friend, she told you wrong. She sent you here to do her bidding. How does that make you more powerful?"

"Just look at the lifestyle of the Gods and the Titans. You have nothing compared to them. Where is your throne? Where are your courtiers? Where is your treasure? Their power is far superior to yours. They are using you. You are expendable!"

Peremptoriness realized that Rama was right. "I want more power!" His voice shouted to the sky. His thunderous voice echoed off the waves, off the boat, and off the cloud he was enshrouded in. His voice pierced everything and was felt everywhere, even back to Piperi. The cloud lifted, and waves splashed against the boat. The sun was able to break through his burgeoning mass. Peremptoriness had been distracted. Rama had won.

Rama concluded her conversation with the Titan, "Be off my good fellow. Find more power elsewhere. A victory here will mean nothing to you. This boat, this crew, we mean nothing to your power, might and your glory. There is nothing here that will give you more power!"

Rama then encouraged him to leave. "Peremptoriness, the gods of Olympus, should be your next stop; they have all the power you seek. They control the power of the Universe."

Again, Peremptoriness realized that Rama was right. The fog lifted and the sun began to shine in its strength. It was a new day.

"It will be the last day for Zurenda," Arjun said smugly as the conversation between Rama and Peremptoriness ended.

"We dodged another attack." Rama sighed with relief.

Arjun and Lycos lowered and re-sheathed their weapons. Everyone breathed a sigh of relief, except Zooey, who managed to sleep through the whole thing!

CHAPTER SEVENTY-SIX

Zurenda

"**P**eremptoriness has failed! That big stupid marshmallow will listen to anyone!" Zurenda lamented.

Eris was quick to reply: "He listened to you, my dear. There will be other Titans to train," Eris stated reassuringly; "There will be others. Have patience, my daughter."

Eris continued: "Our ally, Poseidon has two more woes in store for this little band of misfits. You will see my dear. We will prevail." With those comforting words,

Eris whipped herself into a thin black cloud and then vanished into the dark air of the palace corridors.

Zurenda would not, however, be comforted. She decided to take matters into her own hands. She went to the only mortal friend that she could think of; she went to confide in Talia.

Talia knew nothing of the dark magic that Zurenda was capable. She did, however, have a good listening ear.

"I need to have my domain secured," Zurenda told Talia in the breaking light of day. The rays of sunshine seemed to bounce off the black tar that covered Selene's statue in the grand hall. Talia noticed this phenomenon too. Both she and Zurenda stood and marveled at the sight of the sun's rays burning tar away from the monument, leaving a puddle of the substance on the floor beneath the marble statue of Selene.

"What could it mean?" Talia asked her Queen.

Zurenda was quick to answer. "It means that we will have visitors who intend to wipe the stain away from the Goddess. Let's make sure that it does not happen."

Zurenda directed that another coat of tar be painted onto the image. I don't want Selene to have any influence in this palace, not now and not ever!"

Talia dispatched her guards at once.

CHAPTER SEVENTY-SEVEN

The Sporades

Zooey cried from the bow of the boat. "Land Ho!" This morning she had turned herself into a Raven and was busy vetting her new black wings in the thin column of warm air rising from the sea.

Arjun squinted into the distance, the palm of his hand flat-out over his eyes, like a visor. It was the last island of the Sporades alright. Piperi. "We are almost there." Arjun confidently announced. The whole gang moved port side to have a better look, inadvertently tipping the boat in that direction.

Piperi was just as he remembered leaving it months ago, a naked chunk of rock jutting out of the sea with a little grass and few trees on top, they grew closer, Arjun could see the Palace. They were nearly there!

This approach seemed all too easy. However, just as he said this, a loud hissing noise could be heard from across the water. "Oh boy!" Arjun said as he gripped the helm a little tighter. "Someone better check out the source of that sound."

Zooey was the perfect fit to check out the hissing noise. After a big leap into the air and a few false flaps, Zooey took to the air and started to scan the sea for anything that would make that strange noise.

"Found it!" Zooey said in her high squeaky bird-like voice.

"Found what?" Kiera asked. "The serpent, the monster! You know, the giant snake! Right over there behind the boat." Zooey pointed with the black tip of her left wing.

Everyone turned around to have a look aft of stern. The monster was just breaking the surface of the water in the wake of the boat.

"A colossal sea snake!" Fabian shouted to the crew.

"Told ya!" Zooey stated with full confidence.

The snake began to open its gaping mouth wide in the attempt to swallow the ship whole, in one gulp.

Rama observed. "One bite, game over!"

Fortunately, Kiera was able to get a silver arrow off in the beast's direction before that happened. The arrow hit its mark, right between the eyes, but the desired effect was not as planned or as expected.

Instead of the arrow vaporizing the beast, the snake caught the shaft right between its cat-like slit-black eyes.

Seconds later, the snake turned into a multi-headed monster! A Hydra! Now five hissing heads bore down against them.

Kiera noticed another arrow glowing in the quiver.

"Aim! Fire!" Arjun commanded Kiera. She did as directed and maters only got even worse. Now ten hissing heads faced them just off the port side of the boat.

The snake strategically positioned itself between the ship and the shore while the tail end was starting to coddle the starboard side with its coils, pushing the boat into a squeezing, pre-crushing position.

There was no good way out!

Quin was the only one who recognized that this might be magic and not reality. She started in on one of her incantations.

Zooey was circling high above the boat and watching the whole disaster unfold from a safe distance in the air.

Fabian, Arjun, and Lycos were all reaching for their swords and trying to figure out how best to attack this thing without getting killed.

Quin did the unthinkable! Rama, out of the corner of her eye, caught a glance of what Quin was about to do. She shouted a long and piercing "NO!" at the top of her lungs, but it was too late. Quin jumped off the deck of the boat into the sea, hooves and tail flying. She was heading for the beast!

CHAPTER SEVENTY-EIGHT

Quin

Kiera watched in horror as Quin swam straight for the serpent. Hydra was so pre-occupied with crushing the boat in its coils that it had not noticed the little nostrils breaking the shifting and ever-changing surf. The sea snake thrashed about in the shallows of an off-shore reef, pulling the boat back into deep water and trying to get a better grip on it. Quin ducked below one of the waves and disappeared. In her haste to do something, Kiera shot another silver arrow.

Arjun, Lycos, and Fabian took defensive positions with their swords. Kiera tried to shelter Rama's eyes, but it was no use. She insisted on watching the whole thing.

It seems they all had a front-row seat.

Zooey was still circling high overhead, and providing a useful blow-by-blow announcer-style commentary on the battle from her lofty perspective.

A few minutes after Quin disappeared beneath the waves, to everyone's surprise, a Giant Cyclops reared its head out of the water near the reef. The Cyclops was chest-deep in water and stood thirty cubits tall. The giant was heading towards Hydra, taking one wet step after another.

After the initial shock of beholding this…this giant, Kiera realized that it must be Quin in disguise, a new alternate form of the faun.

She was right! Zooey confirmed her suspicion with a screech from the air. "Look," she said, "Quin just got ugly and one-eyed!" This announcement drew a strange look from Quin, but she managed to stick to her task.

The Cyclops spoke with a familiar voice. "Come here you slippery green snake." With that invitation, the serpent released its grip on the boat, at least partially, and headed toward the Cyclops.

Zooey was right. The Cyclops was ugly, more ugly than most, by a long shot. A thick bushy single eye-brow covered a single brown eye. The Cyclops was covered in thick hair from head to toe and was only wearing a ragged tunic and loincloth.

Quin, the Cyclops, was able to grab the snake by the throat and meet the serpent eye to eye, thus leveling the playing field.

The rest of the crew watched with gaping jaws as Quin took the snake by the throat and began to bite off each head one by one with her enormous mouth and jagged, razor-sharp teeth. Thick green blood poured out of her mouth with each bite. Blood that hit the sea water boiled the sea in pockets of green fire. The serpent's blood that dripped onto the deck of the boat flashed into balls of green fire as it hit the deck.

This kept the rest of the crew busy bucketing water across the deck to douse and wash the flames into the bay.

The severed heads that Quin spat out began floating by the boat in gristly detail; several of the forked tongues still actively sampling the air as they drifted by in steamy balls of green flame.

Finally, the last head was severed, ripped off, bit off, and removed. More green blood oozed out of the severed heads igniting green fires as it hit a receiving surface, cauterizing the multiple serpentine necks, effectively suffocating the monster. After the last snake-head was severed, the tail of the serpent released its grip altogether on the Warrior from Olympus.

Quin then took the limp body of the snake and with both of her hairy hands, tied the creature into a giant pretzel. The tidewater calmed down, and the upheaval and thrashing sea came to a stop. All was calm for a full Athenian minute.

Quin was splattered with snake blood. Some of the blood spilled onto her hairy legs and arms, burning as it went trickling down her leg. To wash off and to clean up a little, she took a deep immersing plunge into the ocean.

Quin's wake caused a rather big wave heading for the boat, but the craft did not seem to mind. After several minutes Quin re-surfaced as a faun, no worse for the wear. Fabian and Lycos helped her back into the boat and handed her a towel.

"You saved us!" Kiera told Quin as she was drying off, giving her a big hug in the process.

"How did you know it was magic?" Lycos asked.

"It was not real magic." Quin corrected. "It was a real serpent, and no doubt another gift from Poseidon. He's trying to keep us from making landfall at Piperi."

Fabian asked the other question that was on everyone's mind: "How did raw snake flesh and blood taste in your Cyclopoid mouth?"

Quin replied with a wry smile. "Like chicken, only worse! A lot more crunchy!"

Kiera had the big question of the day: "Why didn't my arrows work on this beast. I thought I shot one of the glowing silver ones during the heat of the battle?"

The answer from Quin was spell-binding: "The Olympic arrows you shot were not glowing. Olympic arrows only work on all creatures that are connected to Olympus in some way. They don't work on the earth giants that have vowed allegiance to Gaea. Earth Giants are immune to their power."

Kiera had a follow-up question for Quin: "Why did you go fight it then?"

"Oh," Quin said, "I didn't know that when I jumped in the water. I thought it was all magic. I had to figure it out while I was submerged in the sea."

"What were the clues?" Fabian asked.

"Green blood," Quin said. "When I was underwater, I swam over to the serpent and made a small cut on its underbelly with my dagger. When it started bleeding green blood, I knew that I was dealing with an Earth Giant, not magic and not a creature tied to Olympus.

"Traditionally, those creatures or beings bleed red blood. My only defense, at that point, was to turn myself into something bigger. I chose to be a Cyclops."

"Well, it worked," Arjun confirmed. "We are all glad you won that battle."

While the mini-reunion was happening on the deck, something else was happening in the sky. A huge black cloud of ravens came flying out of the black cliffs of Piperi towards the boat.

"Here we go again," Arjun said, regretfully. "We have more unwanted company!" Even as close to the shore as they were, it was useless to try and make landfall with this black cloud of birds descending upon them.

It was time to take cover!

Everyone went below deck. Everyone, that is, except Zooey. She was still circling the boat from a comfortable altitude above the ship. The cloud of ravens swooped down on the boat, hundreds of them. Each raven was dropping small live coals and other nuisance objects on the craft, anything they could get in their talons.

The live coals were the worst. They would hit the deck and start to burn the paint, varnish, and other finishes. Several of the coals burned holes in the sail, starting it on fire. Other live coals then bounced into the galley and began melting holes in the ice pack over the leak. Fabian grabbed a bucket of water and doused the flames on the sail.

Arjun was not that worried about the pay-load, knowing that they could all swim to shore from this distance if they had to.

Some of the ravens were dropping live fish that would flip and flap struggling to make it back into the water. Some of them found their way into the galley, making a mess of the place in the process.

Other ravens delivered a more sinister pay-lode, dropping assorted dead snake parts all over the deck. The green fires were spontaneously combusting with each unwelcome delivery.

"Yuck!" Kiera found the gifts to be disgusting and unwanted. She took matters into her own hands. With the deck mop, she swung at any ravens that were within range, knocking a few of them off the deck and into the water.

Her efforts were useless, however, there were just too many. They would just have to endure the attack and hope the boat did not get destroyed in the process.

The boat began to sit low in the water and was in danger of taking on water if this onslaught did not quit.

With each pass of the Ravens, the boat grew heavier and heavier with the sordid payload.

After the third pass, the boat would not move in the water anymore, being so laden with debris.

"We have a problem," Arjun stated the obvious. "We may have to swim for it."

Everyone pitched in at tossing garbage off the boat, but their efforts did not seem to be very effective.

Everyone pitched in, except for Zooey. Zooey was gone!

CHAPTER SEVENTY-NINE

Amazons

T he climb up to meet the piercing ray of light was nearly complete! Just a few hundred more cubits and they would be there! The only question was this: "Where was there?"

Suddenly, the girls all heard a voice all together ringing in their minds: "My faithful Amazons! I'm so glad you ladies have come to join the party!"

The voice was the unmistakably soothing voice of the Goddess Eris. She continued: "You have arrived just in the nick of time! We will require your services momentarily." The warriors had made it up from Hades to Piperi by sheer chance or by design, right into the middle of the palace courtyard. Cracks in the stone floors allowed the source of light to penetrate into the abyss of rock below.

Following the cracks and the fractures of the solid rock, allowed the girls to get back to the palace. Inside the courtyard, they had perfect vision, and could see the piles of bones in the lion's den, gathered up into one corner of the pit.

"Ladies," the soothing voice came again. "Please gather up the bones and tidy up the pit for our new guests."

Without any hesitation, Kendra and the girls began swirling around the pit enclosure. With each pass around the space, the musty air, bones, and debris started to form a vortex above them. The pit was a cylinder in shape, allowing a cyclone of swirling and spinning air, bone shards, trash, and broken stone to spin without much resistance.

On cue, the ceiling panel opened. The sheer force of the wind in the chamber ejected the debris out of the pit and through an open skylight, with a trajectory that emptied the chamber. The debris flew down off the cliffs and onto the water-washed rocks far below.

The arena was scoured and sandblasted clean with the exception of a few shards of bone, jammed into the corners of the room.

This movement by the deceased Amazons also had the additional effect of re-arranging the labyrinth walls within the dungeon. Walls shifted into a new arrangement, a new configuration. Even the guards posted at each location had to stop and figure things out.

After that task was done, Eris used the girls to do other things their current form or condition would allow. They were sent to check out the success of the giant sea snake.

Kendra returned and reported this news: "The serpent Hydra is dead." She told Eris. "The snake was apparently defeated by magic, your Grace." Surmising that one of the shipmates seemed to possess a remarkable level of magical power. Kendra confessed that she did not know which one it was.

By this time, Zurenda joined the conversation between the spirits of the girls and the Goddess Eris. "Let's have the ladies place a new layer of tar on our soiled statue of Selene."

Eris revealed in the insult. "I would like to see the entire statue covered in black pitch again. The sun keeps melting the tar away for some reason, and I don't want to exert any influence coming from that statue as we make final preparations to welcome our guests. They will be insulted as well by our gesture to the goddess whose temple this is!"

Forthwith, the Amazons flew down the hall and began dumping buckets of prepared tar all over the image of Selene. Indeed the statue was not recognizable after this latest dowsing, especially with the image already leaning badly.

"The preparations for our guests are now complete!" Said Eris.

Zurenda agreed, adding: "They should be here within hours."

Had Arjun known that there would be a welcoming committee at the landing on Piperi, he would have called off the attack. Re-grouped and implemented "Plan B."

This was going to be simple, He thought to himself. *Just like the raid on the palace when we rescued the sailors.*

As it turned out, he was not aware of the counter-attack planned by Zurenda and company. Perhaps it was the will of Selene that his mind was oblivious to the danger the lay ahead.

Artemis was the only goddess that perceived the dangerous circumstances that lay ahead for the team. Instead of warning Selene or Arjun, instead of calling off the attack, Artemis was all too willing to allow the battle to go forward, attributing her premonition about the outcome to her nerves, the jitters, and to worry. Or, could it have been to satisfy her own vain ambition of a proper sacrifice even though she never let on to anyone about this desire. No. Not even to Selene.

CHAPTER EIGHTY

Poseidon

ı

T his crazy mixed-up day turned into a terrible and torturous night. Not yet ashore and still laden with debris from the flock of Ravens, the Warrior from Olympus was having new problems.

With all the debris that the ravens dropped into it, the hold still had some smoldering embers. In addition to that, the ice dam that was keeping the leak in check started to melt. Water began seeping in again as the ice melted.

Something had to give.

That 'something' came in the form of another attack.

Water started to boil all around the boat. Huge bubbles of clayish white liquid began to boil and pop with an exploding shot of sound.

Instinctively, Arjun raised his sword and invoked the power of Zeus upon the waters. Lightning sprayed across the surface of the deep, but nothing else happened. Lycos did the same thing with his sword, only invoking the power of Ares. Again nothing happened.

"What is going on?" Arjun asked the question, to no one in particular.

"Maybe the Gods are not pleased with our handling of Hydra, the multi-headed Serpent?" Rama worried.

"Maybe one god in particular." Quin quickly replied.

Rama added this reassurance: "Guys, it's not that." However, Rama continued, "I perceive that this may be the last attempt that Poseidon will use to attack us from the water."

Suddenly, the entire boat began to rise into the air. Huge white globs of caked mud-slurry started dripping from the hull. The mud was dripping from the stern to the bow and everywhere in-between.

Lycos realized that something was pushing the boat up out of the water. *Well, that may solve our leak problem!* The fleeting thought quickly crossed his mind. Before he could finish that thought, and begin a new one, everyone on board realized that they were being pushed up out of the water by a giant human-like hand. A human hand so massive that the entire boat was being cupped into the palm of the Giant's out-stretched hand. More sea mud began washing off the hull, stern and bow. More of the giant's body was beginning to be revealed as the boat came up out of the muddy seawater.

Being raised up out of the water a good forty cubits, the hand, arm, and part of the shoulder was visible over the sides of the boat.

"The beast looks like a giant man," Arjun said at the first glimpse of the new terror.

The beast was covered in body armor, holding a forked shaped dagger in his left hand. In the afterglow of a very ordinary sunset, the creature stood erect on two feet and raised the boat to the level of his blazing red eyes.

The giant muscle-bound, dark-skinned man was enormous; big enough to darken the sky all around them. The Giant looked at them with his piercing eyes, just a few cubits off aft. He had smoking white vapor for breath and was armored with a golden six-pack breastplate. The Giant came to a resting position while holding the boat and the team within it, treading through waist-deep seawater.

Rama called it correctly: "It's Poseidon himself!" She whispered. Terror gripped each heart!

"Now what are we going to do?" Kiera asked, and then, answering her own question, looked into her quiver and noticed that two arrows were glowing white hot. In an instant, the two arrows were made ready to fire.

Swoosh! And off the arrows went, together.

Poseidon saw them coming and held up his left hand and blackened forked trident to the on-coming arrow attack. The arrows disintegrated in mid-flight. The only thing that reached Poseidon was a puff of silver Olympic smoke.

"Arrows are not going to work!" Kiera called from the front of the boat.

Quin was invoking her magic, but all it did was slow the giant down. By stirring up the sea bottom sediments, Poseidon brought on more sloshing, white mud, and a host of unnatural waves, splashing and crashing everywhere.

There was no stopping him!

Even from the relative safety of the clouds, Selene and Artemis were powerless to do anything against his threats.

Poseidon's thrashing continued for several minutes. The boat's hull began to crack under the crushing grip of Poseidon's right hand. She was breaking up!

Poseidon took the boat and began crushing it into splinters.

Fabian was the first to jump out, and abandon ship! He took a flying leap off the deck and landed in the water near the feet of the giant. Hoping to go unnoticed he dove into the water and tried swimming to shore. Rama and Quin were the next to bail out. Both in their natural form, they held hands as they leaped off the boat headed in a free-fall to the foamy brine. On the way down, Rama turned herself into a spinney puffer fish. Quin first transformed herself into an octopus, and then into a shark, and finally settled on the shape of a seahorse as she hit the water.

This action left Arjun, Lycos, and Kiera still on the boat. Lycos and Arjun made for the galley. "This has to be the safest place to survive this beating." Lycos reasoned. Kiera was too far forward in the boat to make it to the galley. Poseidon began tipping the craft to a nearly vertical position. In defense of this, Kiera found a rope and tied herself to the mast.

Now, inverted, the rope slipped, and Kiera found herself dangling from the ship by one foot.

"Kiera!" Shouted Arjun. "HOLD ON!" I will come and get you! Arjun fastened a galley rope to his waist and kicked open the galley doors. Another leeward jerk by Poseidon left both Kiera and Arjun dangling from ropes, up-side down in the air, at different heights, and at the mercy of Poseidon's brutality.

Poseidon noticed that several of the victims had abandon ship! The giant could see that the others had taken refuge somewhere on the boat itself, trying to ride it out. Poseidon decided that his fun was almost over.

Arjun and Kiera were both hanging up-side-down nearly parallel with the current position of the boat, (the vessel's bow pointing to the open sky). Even as bad as that was, the worst thing was about to happen. Gravity took over.

Kiera's quiver of arrows, the remaining six, fell out of the quiver, like a slow-motion nightmare, the weapons tumbled down into the sea.

Kiera screamed! "They are gone! They are gone!"

Arjun still had his sword at his side, and he kept trying to reach it thinking it would help to stop this madness. However, his hands were too busy hanging on to the rope.

Arjun was too far away from Kiera for her to reach his sword. Lycos could see all this happening through the cracked galley window. He struggled to the doorway to try and help. With his sword in his hand, Lycos invoked the power of Ares. Lightning came streaming from every corner of the sky.

Poseidon was stunned and a little shocked by it, but not entirely disabled. He took the boat and prepared to fling it like a javelin into the pile of sea rocks that lay just at the water's edge.

"THIS WILL BE THE END OF YOUR HERO!"

Poseidon's baritone voice boomed and reverberated off the water, the cliffs, and the shore. Poseidon looked up skyward as if to mock Selene and Artemis, whom he sensed were up there watching, waiting.

The Sea God wound up his arm to deliver a fatal blow to the puny craft, allowing, for a split second, the ship to assume a somewhat level aspect.

Kiera and Arjun both were still dangling upside-down, hanging off of the starboard side of the boat, fighting a tightening rope on their bodies and trying to break free.

Lycos did the unthinkable! He sprang out the galley door and with his sword blazing he cut the ropes that held Kiera and Arjun fast to the boat and then he jumped off the deck into an uncertain fate.

All three of them fell head-long into the water.

This action was all done while the boat was being pulled back into an over-the-shoulder throwing position by the sea god.

All of them splashed into the water and dove out of sight.

Poseidon, unaware of the escape, his eyes full of fury and a heart full of rage for what Arjun had done to his peaceable sea creatures, and also to fulfill his oath to Hades, catapulted the boat forward on to the rocks of Piperi's southern shore.

The Giant had accomplished the desired effect, exploding the small craft it into a million pieces as it came in contact with the rocks.

As Poseidon turned around to recede into the depths of the sea, they could hear the unmistakable voice of the god uttering this epitaph:

"THAT IS THE END OF ARJUN AND HIS BAND OF MISFITS!
"THAT IS THE END OF THE WARRIOR FROM OLYMPUS!"

CHAPTER EIGHTY-ONE

Kiera

The night had set in. Everyone was sloshing their way to shore. Rama and Quin were already there. They had reverted to their usual selves, and Fabian was drying off as best he could at the water's edge with a vigorous shakedown. Lycos and Kiera were on the beach trying to make sense of the whole encounter with Poseidon. Arjun was passed out in the sand.

As soon as she could speak, Kiera broke the silence, which felt like the silence of defeat, the kind of silence you feel when everything you have tried to do has failed, turned to ash and fizzled away.

"I can't believe I was so stupid!" Kiera complained. "I have lost the remaining six arrows to the sea. Now, what will happen to us?"

Lycos, acting a little more positive: "At least we are here at Piperi!" Lycos cracked a half-smile barely visible in the dim starlight. "We just have to figure out how to get to the palace, kill Zurenda, and then implement the escape plan. Simple!" Lycos' smile widened a little more.

Kiera replied with a reality check: "You don't understand," she said, "I need those arrows to do the job. Your swords alone will not work on Zurenda!" This revelation came as a 'news flash' for Lycos, not knowing or realizing that the arrows were that important.

"I have to kill Zurenda!" Kiera clarified. "I can only do it with those arrows. She will not fall otherwise."

"How do you know this?" Lycos pressed while Rama came over to warm them up.

"Artemis told me," Kiera confessed. "We need the silver arrows. We need at least three of them." She said.

Arjun was starting to wake up. He got up on his knees and then steadied himself to his feet with the help of Quin.

The group gathered together and huddled to stay warm. The night air was cold, and they were all in various stages of shock after what had happened.

Arjun did a head count. "We are missing someone," he said while holding his hand to brace his aching head.

"Where is Zooey?" Questioned Fabian. "Oh, yea," he now remembered. "The last I saw her she had turned into a raven."

Quin added: "Zooey was swept up in the flock of ravens that bombed our boat. We don't know what happened after that. I hope she is Okay."

Rama spoke with a little stress and worry in her voice. "The ravens all went back to the palace."

She might already be inside the palace compound." Lycos observed: "Maybe that will help us." Rama nodded her head in hopeful agreement.

In the dim light of night, the team went over to observe the damage to the boat.

"It is toast!" Fabian stated the obvious. "We should just call it the 'pile of toothpicks,' that appears to be its only use at this point."

Arjun, now slightly coherent, went to grab the sail. It too was burnt and in tatters. "Maybe we can use it to make a shelter tonight," he said.

They all pitched in. Within a few minutes, they had a small shelter pulled together next to the splintered hull.

"At least it will be a place to get out of the wind," Kiera said. The rest of the boat lie scattered in a debris field across a large section of beach.

Arjun realized that there was no going back to sea in that vessel. Poseidon had taken his revenge.

CHAPTER EIGHTY-TWO

Survivors

The morning light came too soon. "Look over there!" Talia and Ada took their compliment of guards and began to search the wreckage of 'The Warrior from Olympus.'

"See if there are any survivors!" Ada ordered.

Arjun and the team, anticipating there would be some sort of search, therefore, they hid themselves down along the shoreline far enough to see and not be seen.

"We need a better place to hide!" Fabian whispered to the group.

Rama piped up, "Let's make this simple!" She turned herself into a hollowed-out rock, matching the stones on the shore around them.

"Hide inside of me!" Rama encouraged. With that invitation, the group crouched down inside of Rama 'the rock.'

The disguise was perfect! Quin muttered some magic words to help conceal and erase their tracks on the sand. It worked!

All of them were dead quiet inside Rama. They managed to stay hidden and silent while the detachment of Amazon guards walked all around them combing the beach for any sign of survivors. After several tense minutes, the warriors moved on to a new section of beach, and then back up the narrow and rocky path that led to the palace.

"My Queen," Talia addressed Zurenda with the customary bow, drawing her right arm in a circular motion across her chest. "We have searched the coastline and have found no survivors from the shipwreck last night."

"Did you find any bodies?" Zurenda pressed.

"No, my Queen," Talia clarified. "We have found no trace of anything living or any dead on the beach."

Talia continued. "The scene of the wreck was so hor-
rific that I doubt anyone could have survived the wreck
and escaped on foot. Perhaps the dead were carried off by
Poseidon himself."

"Perhaps." Zurenda acknowledged. "Very well my
faithful young Captain." Her eyes flashed. "Carry on with
your duties."

Zurenda considered Talia's report and mused with
smug satisfaction. "Perhaps Poseidon has completed his
oath."

After the coast was clear, the gang was relieved that
Rama's deception and the magic had worked.

"Whew!" Was all Quin could think to say.

"We dodged another disaster." The more realistic
Fabian expressed.

Once outside of Rama's Rock, Kiera went over to the
shoreline where she had crawled out of the water the night
before. Wading out in the water chest deep, she looked at
the sandy bottom for any sign of the remaining silver
arrows. Nothing!

Lycos realized what she was doing and swam out to
help. Both of them dived several times in the shallows
looking for the arrows. Lycos, the stronger swimmer,
found one, and then another. *If I can just locate a third, we*

may have enough to complete this mission. He thought to him-self.

Lycos clawed around at the sandy bottom. Nothing turned up but a few seashells and some kelp.

"Maybe they fell into the water further offshore." Ly-cos reasoned. And then, as if by a stroke of good luck, he found the remaining arrows. The arrows had been wedged in between two deeply submerged rocks and covered with dozens of orange starfish. Lycos felt relief with this dis-covery. Relief - just incredible relief!" All six arrows were recovered. Lycos managed to swim back to shore without being detected, except for a brilliant school of ophiuroids.

After dripping dry in the sand for a few minutes, he went over to where Kiera was; she was bent over with worry. "Here are your arrows." He presented the rest of them to Kiera. She gave him a big hug, and they both helped each other over to where the rest of the group was now gathered around.

"Here is your breakfast!" Fabian said as he encouraged the group to eat something.

After a few minutes, still soggy and dripping, Kiera and Lycos showed up to join the meal. It was simple. A few scraps of dried bread, olive oil, and some salted fish. That was all that Quin could round up from the wreckage of the boat. She quietly said to the team: "Eat up!"

CHAPTER EIGHTY-THREE

Zooey

Zooey, by sheer bird-brain luck, or dumb luck, ended up with a bird's eye view of Zurenda's palace and the whole operation. After getting caught up in the frenzy of ravens dropping debris on the boat, and then being whisked away by the flock back to the palace, Zooey was able to do some reconnaissance for the team without being detected as an intruder.

Still learning to fly, she flapped her way right into the palace with all the other ravens. The only downside to this was that she had to eat raven food, and had to pretend to like it, which even for Zooey, was not that appealing: "Raw roof rat. Yuck!"

While in the palace Zooey winged her way through the labyrinth memorizing the current configuration of walls and dead ends. From the tour through the dungeon complex, she could see that there were still several unlucky sailors, prisoners, awaiting their executions.

With a quick flight high over the lion's den, Zooey discovered that there were a total of eight lions in the cages. She thought that was strange because she remembered Arjun talking about only three.

Useful information to know, she thought. Zooey then flew down the cavernous hallway that led to the docking cave; her black wings nearly touching each side of the tunnel walls. Zooey could see that there were four ships lying at anchor in the docking cavern. *Again, excellent information to know,* Zooey thought.

With her confidence peaking, she felt even more birdlike. Zooey winged her way to the palace entrance. A few other ravens were flitting about in the vicinity. Maybe she could get a good look at the palace's grand hall.

This was a daring move on her part; she could see Zurenda in there with her smoke and mirrors talking to a black pool of water. Thinking this was bizarre behavior, even for a demi-god, to be talking to a pond full of smoky water, she closed in for a better look. From a perch behind the throne, she could see Zurenda's reflection in the water.

This too was a little unnerving, because Zurenda could also see her. Tense seconds passed, and then Zurenda turned and looked Zooey right in the eye.

"Come here my pet." Was the gentle call of a master to a faithful winged servant. Reaching her arm out to allow for a perch, Zurenda expected the raven to come down and rest upon it.

Zooey was really nervous. Could she pull this off? Was this happening? Swallowing her fear, with a Raven like cawing: "Cawaa, Cawaa," Zooey jumped off her perch behind the throne and glided ever so slowly down to land on Zurenda's left arm, her talons anchored firmly on the golden band that covered her forearm.

Zooey tried not to make eye contact, but it was no use. Zurenda wanted to talk.

"My pet," she said to the raven, stroking Zooey's black beak with her right index finger. "Talia has assured me that last night's intruders were neutralized with a little visit from Poseidon. I am not completely convinced. I want you, my pet, to survey the cliffs and the beaches of the island and see if you can spot them."

Zooey glared right into Zurenda's eye. Her black and grey eye belied no deceit that Zurenda could detect.

"Cawaa, Cawaa, Cawaa," was the only reply from her "Pet."

With that, Zooey sprang into the air and headed for the nearest open window. *I can't believe I pulled that off!* Thought Zooey's little bird brain. *Maybe I should stay in the shape of a bird.*

A few minutes later in Zurenda's great hall, Mara, one of her faithful Amazons, reported at the behest of the Queen.

"Mara!" Zurenda ordered. "Follow that bird!"

CHAPTER EIGHTY-FOUR

Chimeras

Being shipwrecked again was nothing new for Arjun or Lycos for that matter. The hours passed. They needed to wait out the daylight and attack the palace under the cover of darkness. From Quin's point of view that seemed to be their best idea going.

To everyone's surprise and delight, a lone raven came into view; the bird was coming from high above the cliffs of Piperi.

The raven was decidedly alone, and everyone hoped it would be Zooey.

After Zooey caught up with the group, they still kept out of sight as much as possible. Zooey turned herself back into a fig tree.

"It's Zooey!" Rama went over to give her an enthusiastic satyr hug.

"Please, tell us where you have been and what you have been up to." Rama encouraged.

Zooey began the debriefing. She told them everything that she had learned about the palace, including the dungeon, the lions, the labyrinth, and the boats.

Arjun nervously dipped a piece of bread in a bowl of olive oil while listening to her report. Kiera was eating too, but only because she was starving, not because she was nervous.

Zooey got to the part in her story about eating the rats. This made everyone sick, starting with Quin, who, at just the thought of eating raw rat meat, became nauseated and she threw-up right on the beach. Kiera was not much better. She only gagged a little, managing to keep her food down. Fabian paid no attention to this detail, and neither did Lycos.

"We need to attack tonight," Arjun stated. "Zurenda may already know by now that we survived the wreck and the other Poseidonic surprises."

No sooner had he said these words, than a detachment of Amazons, Mara's warriors, could be seen on the skyline above them and to the east.

"Take cover!" Arjun commanded. Arrows started flying from the Amazons' high position off the cliff above them.

"This is not a great location for defensive measures," said Arjun. "How will we ride this out, if they already know we are here?"

A quick team huddle was in order. Arjun whispered to the shapeshifters: "Rama, can you, Zooey and Quin turn into battle-clad dragons?" he asked. Then a better thought came into his mind. "Better yet, can you three change into flying, fire-breathing Chimeras?"

Quin and Rama looked at each other, and then they both looked a little worried, "I've never done that before," said Quin. "I've never tried it either," confirmed Rama.

"I just got finished being a bird," her confidence building, "I'll bet I can be a Chimera," said Zooey.

Arjun encouraged them to try. The three shapeshifters huddled in a circle, with arms locked together; they started a clockwise movement in the sand while Quin began chanting words that went something like this:

Those of Zurenda who oppose us,

Shall feel the wrath of the fire,

Cliffs and forest shall burn,

Warriors shall turn while,

the Chimeras shall conquer all.

Our talons shall tear them to pieces,

From the face of the earth, they shall go,

Olympic fury shall rain down upon them

The depths of Tartarus they shall know!

Arjun, Lycos, and Kiera were all stunned at the outcome of this magical chant. Before their very eyes appeared three of the strangest chimeras that anyone could ever imagine.

Zooey looked like a lodgepole with a pair of transparent wings, a tail and two talons beneath her spindly legs. Zooey's mouth was filled with fire like the smoking end of a gun, and black smoke was already pouring out.

Quin looked like a real winged, but excessively large green chimera; complete with all the trimmings. The only strange part was the eagle's beak located where there should have been something else.

Rama looked like an oversized fire-breathing, winged, goat with an extra goat head sticking out of her back and facing backward. She sported long curled horns and a long curly tail.

"Okay, ladies," Quin gathered them and got their attention. "Let's go Bar-B-Que some Amazon warriors."

Fabian and Lycos were still pre-occupied, shooting arrows at the warriors on the cliff, trying to cover the group until the transformation was complete.

The Chimeras tested their wings against the sea breeze in preparation for flight. This action also caught the attention of Mara's warriors, who were utterly stunned and unprepared for such an attack.

Mara's warriors all instantly started shooting arrows at the three very odd looking chimeras, but it was no use, the arrows that did make contact, just bounced off the Chimera body armor.

Zooey was the first one airborne, making her first dive-bomb at the warriors. She let out a fireball from her snout so terrible that all the trees and grass surrounding the warriors immediately ignited in flames. Several of warriors caught on fire and went running off the cliff, screaming in a frenzied attempt to escape the flames.

This left the rest of the warriors unprotected at the edge of the cliff. Fabian was able to pick a few Amazons with conventional arrows.

Rama, bless her heart, was decidedly uncomfortable being a chimera, she held back far enough away from the cliff to observe the carnage, managing not to get involved in the battle.

Quin, testing her firepower learned quickly how to be a chimera. Quin executed the second dive-bomb sortie. She came cross-wise to the warriors, swooping low, and began seizing several of them with her talons and dropping them far out into the sea. Quin left a swath of scorched earth in her wake, putting a smile on her face.

It did not take very long for the Chimeras to complete their work on Mara's detachment. However, the battle was not yet over. Zooey could see more warriors coming across the field from Zurenda's Palace. This time the warriors were well armored and on horses.

The fighting was just beginning! The next detachment of Amazon warriors were coming, led by Ada. She was, equally as unprepared for the chimeras as was Mara, but she was a skilled equestrian.

Rama finally found her confidence building before she was caught in an updraft from the cliffs which took her by surprise. Once stabilized, she made a dive-bomb run towards Ada and her equines. Though Rama was not as big as Quin and Zooey in their chimeric state, Rama was still large enough to pick off pairs of warriors on a galloping steed. Each pass proved her efforts were effective.

Rama found herself flying in low and butting heads with the warriors. This action immediately knocked them right off their steeds and knocked them out cold as they fell to the ground. One of the warriors was caught by the stirrup of her saddle and found herself and her mount charging right over the cliff into the abyss.

There was no one else to fight, at least not at the moment. The chimeras circled back around to Arjun and the rest of the group, landing just in front of them on the beach.

"Better climb on!" Quin encouraged the others.

"We can fly you right up to the heart of the action."

Arjun, Kiera, and Lycos wasted no time in getting a chimeric ride to the top of the plateau.

Fabian was the only reluctant one, choosing to 'hoof it' all the way to the top of the plateau. "With the warriors neutralized on the cliff, I should be able to make it up there by myself," he said, not wanting to deal with the awkwardness of trying to climb on to a chimera and then the additional awkwardness of trying to climb off of one. "Too weird," Fabian explained to no one in particular.

Once the group was re-assembled at the top of the cliff, Arjun could see the front door to Zurenda's Palace for the first time.

"Our cover is blown," Arjun confessed to the group. "No doubt, Zurenda will be waiting for us now."

Lycos observed: "So much for the element of surprise under cover of darkness."

Kiera added: "Zooey knows how to get into the palace from several directions. Maybe we can still surprise the queen."

Arjun considered this proposal. If they attacked the palace from several directions, could they keep the rest of the guards busy and distracted long enough to gain access to the queen? It was a tempting thought. Arjun looked at his sword. The reflection in the blade showed nothing that would indicate an attack one way would be better than another.

"What would Selene want me to do?" He said, keeping an open mind.

"The blade will show you nothing," Rama said. "The blade has gotten us this far; it is up to us to complete this task. The gods have done their work."

CHAPTER EIGHTY-FIVE

Amazons

After scouring out the lion's pit and placing a spit shine on the doors and hardware, Kendra and her warriors were ready for a new assignment. They communicated with Zurenda by using the reflection in the Palace pool.

"What would you have us do now, my Queen?" Kendra inquired.

A wisp of grey smoke came up around the queen's person as she formulated a reply. Zurenda spoke. "I would have you and the warriors prepare a roadblock for our intruders."

Zurenda continued. "Arjun and his friends are coming down the path from the plateau; we want to welcome them with the most unearthly fury that can be conjured up."

Kendra, ever loyal, replied: "Yes, my Queen. We will prepare a most unlikely welcome."

Before Kendra and the Amazons could leave the palace, Talia, Coreen and the last detachment of warriors came to report on the on-going battle.

"My Queen," Talia and Coreen stood together in the hall as Talia addressed her leader: "We have shifted the labyrinth once again, should the intruders try to enter through the docking tunnel. We have also posted guards at each ship in the cavern to prevent any unauthorized use." Talia continued her report. "The few remaining prisoners held in the dungeon have been placed under a double guard. There will be no escapes, my Queen." With that, Talia and Coreen made the parting gesture with their right arms and then they were dismissed from the great hall.

"Ladies," Zurenda asked them as they were about to leave, "would you kindly return to my throne for a follow-up question; "how are you at fighting chimeras?"

Talia responded: "We have the trebuchet weapon; we have many large cross-bows and an assortment of spears."

Zurenda suggested to her Captain that there should also be a way to include fire in her arsenal.

"We will find ways to use fire, my Queen," Talia promised.

With that Zurenda's leaders were both dismissed to carry out more mischief for Arjun and his band of misfits.

Zurenda turned to her Mother for additional help. Throwing her hands high in the air with fingers outstretched she prayed to the one person who would listen.

"Eris, Goddess of Contempt," she implored. "Help us win this fight against the chimeras, and repulse the man who carries the Sword of Olympus. Help us render Cassandras prophecy null and void. Help us defeat the Warrior from Olympus!"

My daughter, Zurenda heard the words of the Goddess clearly in her mind. *The chimeras are an illusion. Pay them no heed. This day shall I deliver the man Arjun into your hands.* Her arrogance piqued. *I have decreed that you shall have the pleasure of killing him yourself!* For Zurenda, this message was clear. She would prevail.

CHAPTER EIGHTY-SIX

Hadrian and Zedra

The rock blasting was getting old! "We are making little to no progress," Hadrian lamented with plenty of discouragement in his voice.

"Keep trying," Zedra encouraged. "The rocks are breaking up into fragments now, unlike before. We are getting closer to the surface."

The sword blasting continued all afternoon, in spite of the dust and debris field that they were creating and leaving behind.

The debris was like a pile of small head-sized stones stacked up from the center of the earth, and then it happened! A new strike at the rock revealed a thin sliver of daylight that could be seen.

"You were right, Zedra, we are almost to the surface!" Hadrian confirmed while leaning on his sword with both hands to take a much needed, but brief rest. "I wonder where we will come out in the mortal realm."

Zedra replied. "Don't know."

Hadrian responded by adding, "But it's going to be better out there than being cooped-up in here."

Hadrian made another observation: "The tunnel we made is almost big enough to drop a horse through, and have it fall all the way down to Hades."

Zedra nodded her head in agreement. "Maybe it will somehow prove useful."

The pair kept plugging away. The sliver of light grew bigger and brighter. They knew they were near the surface of the earth when a smattering of bone shards came falling down upon them during the blasting. Hadrian thought that to be strange, but then he realized that they may be closer to the dungeon of Zurenda than they first thought.

CHAPTER EIGHTY-SEVEN

Fabian

The assault on the palace was not going to be easy. From their vantage point on the plateau, Arjun could see that the guards were making preparations to use trebuchets against them and who knew what else. With twenty-two guards already neutralized, it was anybody's guess how many more they would have to face.

Zooey, Rama, and Quin were still in their chimeric form. Maybe they could get a look at the palace defenses and see if any more resistance could be spotted.

The flight over the palace courtyard was a bad idea. The guards were launching flaming arrows and spears at the girls from the center of the courtyard and all the towers.

"No sign of the Queen," Zooey reported, and Quin and Rama both confirmed that report.

"Perhaps the best way to enter the palace is from the air," Rama suggested. "The path that led to the front gate is already steeped in defensive measures."

Quin suggested they wait until the cover of darkness, which wouldn't be too much longer. "We could conduct an air raid after the sun goes down."

Fabian liked the direct approach. "Let's drop fire rocks through the roof of the palace and see what burns!"

Arjun was a little worried about that idea as his Mother's colossal statue was still in there in some form of disrepair. He did not want to make it worse.

Arjun, Kiera, and Lycos finally agreed on the 'wait till dark' approach, even though they felt somewhat exposed on the plateau so close to the palace entrance.

Their only defense, at the moment, was to hunker down behind a thick grove of olive trees.

"How will we defend ourselves from a frontal attack here?" Fabian asked a fair question. "Worse yet," Fabian continued. "How would we defend ourselves from a sneak attack to the rear; or an attack to our left or right flank?" Fabian, registering his concern on 'the plan.'

"Our best hope is to attack under cover of darkness," Arjun reasoned. "Maybe the gods will be with us."

All the team could do was to wait. There was no other sane choice. "Anything else would be suicide, and we don't want anyone to get hurt or captured. We need everyone," said Arjun.

"Where is Artemis? Where is Selene?" Fabian asked. "Their absence is more than just apparent." In his mind, the Goddesses are needed for this stage of the mission, the invasion."

He was hoping that they would come out of no-where and magically make this fight go away. Fabian had the most to worry about. He was after all a Centaur, and the Amazons hated his species. The history books were full of conflicts between the Amazonian Warriors and centaurs over the last several centuries. If they wanted someone to fail in this battle, it was Arjun, and if they were seeking revenge for past wrongs, then they surely wanted Fabian dead. Fabian was not new to this knowledge of the fates. He lived with it every day of his life. The only problem that made this contest different was that there could be one hundred of them and only one of him. In his heart, he felt out-numbered.

Fabian was out-numbered, they were all out-numbered. In spite of what Rama had said, 'about the gods having done their work,' Arjun kept an eye on his blade, perchance there would be revealed a message from mother, a message from home.

CHAPTER EIGHTY-EIGHT

They Are Coming!

Kiera was having a bad hair day. Her braid, the one that Quin did for her, had come undone and uneven locks of hair kept blowing in her face obscuring her view.

"There is not much to see anyway," Lycos noticed her golden mop. "Just the rear ends of three chimeras." The girls were good sports to volunteer even if reluctantly, to double as a defensive bunker in the olive grove.

For the first time in weeks, everyone was waiting for the sun to go down. It seemed like it never would.

While waiting, Kiera and Arjun hatched a fantastic idea. "What if we fly one chimera, circle wide, and swing into the docking cave and then have the other two chimeras attack the front gate with fire. That may pose enough of a distraction that we could enter the docking cave tunnel as we did before, and it may give us enough time to work our way through the labyrinth." Kiera suggested.

"What are the odds that we will have an opposite reaction?" Arjun quizzed. "They may be expecting us to do just that. If we fall into their hands, we will have an epic disaster."

Arjun considered these options while gathering and tying back Kiera's hair with a piece of leather string he pulled off of Zooey's armor.

Fabian, overhearing the conversation, suggested a plan that already sounded familiar. "The chimeras could be used to drop huge stones, trees, whatever, on their equipment and all who would oppose them."

Lycos said, "This idea sounds like a plan that makes sense." The more he thought about the plan, the better he liked it.

Chimera Quin abruptly interrupted. "I need a snack!" She said. "You know, like a side of beef!"

"Our shapeshifter has a point." Lycos agreed with Quin, "we are all hungry, but there doesn't seem to be a good source of food at the moment."

"Food!" Rama added, "I wish we could eat well before this fight, but I don't see it happening."

Understandably, the gang was all starving. Arjun brought the focus back to why they were there. "We need to stick to the plan to get this mission accomplished, or we may never be able to complete it."

The good ideas about food were interrupted.

"Look toward the palace gates everyone!" Quin announced. "They are coming! The Amazons are coming!"

Talia and her warriors were charging at them at full speed ahead with battle-hardened horses. There were ten of them. It was time to move!

Fireballs of burning coal were being slung at them one right after the other, with the trebuchets. Their protective location in the forest would be overrun. The whole area was given up to fire and flames.

"We have to go!" Arjun commanded! "The attack on the palace front gate is no longer an option. Everyone mount a chimera. Yes, even you, Fabian!"

Seconds later the chimeras were ready, Lycos, Arjun, Kiera, and Fabian were airborne, and the chimeras bore down on the war-mongers using the full fury of the beasts!

Streams of fire scorched the trebuchets, burning them and catching their surroundings on fire. The equipment and the warriors that operated them burst into flames. Thick smoke billowed upward.

After that foray, they circled over the cliffs to the northwest edge of the island. Another round of fire and destruction was laid bare upon the Amazons in their wake.

The Warriors returned fire with arrows and cross-bows loaded with long spears.

Luckily the spears missed their mark, and the fire-breathing trio went back for one more pass on the warriors before they all made a full circle to the west, and then to the south and coming in for a landing near the docking cavern.

From the tail end of a chimera Kiera could see that there were several warriors down, and the rest of them were running in random chaos for the safety of the palace.

Maybe the attack was working, she thought.

As they all came in for a landing at the docking cave, Zooey belched a fireball towards the stone tunnel to make sure there were no guards near its entrance. Rama and

Quin lit up the cave with more fireballs, turning the sunset into a display of red ash and black smoke silhouetted behind them in the cave's opening.

The only individuals in the docking cavern appeared to be them. "It looks like everyone else was drawn off to the fields above," Quin observed.

Kiera and Arjun jumped off of the leathery back of Rama on to the stone floor next to the boats. Quin and Fabian landed a little closer to the tunnel entrance. Lycos and Zooey landed right on the deck of a ship, causing it to list forward and then side to side as it stabilized.

"Okay, gang! Let's do this!" Arjun, the eternal optimist, shouted. "Quin, Rama, and Zooey turn yourselves into something useful that will fit into the tunnel."

And then Lycos suggested: "Like a lion or a wolf!"

Zooey counter-offered. "Like a fire-breathing snake?"

Quin suggested: "Like a wild boar?"

"I know," said Rama, "I will turn myself into a rabid three-headed wolf."

So much for committee work, Kiera made the final decisions:

"Rama, you will be a three-headed wolf."

"Quin, you will be a fire-breathing snake."

"Zooey, you will be a roaring lion."

Fabian just rolled his eyes. "We need swords too." Fabian reminded the group. "All the ones we can carry."

"That's why you, Arjun and Lycos are here," Kiera answered. "I have the arrows!" Kiera announced, stating the obvious.

Kiera added, "None of my arrows are glowing, so we must be in a safe place at the moment."

Arjun looked at his blade. The reflection seemed dark and foreboding, but there was no vision upon it. "Guys, I'm still uneasy about this approach."

"We have no choice!" Rama observed. "We were going to get incinerated up on that plateau; this tunnel is our best option, even though we have to face the labyrinth."

Rama added her approval of the plan with an additional word of encouragement: "Arjun, trust your instincts."

CHAPTER EIGHTY-NINE

The Labyrinth

The coal fires did not stop burning at the edge of the plateau. "Looks like there is more where that came from," Kendra announced. "We'll feed them buckets of melting scalding rocks."

The elements were being pushed up from what seemed like the center of the earth, following the path that Kendra and the girls took to get back to the palace.

Steam poured out of every crack in every rock that had so much as a hairline of a fracture.

Zurenda waited with anticipation to deploy Kendra's forces by using steaming hot rocks that could be dropped into the labyrinth.

"This should stop them!" Phoebe proudly announced.

"Change the labyrinth again." Ordered Kendra. "We will stop them for sure."

Zurenda joined the conversation, "By the end of the night they will pay dearly for their arrogance. They will all be well steam broiled and on their way to Hades!"

Aeila, also one of Kendra's warriors, flooded the labyrinth with water from the palace fountain which instantly became a steamy sauna clouding the pathway and created an additional obstacle by blocking the passageway, either going in or out.

"They will be trapped forever!" Kendra gloated, the steam rising past her almost transparent face and casting a strange and faint shadow on the ceiling above her head.

Zurenda added to the boast! "I will have my revenge upon the Warrior from Olympus and his band of misfits!"

In a bold act of blasphemy, Kendra looked skyward shaking her clenched fist she cursed Artemis and Selene in the name of Poseidon for what they had done to her and the girls!

It must have been enough. The entire mountain shook. The whole island trembled.

New cracks were visible in the solid rock. Shards of rock fell into the tunnel and began blocking the way for Arjun and the rest of the gang. The only way for them to go was up; there was no turning back!

Zooey roared like a lion. The sheer volume of her sound made the walls creak and pop some more. Quin took a more practical approach. She slivered in and out of the fallen rocks and the ones that Kendra had put there to find the way through this rat maze. The heat and intensity of the steam was getting to be a problem. Everyone was sweating, and the air was getting almost too thick and too hot to breathe.

"We need some relief from this steam." Kiera pleaded.

However, there was no relief, only more steam that poured into the passageway through every crack and added to the pain of scorching hot rocks in every direction.

Quin used her snake fire to light the way. "Over there." Quin pointed her forked tongue to the right passage.

Kiera had her bow loaded and ready to react to any surprise.

"Keep going." Rama was following the group at the rear. "I sense that there is fresh meat ahead." Rama's three super-sensitive noses detected something in the distance, this made Fabian a little worried, and a bit self-conscious that she might think he was on the menu.

"Focus!" Arjun told everyone and then asked Quin. "Quin, what about this passage up ahead and to the left?"

The group had just come to another junction. No choice looked better than the other. Quin sampled the air. She sampled it again. With a hissing sound in her voice, she suggested that they take the right passage.

The right-hand passage turned out to be a dead end. "We have to turn around," Quin said regrettably.

Turing around was not so easy when you have seven individuals in the same tunnel. "Okay," Kiera said as she squeezed by Fabian and under Zooey's mane, which tickled by the way, between Rama's second and third head and then over the back of Quin's scales. Each one had to negotiate the backup, and turn-around in a similar manner.

It was incredibly claustrophobic, to say the least!

This maneuver was followed by a few left turns down an unlit passage, followed by a right turn and then another left.

Lycos almost felt like they were making progress. "The walls have just shifted again," Lycos observed. "We need to keep together, or we will get hopelessly separated."

This statement made everyone worried about getting lost.

Zooey, who did not like being alone in the least, was the most worried about getting lost.

The whole mountain of stone they were in started to tremble again. Plates of solid rock kept grinding against each other belching dust into the sordid mix of steam and sweat.

"It's like this whole place will come down on our heads if we don't get out of here." Fabian worried. "Lycos, do you see what I see?"

Hopes began to rise as everyone looked forward to a light at the end of the tunnel.

"We have almost made it!" Rejoiced the three-headed wolf. "I so need some fresh air!" Head One of Wolf Rama said. Fabian just rolled his eyes again.

Lioness Zooey cautioned the group: "I smell more trouble ahead. I smell the makings of a trap!"

Just then, the earth shook again, a large slab of rock fell from the tunnel's roof and down onto the last few inches of Quin's serpentine tail. "Ouch!" Quin hissed in pain.

"Luckily you did not get trapped under that stone," Kiera observed.

"Look at the light; it's getting brighter." Arjun smiled. "Maybe we are about through this rat maze; I for one am very much done with it!"

Fabian looked at the passage behind them. The tunnel that they just passed through had closed.

There was no going back!

CHAPTER NINETY

Zurenda

"**B**y all the Gods! What is going on! Why is this whole island shaking? Is it an earth-quake?" Zurenda questioned as she held on to a column in the palace hall for support and to keep from falling inside the trembling building. This support post was the same column that supported her during the last set of tremors. The earthquakes finally broke up the exterior wall of the dungeon. Stones and large boulders separated from each other leaving an open pathway to escape. The few remaining prisoners were able to squeeze out of the opening and go free, and like seasoned sailors; they headed straight for the docking cavern in hopes of procuring a boat. Zurenda was not aware, neither were any of her warriors aware of the escape. Arjun and company had their complete focus, and nothing else seemed to matter.

With a signal from the delta necklace emblems, Zurenda commanded the warriors to retreat from the plateau. There was no place left for them to take cover. The olive grove, incinerated. The tall grass, burned; the sky, blackened with smoke.

Talia reported to her queen: "They are coming up through the labyrinth. All of them!" Then to her warriors, Talia made the battle cry: "Be ready!"

Zurenda told her warriors that the intruders could assume any form that could be imagined. "We last saw them as chimeras going into the docking cave; we know they have shapeshifters with them."

Talia added this observation: "Maybe they will be something else when they come out of the labyrinth. Be prepared with arrows, swords, spears, and fire! Anything could happen!" Talia ordered her guards: "Shoot to kill whatever comes out! Be it a mouse or a monster, kill whatever you see!"

Even the lions in the pit were nervous. The rumbling of the earth had set them on edge. Each one was clawing at the iron doors that led to freedom. Unable to escape their cages, the Lions resorted to an ungodly high-pitched screeching noise that sent shivers up every spine within hearing distance.

Due to the earthquakes, Zurenda worried that the sliding floor of the pit might not work when she needed it the most.

There were so many things to think about. *Would she be able to capture and kill Arjun? Could she kill the rest without too much resistance? How would this fight end?*

There was no added reassurance from Eris. It seemed that the gods had grown silent on this eve of battle.

"Why?" She said.

Eris was watching from a safe distance, so were Selene and Artemis.

There would be no help from the gods. This battle was a mortal contest; it had to be. It was the only way that a true victor could be determined.

Eris reasoned that the winner would be declared by the gods, and the news of this battle would echo down the canyons and over the rooftops of Greece. The winner would be the undisputed demi-god, and everyone would know it. Selene, on the other hand, was not that bold.

For this reason, it had to be a fair fight. At least that was the way that the gods viewed it.

Zeus himself stated in the last meeting that he would not interfere with the demi-gods at this stage of the conflict. He wanted to see for himself how resourceful this son would turn out to be, this 'Warrior from Olympus.'

Eris on the other hand, wanted her daughter to win because there was so much at stake in the world of conquest and domination. "Surely, this outcome will seal my position as the Queen of the Universe," she told the black cloud that was beginning to swirl up around her. "My revenge against Zeus and Selene will be complete!"

Hidden in the cloud high above the palace, Selene's motives for a positive outcome for her son were much less self-centered. She wanted global peace and harmony. "Is that too much to ask?" She looked to Artemis for an approving reply. Artemis was busy holding on to the reigns of the chariot. Crystal and Starlight were restless.

Artemis, though distracted, was very much in favor of Selene's desires and outcomes as well. The goddess did, however, seek a proper sacrifice to fulfill her own self-interests from missed opportunities in the past.

Would everyone get their wish? Would no one get their wish? Only time would tell. And Father Time waits for no one, not even for the gods.

CHAPTER NINETY-ONE

The Labyrinth

The entrance into the labyrinth from the great hall was from the west door about halfway down the corridor. Columns of grey smoke-white marble lined the corridors along the great hall. It was truly an impressive structure. The door to the labyrinth was not that heroic, however. The door was about five cubits tall and about two and a half cubits wide. The door itself was made of thick mahogany planks and had a high polish or shine on it. The door was also fitted with a small hand-sized view-window covered with iron bars. The whole door was covered with broad iron straps that bound the planks together.

It was at this location that Talia and her guards took up a defensive position. It was this location that Arjun and his crew had to come out. There was no other choice.

As Zooey correctly observed, "it was a trap!" Shape changing was only going to help three of the seven individuals in the Labyrinth. How could the rest of the group survive? There had to be a way forward, but how?

Arjun was leading the group when they got to within twenty cubits of the entrance door. There was only one bend left in the maze, and they were at the end.

Lycos peeked around the corner. He could see the wooden doorway, the small square window, the iron bars and through it, and the welcoming committee. "We can't do this as a frontal assault," Lycos whispered to the group. "We will be cut down before we make it through that door. We need to have Zooey, Rama and Quin figure out how to help us get out of this maze and manage to survive."

Rama had an idea: "What if I change into a large rolling stone and you four climb inside of me as I roll through that door?"

Arjun commented: "I like where you are going with this idea, Rama, but once through the door, there will be maybe twenty guards to fight and only a few of us. I don't like the odds."

Zooey offered another idea using her high squeaky voice, which sounded really weird coming from a lion.

"How 'bout we turn ourselves into something tiny, like gnats? The guards will never see us come out. We can fly or crawl past them and get behind them and then turn into something else, like a giant of some sort, mop the floor with these warriors, and then you guys can come out of the door when it's safe."

Kiera liked that idea a lot, glancing at her quiver. "All my arrows are glowing. We have to decide right now!"

Arjun made a decision: "Let's do a combination of the two ideas as follows: Let's have Zooey and Quin turn themselves into gnats, and fly to the opposite side of the hall. Then, turn into a giant monster or something that does not mind having a dozen arrows stuck in your butt. After the initial attack is over, Rama comes out of the tunnel like a bowling ball, rolling over any remaining survivors.

"Once that is done, the rest of us come out of the tunnel and take-on the demi-god and any monsters she may come up with."

Arjun looked at the group for approval. "What do you guys think?"

"Sounds like a plan," Fabian said.

Everyone else agreed.

"Okay guys, let's do this!" Lycos said with enthusiasm.

"May the Gods of Olympus help us!" Arjun exclaimed.

"Mother, help us!" He added with an earnest tone in his voice.

Kiera peeked around the corner. "We have to start this plan now!" she said, "they are setting fire to the arrows!"

CHAPTER NINETY-TWO

Arjun's War

Who would have ever thought of sending an insect into battle? No one! No one, but Arjun that is. Zooey turned herself into a gnat. Quin turned herself into a tiny black sugar ant. Both of the girls made for the crack under the door.

Quin crawled slower than Zooey, but that may have been an advantage. Once Zooey was under the threshold of the door, she kept a low flight pattern and made it past one, two, three, up to eight guards. Quin was crawling along at a snail's pace, well, at an ants pace, to be exact. But the dark granite floors were the perfect cover for her.

It took several minutes for them to get into position on the opposite side of the hall. Fabian and Rama were next. Once Rama became a large round stone, Fabian climbed inside her and prepared for the ride of his life.

"Lucky for us, rocks are not flammable. Ready!" Rama whispered.

"Ready!" Fabian confirmed. Rama began rolling toward the locked labyrinth door.

Zooey hit a snag. One of the hazards that she forgot to anticipate was spiders. After getting behind the guards, she flew up into the rafters to have a look around and managed to get herself tangled up in a spider web at the cornice of one of the columns.

This was not part of the plan! Zooey had to think quickly! A spider fifty times her size had taken notice of her in its web and was coming over to do what spiders do best.

Zooey started to panic. *I need to change into something big! A Rhinoceros!* She thought. Transforming into something that big took several seconds. She narrowly missed getting bitten and poisoned by a spider only to find herself as a two-ton Rhinoceros clinging to the ceiling cross-beams.

Zooey blinked. Gravity took over! A split-second later, Zooey came crashing down from the rafters as a huge grey Rhinoceros! Her entrance, (stage left), was not at all graceful. "BOOM!!" She hit the floor, backside first, with the full weight of her massive body.

The whole palace shook under the impact, crushing a few of Zurenda's warriors in the process.

Other warrior guards turned around to look at this spectacle. In disbelief, they beheld the sight, but their arrows were ready and already on fire. They started shooting at her.

Each burning arrow seared her hide, but none of the weapons were able to penetrate her thick skin sufficiently to do any damage.

Just then, the obscure tiny ant in the corner of the room became a Giant Cyclops. The Cyclops reached out with its long hairy arms and hands, grabbing warriors one by one crushing them like tin cans in each clenched fist. Arrows and spears were utterly ineffective on her protective coat of ethereal.

Quin discarded their bodies, Amazons and weapons onto the floor. Using some of the Amazons as clubs Quin began swinging them around as projectiles, indeed weapons, against any other warrior guards who would dare challenge her.

There was little in the way of defense that the guards could do in the face of this challenge. Quin's carnage continued for several minutes.

This "Quin rampage," and a full grown rhinoceros running loose in the palace hall, gave Rama and Fabian the chance they needed. Rama rolled right up and out of the wooden labyrinth door crashing it open with hardly any effort whatsoever. Once through the door, Fabian jumped out of the stone and began hand-to-hand combat with the few remaining warriors that Zooey and Quin had not managed to kill already.

Guards were running everywhere! Arrows were flinging and then bouncing off of walls, rhinoceros skin, and thick cyclops hide.

Chaos reigned! Confusion was on every hand!

Lycos, Kiera, and Arjun all ran out of the labyrinth door, well, what was left of it. (The door had a few fragments of wood swinging back and forth on half-destroyed iron hinges). The team had most of the warriors under control.

Zooey went around crushing fallen warriors just to make sure they were dead. She pressed her full weight upon them until she could hear their rib bones crack and pop, after that, she got up and went to the next victim. "This is war," Zooey reasoned, completely unapologetic, "I will take no prisoners."

Quin had Talia by the hair of her head and was pulling her, dragging her, across the great hall. Quin, like a clumsy cyclops, stepped on Talia's left arm breaking it badly in two places. While being dragged across the floor, by the hair of her head, Talia reached up with her sword and cut off her own hair to escape Quin's grasp. Quin pulled up the lock of hair to her eye level in surprised disbelief.

Talia managed to roll away and escape Quin's grasp, with only a broken arm and the loss of her long hair. Talia ran down the great hall, with her left arm aching in intense pain. She reported the news of the battle's progress to Zurenda.

Zurenda was not pleased! Neither was she amused. "I will take matters into my own hands!" She said. "Talia, you wait here," leaving her Captain alone near the throne room.

Before Zurenda could draw her sword, Kiera was poised and ready to shoot at a distance of fifty paces. Kiera had loaded not one, but three glowing arrows into the bow, all trained on the demi-god's heart. She was not going to miss.

The launch would have been perfect, but Lycos and Fabian who were protecting Arjun and Kiera from the rear, stumbled over one of the dead warriors, causing them to both fall backward onto Kiera. She fell to the floor. The arrows went flying out of her bow to an uncertain target.

Seeing this, Zurenda motioned to the arrows and also to Kiera's bow with a turning-twisting gesture of her right index finger. The bow and arrows began hovering between Zurenda and Kiera in mid-air, just out of reach!

"The Bow of Artemis!" Zurenda observed, "You won't be needing that anymore, my dear!"

Kiera reached for her dagger, which she wore on her belt; again, Zurenda's magic took over. The knife left her hand and went flying upward to impale itself into the ceiling rafters.

Next, Kiera found herself being lifted into the air and thrown across the great hall, at the speed of an arrow, and into the stone wall on the opposite side.

Upon hitting the wall with a thud, Kiera hit her head and passed out, slumping to the floor, in a helpless heap. Kiera's bow and her three launched arrows were then carried through the air, where they found their mark in the heroic statue of Selene, the arrows, sticking into the thick paste of tar at three different places around the Goddess' statue.

The other three arrows remained undetected in their quiver. Kiera lay motionless against the corner of the hall.

After collecting their senses, Arjun, Lycos, and Fabian found themselves on their backs, on the marble floor, looking straight up at the Demi-Goddess. Shock and awe filled their eyes, at the sight of finally laying eyes on their foe. Zurenda stood before them! She was as terrible and fearful as she was beautiful.

Zurenda took both her hands and motioned to them, with her index fingers. Making a quick circular motion with her right index finger, she pulled the Olympic sword right from Lycos' grip. He could see this all happening, and yet he was powerless to do anything about it.

"The Sword of Ares!" Zurenda observed, reaching out for the swift flying sword and then grabbing it by the hilt mid-flight with her right hand. "You Lycos, my youthful and fine sailor from the Aegean, you will have the pleasure, indeed the honor, of being the first one I kill today with the Sword of Ares!"

Zurenda continued her lecture to Lycos. "The sword that you have carried these many months as Arjun's trusted companion, will provide a fitting end for you, my brave and youthful warrior. Your demise will also be a fitting spectacle for your companion Arjun to see, as you are killed with it!" Zurenda caressed the sword in her left hand, admiring its craftsmanship, finishing the thought with an evil look that flashed across her eyes, and made her smile!

Lycos gulped as he tried to find his feet.

Arjun turned, drawing his sword as he spun in slow-motion to face the Queen while shouting a long and painful: "NOOoooo!!!!" in the process.

Zurenda, with the other hand and with another finger gesture, took Lycos and flung him vertically through the air into the ceiling rafters. His backbones cracked against the timbers. Pain shot through his body as he was held there, pinned upside down against the beams.

Arjun did the only thing he could think to do. He reached for the dagger in his belt and flung it toward the demi-goddess, narrowly missing her body, but cutting her clothes. This action broke her concentration away from Lycos for a split second as the dagger passed by her and connected with the Sword of Ares creating a hail of sparks and a plume of white smoke.

The earth shook again. The shaking was so hard this time that several of the stained glass windows in the great hall were shattered and fell out of their frames. Shards of colored glass came tumbling to the floor. The columns shook, and the ceiling dust formed a white cloud that began to hang over the rafters. The beams were giving way.

To Arjun's surprise, something unexpected happened. Fabian rammed Zurenda with his head down at full gallop from across the hall. He hit her from behind, taking her on his back and sailing down the hall some fifty paces until his hooves finally caught some traction, and he skidded to a stop. The sword of Ares went skating across the floor to the foot of Arjun.

"I will kill you for this!" Zurenda screamed at the Centaur with all the fury she could muster.

Fabian replied with more head-butting treatment and another trip further down the hall, dragging Zurenda under his body with one arm, and reaching for a spear with the other.

This action bought Arjun and Lycos some time. Lycos was still pinned on the ceiling, his back still in pain, while being pinned to the rafters by Zurenda's magic. However, with the Fabian diversion, Arjun was able to retrieve the Sword of Ares and heave it up, butt-end first, to Lycos' awaiting hand.

Meanwhile, the rest of the team was becoming oriented to the marble walls they all were flung up against. Lucky for the shapeshifters, Quin took the precaution to place a spell on each of them before the fight began that would protect them from sharp objects like arrows, swords, spears, and daggers.

Kiera was not so lucky. She had a knot on her head the size of a walnut. Her head was cracked and bleeding between her left eye and ear, but it was not a fatal wound, at least according to Quin.

"We have to get to Arjun!" Kiera muttered half-conscious to Quin and Rama.

"Yes, we know Kiera, but let's get you to a safe place."

Rama did the only thing she could think of. She turned herself back into a satyr. Picking up Kiera and slinging her over her back she carried Kiera down the length of the great hall and right out the back door, unchallenged.

"The Amazonian Warriors must all be dead!" Rama mused. Quin and Zooey gathered up Kiera's bow and the remaining three arrows and followed Rama out the door. Once in the courtyard, Rama let Kiera down to rest in the flower bed next to some hedges. She suggested that Zooey and Quin stay with her while she went back to the palace and helped the others. Rama then turned herself back into a Cyclopes and headed back into the fight.

The fight inside continued. Zurenda had finally gotten the upper hand with Fabian 'the snowplow!' They skirted the palace and mopped every floor with Fabian's hide and Zurenda's cape. While passing through the throne room, Fabian was severely slashed on the right shoulder by Talia, who was sitting on the edge of the reflecting pool, with a long spear propped up against the throne.

After that brief encounter, Talia tossed Zurenda the spear. Catching the spear mid-flight with her right hand without even so much as a flinch, Zurenda lunged the spear into Fabian's already bleeding chest. Fabian let out a huge centurion cry, skating down the corridors until he hit a column head-on. This impact was followed by a centurion groan that could be heard all over the palace.

The centaur fell silent. Was Fabian dead? None of the shapeshifters could tell.

Zurenda's eyes flashed, "Now to kill-off the rest of these uninvited intruders!" She shouted, looking somewhat disheveled, she left the spear stuck squarely in Fabian's gut and shook herself off.

Marching back to the throne room, and passing by the heroic statue of Selene, completely covered in white dust and black tar, she did not even notice the three Olympic arrows sticking out from the mixture of goo.

Zurenda stormed forward, to an awaiting Arjun and Lycos. Arjun was there near the throne, trying to help free Lycos, who was still helplessly pinned to the ceiling by Zurenda's magic.

Talia managed to get there as well, broken arm and all. She tossed a sword to Zurenda at which Arjun reacted by trying to catch it in mid-air missing in the attempt.

Speaking to Arjun, Zurenda stated: "Talia has a good aim, even with a broken arm, my handsome Nemesis from the North."

Zurenda continued, "At last we meet, Arjun son of Selene, son of Zeus!" She stated with bitter contempt.

Arjun was not surprised that she knew him, after all, he knew about her.

"Zurenda," Arjun addressed her, "Your days of discord and contempt are coming to an end."

Lycos was on the ceiling watching the whole thing, but powerless to take any action.

"You will release Lycos this instant!" Arjun demanded.

"And why should I?" Zurenda retorted. "You have invaded my palace; you have brought carnage to my house! I OWE YOU NOTHING!" The queen screamed at the top of her lungs.

Zurenda signaled Talia to open the pit. The earth shook again. This time the floor covering the pit would only open halfway before it stopped, producing a large puff of white smoke in the process.

Maybe it would be enough. Talia reasoned while she maneuvered behind the throne and a few steps to the left, placing a few daggers into fixed positions directly beneath Lycos.

Lycos could see this all happening below him, and yet seemed powerless to stop it. At least Lycos had the Sword of Ares in his hand. With both hands, he pointed the sword in the direction of Talia and commanded that the lightning shock her in the name of Ares. Nothing happened. He tried again. Nothing!

Zurenda, seeing this action, and the manner of death that Talia had prepared for him, commanded that Lycos be freed, released.

With a flick of her wrist, suddenly, immediately, Lycos dropped like a rock, heading straight for the daggers!

Rama the Cyclops caught him just in the nick of time, as she fully appeared out of the white cloud of dust that hung in the room.

The impact of Rama catching Lycos with her outstretched arms caused the Sword of Ares to go skating across the throne room, past the foot of Arjun, and then it bounced off the fountain, finally clanking to a rest near the foot of Talia. She picked it up with her right arm.

The Cyclops carried Lycos away from the fight under one arm and collected the body of Fabian under the other. During Rama's retreat, she made her very own new doorway in the exterior wall behind the statue of the goddess, and to safety.

Lycos looked anxiously back at Arjun. He tried to persuade Rama to let him down, but it was no use, she would not listen, she had made up her mind.

Arjun felt alone, and he was alone. He was standing in front of the Demi-Goddess Zurenda and her Captain of the Guard, Talia. Alone! Well not entirely.

Arjun called for Kiera. "KIERA!" He shouted to an otherwise empty hall. Only his echo returned a reply from the queen, Zurenda.

"Your beloved Kiera is dead!" Zurenda calmly stated. "Kiera is dead!" She said again, a little louder to suffocate any of his hope for receiving help from her.

All this seemed to Arjun like a dream. Arjun was so captivated by the Queens beauty that he did not see the treachery that her looks belied. He could not even hear his own heart beating within his chest. He could not even hear his thoughts. All he could see and think about was the beauty of Zurenda, and all he could hear in his mind were the words: *Kiera is dead! Kiera is dead... Kiera is dead!*

Zurenda sensed this overwhelming turmoil within him. She sensed his weakness and played upon his pride, his human nature, and his complete and total confusion.

"Arjun," Zurenda continued. "You are a Demi-God; I am a Demi-Goddess. We need to stop fighting each other and find a way to work together... as a team! We need to take our rightful place in the lofty heights of Olympus."

Arjun clenched his sword's grip even tighter at her blasphemy. "Relax my strong and handsome warrior. I know your reputation. I know your parentage. I know your destiny! You are the famed Warrior from Olympus! You are the embodiment of Cassandra's prophecy. You are the Son of Zeus!" Arjun was stunned by her subtle craftiness.

The message she delivered was in her most soothing and calming tone of voice, "We can join forces and rule the heavens and the earth, the mountains and the streams, the land, and the sea. Stop fighting me! Come join me!" Zurenda encouraged.

Arjun was confused, his clarity of thought had not yet returned, at least not until the earth started shaking again.

Zurenda looked up at the rafters; they were smoking again. Arjun came to his senses. For a split-second, Arjun saw who Zurenda really was and what she had become. She was a mystical witch, a conjurer, a necromancer, deceiver, and an undeserving queen!

"I cannot join you!" Arjun countered, still in a sort of incoherent daze. "I have a mission to fulfill for the goddess Selene. For Mother, for Father, and for Greece."

Zurenda's true colors came flashing out again. With the full fury of her words, she stated simply: "Fulfill your Mission, Arjun! And then die at the hands of a Queen!"

They crossed swords several times, each opponent exhibiting great skill with their weapon of choice. Every time the Olympic swords connected, white-hot sparks scattered in every direction.

Talia's actions changed the course of the fight. She catapulted the Sword of Ares at Arjun. Aiming for Arjun's chest, but missing his upper body while cutting his right arm. The cut was not deep, but blood began oozing everywhere. The Sword of Ares spun down the marble floor and careened into the open pit. It was now out of reach.

This action caused Arjun to lose concentration for a split-second.

With that distraction, Zurenda launched a ninja kick, hitting him in the back with enough power to knock him sideways and down onto his stomach, delivering enough power to slide him head-first toward the opening in the floor.

The Sword of Zeus went skating over the floor to the foot of Zurenda.

He was disarmed!

She slipped her left foot under the sword flinging it up to her right hand with a seamless motion.

Arjun reached for his boot dagger, but could not quite retrieve it while managing to stay concentrated on the Queen. The tables turned.

Zurenda, now holding the Sword of Zeus in the right hand, did the unthinkable! She invoked the power of sword! Lightning splattered all over the room, the ceiling, and the floor in front of him.

Losing his grip on the edge of the slab, with his injured arm, Arjun could feel his feet and legs slide helplessly into the pit.

Seconds passed, Arjun clung on to the edge of the pit with both elbows and then slipped to catch the edge with both hands. Though throbbing in pain, he soon found himself clinging to the edge of the slab with just his fingertips. Zurenda then took her full fury on Arjun. Again, she invoked the power of the sword:

"HA, HA! ARJUN! BY THE POWER OF YOUR WEAK AND POWERLESS FATHER, ZEUS!"
She blasphemed.

The lights went out, and the palace shook again. Sparks of lightning sprayed everywhere. The colossal temple statue of Selene fell over in response to the building shaking, crushing a few more guards in the process. Shards of white marble broke away from the statue and exploded across the floor. The building shook again. Arjun lost his fingernail grip on the slab and slid helplessly backward into the darkening pit.

"THAT IS THE END OF THE WARRIOR FROM OLYMPUS!" Zurenda gloated!

Talia pushed the iron lever up that operated the pit's floor opening, closing it tight.

This fight was over! Zurenda had won! She now had a new prisoner.

"THE PRISONER OF ZURENDA!"

She gloated in victory to her precious audience of one!

"Talia, release the lions!"

CHAPTER NINETY-THREE

Eris

S omewhere from within her veiled location, deep in the halls of the palace, behind the ruined recesses of the statues, came the faint but unmistakable cackling celebration of the Goddess:

Laughing wildly, Eris made a most un-goddess-like outburst: "HA! HA! HA!"

The muted sound gave way to screeching anthems of jubilation echoing throughout the great hall.

Eris' sinister laughter could be heard by the shapeshifters out in the courtyard. Quin shook her head in disbelief, fighting back the tears. Eris' laughter could be heard along the hallowed slopes of Olympus, and all around the forest of Aeolia.

The stinging rebuke! The scorching words of Cassandra's Prophecy unfulfilled! The sound of the Goddess echoing her daughter's triumphal words:

"THAT IS THE END

OF THE

WARRIOR FROM OLYMPUS!"

CHAPTER NINETY-FOUR

Zeus

Selene came running to Zeus' throne after a brief chariot ride back to the mountain with Artemis. The Goddess was visibly distraught.

"Why did you let our son fall victim to Zurenda and Eris?" Selene would not be comforted.

"My dear," Zeus stated, "our son is not dead, and neither are his friends."

The God of the Mountain was actually very upbeat.

"Eris is a fool!" Zeus clarified. "She and her daughter will pay for their blasphemy! This contest is not over; it is just beginning. Cassandra's prophecy is not yet fulfilled, and it surely shall be, or I am not the God of Olympus!"

Selene pressed further. "What assurances, my Lord have your taken to help Arjun succeed?"

"Have I not sent help to our son from the earth below and from the sky above?" Zeus stated confidently.

Zeus then took Selene by the right hand and looked lovingly into her crystal clear eyes of starlight. "Let's see what else our son and his friends can do!"

CHAPTER NINETY-FIVE

The Prophecy

The Prophecy of Cassandra, as recorded by Hermes:

From the ruin of Troy he shall come,

the sword and the bow he shall wield,

The raven and the beasts shall be his friend,

The raven and the beasts shall be his foe,

Euboea shall be his home, and a goddess shall be his queen.

The mighty gods of earth below and sky above,

Shall he combine to overthrow.

The contempt of gods, and the contempt of men.

The Warrior from Olympus, he shall be known.

For the man who can command lightning from a sword,

shall Eris' kingdom overthrow!

And a new constellation shall be to him known.

Keep a watchful eye for the release of Book Two:

The Prisoner of Zurenda

Justice of a Queen

.

Glossary

Ada	Zurenda Warrior.
Aedish	Athenian Sailor.
Allison	Tree Spirit, fixed in one location. Without mobility.
Apate	Apate is the embodiment of deceit and fraud. She wore a golden girdle which was stolen by Rama while she slept.
Amazons	Steeped in Greek mythology, this group is a tribe of women warriors. Zurenda and her warriors are a sub-

group of this fierce fighting band and practice the same contempt for men as the other Amazonian tribes.

Ares   God of War. Ares is the Greek god of war. He is one of the Twelve Olympians and the son of Zeus and Hera.

Artemis   Goddess of the Windland, confederate with Zeus and Selene. Artemis was often considered as the daughter of Zeus and Leto. She was the goddess of the hunt, lover of wild animals, protector of the wilderness. The deer and the cypress were sacred to her.

Arjun   Demi-God. Son of the Goddess Selene and the mortal man, Theseus. After Theseus died, Arjun becomes the adopted son of Zeus when he proves his worth in a heroic rescue. Arjun grew up believing that he was the mortal son of Theseus the famous sailor and warrior, and he was unclear as to

	who his biological mother was until after the shipwreck.
Agamemnon	Brother-in-law to King Menelaus. Agamemnon was the son of King Atreus and Queen Aerope of Mycenae, the father of Zurenda, and also the father to her other half-human siblings: Iphigenia, Electra or Laodike, Orestes, and Chrysothemis. When Helen, the wife of King Menelaus, was taken to Troy by Paris, Agamemnon commanded the united Greek armed forces in the ensuing Trojan War under the direction of the Goddess Eris.
Aphrodite	Self-declared most beautiful woman in the world
Cassandra	The Prophetess which predicted the fall of Troy and the fall of Zurenda and Eris.
Cerberus	Underworld Task-master.
Charybdis	Charybdis is a ferocious sea monster that lives at the bottom of the sea under a rock. This monster regularly swallows ships whole by

	creating a whirlpool, sucking them into the vortex.
Chimera	Chimeras were not uncommon to Greek mythology. This story contains a few Chimeras relating to their classical origin as fire-breathing monsters.
Circe	Circe was known for her knowledge of potions and herbs. Through the use of this knowledge and her magic, she cast spells on anyone who displeased her.
Clytemnestra	Wife of Agamemnon, Sister to Helen of Troy.
Coreen	Zurenda's warrior and detachment leader over ten women warriors, namely: Antandre, Derimacheia, Myrina, Dioxippe, Harpe, Ioxeia, Cnemis, Andro, Trilla, and Coea.
Crystal	Mythical winged stallion belonging to Selene. Pegasus.
Eris	Goddess of Discord, mistress of Agamemnon.
Erastos	Mortal Father of Kiera.

Fabian	Training Spirit, Centaur.
Gaea	Gaea is the personification of the Earth and one of the Greek primordial deities. The primal Mother Earth goddess.
Gregory	Athenian Sailor.
Hydra	Multi-headed water serpent, the child of Typhon and Echidna.
Helen	Helen of Troy. Also known as Helen of Sparta, or simply Helen, was the daughter of Zeus and Leda and was a sister of Clytemnestra, Castor, and Pollux. In Greek myth, she was the wife of King Menelaus. Her entanglement with Prince Paris of Troy, in part, brought about the Trojan War.
Helen	Zurenda's Warrior Guard. (Not to be confused with Helen of Troy).
Hades	Lord of the Underworld. Hades was the ancient Greek god of the underworld, which place eventually took his name. In Greek mytholo-

gy, Hades was regarded as the oldest son of Cronus and Rhea, although the last son regurgitated by his father. He and his brothers Zeus and Poseidon defeated their father's generation of gods, the Titans, and claimed rulership over the cosmos. In this transaction, Hades received the underworld, Zeus the sky, and Poseidon the sea.

Hadrian	Athenian Sailor. An unassuming character, Hadrian plays an important role in this story.
Hermes	Messenger to the Gods.
Hydra	Hydra is a sea serpent with reptilian traits. Hydra is multi-headed with poisonous breath and green blood.
Iphigenia	Daughter of Agamemnon, sacrificed to Artemis, in lieu of Zurenda.
Jacob	Athenian Sailor.
Jayla	Zurenda's warrior guard, subordinate to Kendra.
Jason	Athenian Sailor.

Joshua	Bike riding skeleton - servant of Cerberus.
Kaleb	Athenian Sailor.
Kiera	Arjun's childhood friend. Excellent Archer.
Kendra	Zurenda's warrior and Captain of the Guard. She commanded a detachment of twelve women warriors, namely: Clonie, Aeila, Derinoe, Phoebe, Hippolyia, Antiope, Glauce, Ploydora, Bremusa, Euryale, Menippe, and Lyce.
Lycos	Captain of a Greek Trireme, and best friends with Arjun.
Marcus	Athenian Sailor.
Mara	Zurenda's warrior and detachment leader over ten women warriors, namely: Penthesilea, Evandra, Alcippe, Marpe, Otrera, Laomache, Theseis, Philippis, Tecmessa, and Xanthe.
Paris	Trojan ruler. Paris was the son of King Priam and Queen Hecuba of Troy, who eloped with Helen,

	queen of Sparta, in part, causing the events that led to the Trojan War.
Peremptoriness	Cloud Titan. Peremptoriness is an element of an idea more than an object. A descendant of the family of the Oligarchs.
Poseidon	God of the sea. Brother to Zeus and Hades. Poseidon was hot-tempered and intolerant of mortals and demi-gods.
Proteus	Lesser Sea God. Homer called him "The old man of the Sea." Proteus had the power to change shapes and forms, and restore life from death. Proteus bestowed that power upon Rama with the contents of a Golden Sea Shell given to the satyr.
Quin	Training Spirit, faun, and adopted sister in magic of Circe. Quin was also a shapeshifter. Quin plays a significant role in the story.
Rama	Training Spirit, Satyr. Rama carries a leather pouch con-

	taining a golden seashell with a black pearl inside possessing magical and healing properties. Rama was also a shapeshifter.
Salacia	Female divinity of the sea. Salacia was the personification of the calmness and beautiful aspect of the sea as a whole. The name Salacia denotes the wide, open sea. Salacia possessed power to act on objects that were found in the sea.
Selene	Goddess of the Moon, Mistress of Zeus. She is the daughter of the Titans Hyperion and Theia, and sister of the sun-god Helios, and Eos, goddess of the dawn. Each day, she drives her chariot pulled by Pegasi across the heavens. According to Greek Mythology, Selene had several lovers including Zeus and the mortal Theseus. In classical times, Selene was often identified with Artemis. Selene's Roman name is Luna.

Semon	Fisherman. Working in the Port of Pagasae, operative for Poseidon.
Starlight	Mythical winged stallion belonging to Selene. Pegasus.
Stephanus	"Steve" The Olympic Black Smith. Also known as Hephaestus in Greek Mythology.
Talia	Zurenda's warrior and eventual Captain of the Guard. She commanded a detachment of ten women warriors, namely: Ainippe, Clete, Gryne, Hippo, Myrto, Otrera, Sinope, Marpesia, Alcibie, and Deianeria.
Theseus	Famed sailor of Greece, biological father to Arjun.
Zedra	Zurenda's failed Captain of the Guard, her subordinate was Kendra. Zedra, later in the story, is no longer loyal to Zurenda and helps Arjun's team.
Zeus	The God of Lightning. Chief of the Gods. Zeus played a dominant role, presiding over the Greek

Olympian pantheon. He fathered many of the heroes, and adopted other heroes, including Arjun, when it was convenient to do so and suited his ambitions.

Zooey

Mentor, Tree Spirit, Hegemone, and shapeshifter. As a fig tree, Zooey is not that interesting. However, she does play an important supportive role in the story and sprinkles good humor into difficult situations.

Zurenda

The villainous Queen of this story. Zurenda is a Demi-Goddess. She is the daughter of the Goddess Eris and the not so supportive mortal, King Agamemnon. Left to grow up on the island of Piperi alone, Zurenda turned to the dark arts of magic and sorcery. Her destiny shapes the outcome of the Underworld.

Greek-Aegean Map

Greek-Aegean Map.

> This map provides, as a reference document, for some areas mentioned in the story.

> Authors note:
> The map herein represents general locations mentioned in the story. It is not intended to be a literal representation of the geography of Greece or the Aegean Sea.

Troy

Olympus

Aeolia

Port of Pagasae

Piperi

Aegean Sea

Skantzoura

Skyros

Euboea

Kymi

Athens

Sea of Crete

N

Mediterranean

Listed below are ancient locations and their equivalent contemporary names:

- Mentor Meadows is located near the ancient area Southwest of Mount Olympus called Aeolia.
- Cerythus Village is near to the modern day (Kymi) Kimi on the Greek Island of Euboea.
- Elysian Fields, for a point of reference, this is the Ancient Greek equivalent of Heaven.
- Peparethus Island is also known as Piperi. Part of the Thessalian Sporades grouping of islands.
- Port of Pagasae is near the port city currently known as the Port of Volos.
- Scryros Island is also known as Skyros.
- Skantzoura Island is located between Piperi and Skyros.

Credits:

- Chapter heading and post chapter illustrations and medallion clip art: Licensing agreement through Shutterstock.com.

- Aegean Sea Map – By the Author.

ABOUT THE AUTHOR

Kent A. LeFevre

Kent enjoys authoring books of diverse genres from illustrated children's books, to historical fiction and pure fictional fantasy.

His writing career began around the year 2010. Since then, he has authored and illustrated over a dozen books. He enjoys writing books that are family friendly and crafting stories that will put a smile on your face.

Kent and his wife Christine make their home in the shadows of the Sierras.

To learn more about this author, please visit:
www.squareplatemedia.com

Other Titles by this Author:

- The Sofa Sitters
- Banished to Snake Island
- The Dragon Bride
- Aliens see only the color purple and Cats see only the color blue.
- Tommie's Gold
- Tales of the sea, my new Boat and me
- Fish Tales
- The Great Watermelon Scientist
- Chairs
- My Life without Fingernails
- Zombies don't eat Vegetables
- Zombies Visit the Dentist
- Black & White
- The Artistry of Kent A. LeFevre

Publisher: Square Plate Media.
Published in The United States of America,
© 2018. All rights reserved.